THE
HAUNTED
DOLLS

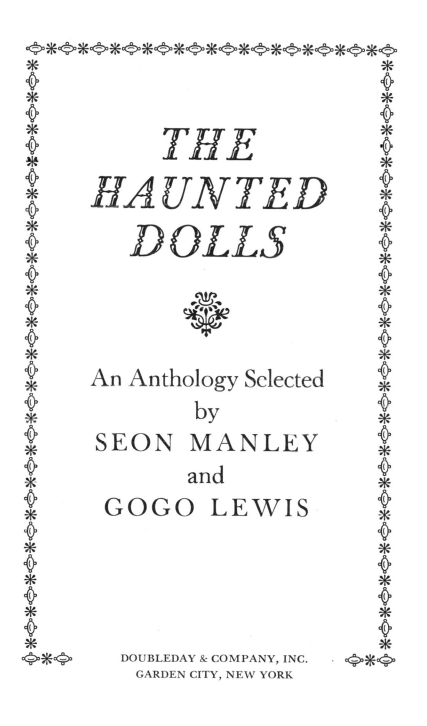

THE HAUNTED DOLLS

An Anthology Selected
by
SEON MANLEY
and
GOGO LEWIS

DOUBLEDAY & COMPANY, INC.
GARDEN CITY, NEW YORK

We are grateful to the authors, agents and publishers who have given us permission to reprint the following selections:

The Dressmaker's Doll, by Agatha Christie. Reprinted by permission of Dodd, Mead & Company, Inc., from *Double Sin and Other Stories,* by Agatha Christie. Copyright © 1958 by Agatha Christie Ltd. Permission to reprint also granted by Harold Ober Associates Incorporated.

The Peg-Doll, by Rosemary Timperley. Copyright © by Rosemary Timperley 1978. Reprinted by permission of the author and the author's agents, Harvey Unna and Stephen Durbridge Ltd.

The Haunted Doll's House, by M. R. James, from *Collected Ghost Stories,* by M. R. James. Reprinted by permission of Edward Arnold (Publishers) Ltd.

The Doll, by Algernon Blackwood, from *Tales of the Mysterious and Macabre,* by Algernon Blackwood. Reprinted by permission of The Public Trustee and the Hamlyn Group Ltd.

The Grey Lady, by Mary Danby. Copyright © by Mary Danby 1978. Reprinted by permission of the author.

The Doll, by Terry Tapp. Copyright © Terry Tapp 1978. Reprinted by permission of the author.

Our thanks also to Betty Shalders; "The Christmas of the Big Bisque Doll." Copyright © 1980 by Seon Manley; Terry Hayes; Bobbie Colgan; the staff of the Bellport Memorial Library, Bellport, New York; the staff of the Patchogue Library, Patchogue, New York; the staff of the Greenwich Library, Greenwich, Connecticut; our husbands, Robert R. Manley and William W. Lewis; and our daughters, Sara Lewis, Carol Lewis, and Shivaun Manley.

ISBN: 0-385-15363-5 Trade
        0-385-15654-5 Prebound
Library of Congress Catalog Card Number 79–7608
Copyright © 1980 by Seon Manley and Gogo Lewis
All Rights Reserved
Printed in the United States of America
First Edition

❖❖*❖*❖*❖*❖*❖*❖*❖*❖*❖*❖*❖*

This book is for our cousin
Dorothy J. Murison
with much love

CONTENTS

INTRODUCTION

What strange creatures they are—dolls. Look at
them crowded together in a window. They stare out
into the world with a seeming intelligence. There
have always been dolls and there always will be.
There are dolls for children to project their fantasies
upon, magnificent dolls for collectors, sweet dolls that
will always be a memory to adults, dolls that comfort
and protect and listen to endless stories.

There are the witches' dolls. These are the dolls of
some menacing cruelty. There are harvest dolls, once
made in the autumn to aid and abet the agricultural
peoples in cultivating the land. Off they go together
—men and women and children—into the fields,
reaping the last of the grain, and the very last is laid
down flat and covered. Then the bonniest lass will
cut this final handful, and it will be fashioned like a
doll and called a corn baby or corn doll. It is
brought home with music, and preserved in a parlor
for a full year.

From farmer to folklorist, from collector to student, from child to parent, the doll has special meaning. Fanciful, beautiful dolls have been made of almost every substance in the world. Made of
papier-mâché, made of pegwood, made of fibers,
made of finest porcelain, made of wax, made—yes,
still, even in the United States—out of cooky dough,

out of apples, out of hay, out of clay. The images of
spirits are represented as dolls in some of our Indian
tribes; they are fashioned from wool in Peru, from
rags everywhere, from gingerbread. There are dolls
all around us if we care to look. And there are collectors looking.

One of the greatest and most enjoyable fields for
the collector—that of dolls and dollhouses—has
furnished all sorts of books, from how-to, to where
one finds and collects these magnificent dolls of other
days. But everyone who has ever looked deep into the
sightless eyes of the lost doll knows it has a story. Because the doll was once made as an image of hu-
mankind, the doll has evoked many human reactions.
Dolls can be menacing; they can appear to be weird,
eerie, strange and mysterious. Indeed, it appears
sometimes that dolls can be haunted. Here, from the
pens of some of our most imaginative writers, are the
Haunted Dolls—in the very first book to explore the
hidden aspects of the doll world.

THE
HAUNTED
DOLLS

Rose Mueller Sprague

These American fashion drawings for the spring of 1890 were accompanied by instructions for dressmakers. They included suggestions for the dress of the doll; leftover pieces from the Gobelin blue India silk used for the young miss on the left. (Manley-Lewis collection)

AGATHA CHRISTIE

✧✧*✧*✧*✧*✧*✧*✧*✧*✧*✧*

THE DRESSMAKER'S DOLL

"When I begin to write," Dame Agatha Christie *once explained, "I must behave rather as dogs do when they retire with a bone; they depart in a secretive manner, and you do not see them again for an odd half hour. They return self-consciously with mud on their noses. I do much the same."*

Although Dame Agatha spoke relatively freely about her detective stories, she was unusually close-mouthed and secretive about her supernatural tales. "The Dressmaker's Doll" is one of her very best and, indeed, one of her most sensitive stories.

Fashion dolls, or dressmaker dolls, as they were sometimes called, are of particular interest in the history, not only of dolls, but of fashion, because they preceded fashion books and patterns by many years. The first fashion doll was probably sent by Queen Isabeau of Bavaria to the Queen of England, the

*wife of Henry IV, in the early fifteenth century. In
this way two royal courts could compare notes on
popular fashions. These dolls were often nearly life
size and were made to measurement. As a result,
they had an unusually lifelike aspect. In addition to
the fashion dolls that were sent to the courts to illus-
trate fashions, these very elegant dolls were often sent
as gifts to royal children.*

*The sophisticated dolls sometimes appeared to have
a life of their own, and so it is not surprising that
Dame Agatha's great skill should find a magnificent
subject in one of the descendants of the fashion dolls.*

THE DOLL lay in the big velvet-covered chair. There
was not much light in the room; the London skies
were dark. In the gentle, grayish-green gloom, the
sage-green coverings and the curtains and the rugs
all blended with each other. The doll blended too.
She lay long and limp and sprawled in her green velvet clothes and her velvet cap and the painted mask
of her face. She was not a doll as children understand dolls. She was the Puppet Doll, the whim of
Rich Women, the doll who lolls beside the telephone,
or among the cushions of the divan. She sprawled
there, eternally limp and yet strangely alive. She
looked a decadent product of the twentieth century.

Sybil Fox, hurrying in with some patterns and a
sketch, looked at the doll with a faint feeling of
surprise and bewilderment. She wondered—but whatever she wondered did not get to the front of her
mind. Instead, she thought to herself, "Now, what's

happened to the pattern of the blue velvet? Wherever have I put it? I'm sure I had it here just now." She went out on the landing and called up to the workroom.

"Elspeth. Elspeth, have you the blue pattern up there? Mrs. Fellows-Brown will be here any minute now."

She went in again, switching on the lights. Again she glanced at the doll. "Now where on earth—ah, there it is." She picked the pattern up from where it had fallen from her hand. There was the usual creak outside on the landing as the elevator came to a halt, and in a minute or two Mrs. Fellows-Brown, accompanied by her Pekinese, came puffing into the room rather like a fussy local train arriving at a wayside station.

"It's going to pour," she said, "simply *pour!*"

She threw off gloves and a fur. Alicia Coombe came in. She didn't always come in nowadays, only when special customers arrived, and Mrs. Fellows-Brown was such a customer.

Elspeth, the forewoman of the workroom, came down with the frock and Sybil pulled it over Mrs. Fellows-Brown's head.

"There," she said. "It really does suit you. It's a lovely color, isn't it?"

Alicia Coombe sat back a little in her chair, studying it.

"Yes," she said. "I think it's good. Yes, it's definitely a success."

Mrs. Fellows-Brown turned sideways and looked in the mirror.

"I must say," she said, "your clothes do *do* something to my behind."

"You're much thinner than you were three months ago," Sybil assured her.

"I'm really not," said Mrs. Fellows-Brown, "though I must say I *look* it in this. There's something about the way you cut, it really does minimize my behind. I almost look as though I hadn't got one —I mean only the usual kind that most people have." She sighed and gingerly smoothed the troublesome portion of her anatomy. "It's always been a bit of a trial to me," she said. "Of course, for years I could pull it in, you know, by sticking out my front. Well, I can't do that any longer because I've got a stomach now as well as a behind. And I mean—well, you can't pull it in both ways, can you?"

Alicia Coombe said, "You should see some of my customers!"

Mrs. Fellows-Brown experimented to and fro.

"A stomach is worse than a behind," she said. "It shows more. Or perhaps you think it does, because, I mean, when you're talking to people you're facing them and that's the moment they can't see your behind but they can notice your stomach. Anyway, I've made it a rule to pull in my stomach and let my behind look after itself." She craned her neck round still farther, then said suddenly, "Oh, that doll of yours! She gives me the creeps. How long have you had her?"

Sybil glanced uncertainly at Alicia Coombe, who looked puzzled but vaguely distressed.

"I don't know exactly . . . some time I think—I

never *can* remember things. It's awful nowadays—I simply *cannot* remember. Sybil, how long have we had her?"

Sybil said shortly, "I don't know."

"Well," said Mrs. Fellows-Brown, "she gives *me* the creeps. Uncanny! She looks, you know, as though she was watching us all, and perhaps laughing in that velvet sleeve of hers. I'd get rid of her if I were you." She gave a little shiver. Then she plunged once more into dressmaking details. Should she or should she not have the sleeves an inch shorter? And what about the length? When all these important points were settled satisfactorily, Mrs. Fellows-Brown resumed her own garments and prepared to leave. As she passed the doll, she turned her head again.

"No," she said, "I *don't* like that doll. She looks too much as though she *belonged* here. It isn't healthy."

"Now what did she mean by that?" demanded Sybil, as Mrs. Fellows-Brown departed down the stairs.

Before Alicia Coombe could answer, Mrs. Fellows-Brown returned, poking her head round the door.

"Good gracious, I forgot all about Fou-Ling. Where are you, ducksie? Well I never!"

She stared and the other two women stared too. The Pekinese was sitting by the green velvet chair, staring up at the limp doll sprawled on it. There was no expression, either of pleasure or resentment, on his small popeyed face. He was merely looking.

"Come along, Mum's darling," said Mrs. Fellows-Brown.

Mum's darling paid no attention whatever.

"He gets more disobedient every day," said Mrs. Fellows-Brown, with the air of one cataloguing a virtue. "Come *on,* Fou-Ling. Din-dins. Luffly liver."

Fou-Ling turned his head about an inch and a half toward his mistress, then with disdain resumed his appraisal of the doll.

"She certainly made an impression on him," said Mrs. Fellows-Brown. "I don't think he's ever noticed her before. *I* haven't either. Was she here last time I came?"

The two other women looked at each other. Sybil now had a frown on her face, and Alicia Coombe said, wrinkling up her forehead, "I told you—I simply can't remember anything nowadays. How long *have* we had her, Sybil?"

"Where did she come from?" demanded Mrs. Fellows-Brown. "Did you buy her?"

"Oh, no." Somehow Alicia Coombe was shocked at the idea. "Oh *no.* I suppose—I suppose someone gave her to me." She shook her head. "Maddening!" she exclaimed. "Absolutely maddening, when everything goes out of your head the very moment after it's happened."

"Now don't be stupid, Fou-Ling," said Mrs. Fellows-Brown sharply. "Come on. I'll have to pick you up."

She picked him up. Fou-Ling uttered a short bark of agonized protest. They went out of the room with Fou-Ling's popeyed face turned over his fluffy shoulder, still staring with enormous attention at the doll on the chair. . . .

* * *

"That there doll," said Mrs. Groves, "fair gives me the creeps, it does."

Mrs. Groves was the cleaner. She had just finished a crablike progress backward along the floor. Now she was standing up and working slowly round the room with a duster.

"Funny thing," said Mrs. Groves, "never noticed it really until yesterday. And then it hit me all of a sudden, as you might say."

"You don't like it?" asked Sybil.

"I tell you, Mrs. Fox, it gives me the creeps," said the cleaning woman. "It ain't natural, if you know what I mean. All those long hanging legs and the way she's slouched down there and the cunning look she has in her eye. It doesn't look healthy, that's what I say."

"You've never said anything about her before," said Sybil.

"I tell you, I never noticed her—not till this morning . . . Of course I know she's been here some time, but—" She stopped and a puzzled expression flitted across her face. "Sort of thing you might dream of at night," she said, and gathering up various cleaning implements she departed from the fitting room and walked across the landing to the room on the other side.

Sybil stared at the relaxed doll. An expression of bewilderment was growing on her face. Alicia Coombe entered and Sybil turned sharply.

"Miss Coombe, how long *have* you had this creature?"

"What, the doll? My dear, you know I can't remember things. Yesterday—why, it's too silly! I was going out to that lecture and I hadn't gone halfway down the street when I suddenly found I couldn't remember where I was going. I thought and I thought. Finally I told myself it *must* be Fortnums. I knew there was something I wanted to get at Fortnums. Well, you won't believe me, it wasn't till I actually got home and was having some tea that I remembered about the lecture. Of course, I've always heard that people go gaga as they get on in life, but it's happening to me much too fast. I've forgotten now where I've put my handbag—and my spectacles too. Where did I put those spectacles? I had them just now—I was reading something in the *Times*."

"The spectacles are on the mantelpiece here," said Sybil, handing them to her. "How did you get the doll? Who gave her to you?"

"That's a blank, too," said Alicia Coombe. *"Some-body* gave her to me or sent her to me, I suppose . . . However she does seem to match the room very well, doesn't she?"

"Rather too well, I think," said Sybil. "Funny thing is, *I* can't remember when I first noticed her here."

"Now don't you get the same way as I am," Alicia Coombe admonished her. "After all, you're young still."

"But really, Miss Coombe, I don't remember. I mean, I looked at her yesterday and thought there was something—well, Mrs. Groves is quite right—something creepy about her. And then I thought I'd already thought so, and then I tried to remember when I first thought so and—well, I just couldn't remember anything! In a way, it was as if I'd never seen her before—only it didn't feel like that. It felt as though she'd been here a long time but I'd only just noticed her."

"Perhaps she flew in through the window one day on a broomstick," said Alicia Coombe. "Anyway, she belongs here now all right." She looked round. "You could hardly imagine the room without her, could you?"

"No," said Sybil, with a slight shiver, "but I rather wish I could."

"Could what?"

"Imagine the room without her."

"Are we all going balmy about this doll?" demanded Alicia Coombe impatiently. "What's wrong with the poor thing? Looks like a decayed cabbage to me, but perhaps," she added, "that's because I haven't got my spectacles on." She put them on her nose and looked firmly at the doll. "Yes," she said, "I see what you mean. She *is* a little creepy . . . Sad-looking but—well, sly and rather determined, too."

"Funny," said Sybil, "Mrs. Fellows-Brown taking such a violent dislike to her."

"She's one who never minds speaking her mind," said Alicia Coombe.

"But it's odd," persisted Sybil, "that this doll should make such an impression on her."

"Well, people do take dislikes very suddenly sometimes."

"Perhaps," said Sybil, with a little laugh, "that doll never *was* here until yesterday . . . Perhaps she just—flew in through the window as you say and settled herself here."

"No," said Alicia Coombe, "I'm sure she's been here some time. Perhaps she only became visible yesterday."

"That's what I feel, too," said Sybil, "that she's been here some time . . . but all the same I *don't* remember really seeing her till yesterday." .

"Now, dear," said Alicia Coombe briskly, "do stop it. You're making me feel quite peculiar with shivers running up and down my spine. You're not going to work up a great deal of supernatural hoo-hah about that creature, are you?" She picked up the doll, shook it out, rearranged its shoulders, and sat it down again on another chair. Immediately the doll flopped slightly and relaxed.

"It's not a bit lifelike," said Alicia Coombe, staring at the doll. "And yet, in a funny way, she does seem alive, doesn't she?"

"Oo, it did give me a turn," said Mrs. Groves, as she went round the showroom, dusting. "Such a turn as I hardly like to go into the fitting room any more."

"What's given you a turn?" demanded Miss Coombe, who was sitting at a writing table in the corner, busy with various accounts. "This woman," she added more for her own benefit than that of Mrs. Groves, "thinks she can have two evening dresses, three cocktail dresses, and a suit every year without ever paying me a penny for them! Really, some people!"

"It's that doll," said Mrs. Groves.

"What, our doll again?"

"Yes, sitting up there at the desk, like a human. Oo, it didn't half give me a turn!"

"What are you talking about?"

Alicia Coombe got up, strode across the room, across the little landing outside, and into the room opposite—the fitting room. There was a small Sheraton desk in one corner of it, and there, sitting in a chair drawn up to it, her long floppy arms on the desk, sat the doll.

"Somebody seems to have been having fun," said Alicia Coombe. "Fancy sitting her up like that. Really, she looks quite natural."

Sybil Fox came down the stairs at this moment carrying a dress that was to be tried on that morning.

"Come here, Sybil. Look at our doll sitting at my private desk and writing letters now."

The two women looked.

"Really," said Alicia Coombe, "it's too ridiculous! I wonder who propped her up there. Did you?"

"No, I didn't," said Sybil. "It must have been one of the girls from upstairs."

"A silly sort of joke, really," said Alicia Coombe. She picked up the doll from the desk and threw her back on the sofa.

Sybil laid the dress over a chair carefully, then she went out and up the stairs to the workroom.

"You know the doll," she said, "the velvet doll in Miss Coombe's room downstairs—in the fitting room?"

The forewoman and three of the girls looked up.

"Yes, miss, of course we know."

"Who sat her up at the desk this morning for a joke?"

The three girls looked at her, then Elspeth, the forewoman, said, "Sat her up at the desk? *I* didn't."

"Nor did I," said one of the girls. "Did you, Marlene?"

Marlene shook her head.

"This your bit of fun, Elspeth?"

"No, indeed," said Elspeth, a stern woman who looked as though her mouth should always be full of pins. "I've more to do than going about playing with dolls and sitting them up at desks."

"Look here," said Sybil, and to her surprise her voice shook slightly. "It was—it was quite a good joke, only I'd just like to know who did it."

The three girls bristled.

"We've told you, Mrs. Fox. None of us did it, did we, Marlene?"

"I didn't," said Marlene, "and if Nellie and Margaret say they didn't, well then none of us did."

"You've heard what *I* had to say," said Elspeth. "What's this all about anyway, Mrs. Fox?"

Sybil said slowly, "It just seemed so odd."

"Perhaps it was Mrs. Groves?" said Elspeth.

Sybil shook her head. "It wouldn't be Mrs. Groves. It gave *her* quite a turn."

"I'll come down and see for myself," said Elspeth.

"She's not there now," said Sybil. "Miss Coombe took her away from the desk and threw her back on the sofa. Well—" she paused, "what I mean is, some-one must have stuck her up there in the chair at the writing desk—thinking it was funny, I suppose. And —and I don't see why they won't say so."

"I've told you twice, Mrs. Fox," said Margaret. "I don't see why you should go on accusing us of telling lies. None of us would do a silly thing like that."

"I'm sorry," said Sybil, "I didn't mean to upset you. But—but who else could possibly have done it?"

"Perhaps she got up and walked there herself," said Marlene, and giggled.

For some reason Sybil didn't like the suggestion.

"Oh, it's all a lot of nonsense, anyway," she said, and went down the stairs again.

Alicia Coombe was humming quite cheerfully. She looked around the room.

"I've lost my spectacles again," she said, "but it doesn't really matter. I don't want to see anything this moment. The trouble is, of course, when you're as blind as I am, that when you have lost your spectacles, unless you've got another pair to put on and find them with, well then you can't find them because you can't see to find them."

"I'll look round for you," said Sybil. "You had them just now."

"I went into the other room when you went upstairs. I expect I took them back in there."

She went across to the other room.

"It's such a bother," said Alicia Coombe. "I want to get on with these accounts. How can I if I haven't my spectacles?"

"I'll go up and get your second pair from the bedroom," said Sybil.

"I haven't got a second pair at present," said Alicia Coombe.

"Why, what's happened to them?"

"Well, I think I left them yesterday when I was out at lunch. I've rung up there, and I've rung up the two shops I went into, too."

"Oh, dear," said Sybil, "you'll have to get *three* pairs, I suppose."

"If I had three pairs of spectacles," said Alicia Coombe, "I should spend my whole life looking for one or the other of them. I really think it's best to have only *one*. Then you've *got* to look till you find it."

"Well, they must be somewhere," said Sybil. "You haven't been out of these two rooms. They're certainly not here, so you must have laid them down in the fitting room."

She went back, walking around, looking quite closely. Finally, as a last idea, she took up the doll from the sofa.

"I've got them," she called.

"Oh, where were they, Sybil?"

"Under our precious doll. I suppose you must have thrown them down when you put her back on the sofa."

"I didn't. I'm sure I didn't."

"Oh," said Sybil with exasperation. "Then I suppose the doll took them and was hiding them from you!"

"Really, you know," said Alicia, looking thoughtfully at the doll, "I wouldn't put it past her. She looks very intelligent, don't you think, Sybil?"

"I don't think I like her face," said Sybil. "She looks as though she knew something that we didn't."

"You don't think she looks sort of sad and sweet?" said Alicia Coombe, pleadingly, but without conviction.

"I don't think she's in the least sweet," said Sybil.

Dolls were as elaborately dressed as their owners.
(Nineteenth-century drawing)

"No . . . perhaps you're right. . . . Oh, well, let's get on with things. Lady Lee will be here in another ten minutes. I just want to get these invoices done and posted."

"Mrs. Fox. Mrs. Fox."

"Yes, Margaret?" said Sybil. "What is it?"

Sybil was busy leaning over a table, cutting a piece of satin material.

"Oh, Mrs. Fox, it's that doll again. I took down the brown dress the way you said, and there's that doll sitting up at the desk again. And it wasn't me— it wasn't any of us. Please, Mrs. Fox, we really wouldn't do such a thing."

Sybil's scissors slid a little.

"There," she said angrily, "look what you've made me do. Oh, well, it'll be all right, I suppose. Now, what's this about the doll?"

"She's sitting at the desk again."

Sybil went down and walked into the fitting room. The doll was sitting at the desk exactly as she had sat there before.

"You're very determined, aren't you?" said Sybil, speaking to the doll.

She picked her up unceremoniously and put her back on the sofa.

"That's your place, my girl," she said. "You stay there."

She walked across to the other room.

"Miss Coombe."

"Yes, Sybil?"

"Somebody *is* having a game with us, you know. That doll was sitting at the desk again."

"Who do you think it is?"

"It must be one of those three upstairs," said Sybil. "Thinks it's funny, I suppose. Of course they all swear to high heaven it wasn't them."

"Who do you think it is—Margaret?"

"No, I don't think it's Margaret. She looked quite queer when she came in and told me. I expect it's that giggling Marlene."

"Anyway, it's a very silly thing to do."

"Of course it is—idiotic," said Sybil. "However," she added grimly, "I'm going to put a stop to it."

"What are you going to do?"

"You'll see," said Sybil.

That night when she left, she locked the fitting-room door from the outside.

"I'm locking this door," she said, "and I'm taking the key with me."

"Oh, I see," said Alicia Coombe, with a faint air of amusement. "You're beginning to think it's me, are you? You think I'm so absentminded that I go in there and think I'll write at the desk, but instead I pick the doll up and put her there to write for me. Is that the idea? And then I forget all about it?"

"Well, it's a possibility," Sybil admitted. "Anyway, I'm going to be quite sure that no silly practical joke is played tonight."

The following morning, her lips set grimly, the first thing Sybil did on arrival was to unlock the door of the fitting room and march in. Mrs. Groves, with an aggrieved expression and mop and duster in hand, had been waiting on the landing.

"*Now* we'll see!" said Sybil.

Then she drew back with a slight gasp.

The doll was sitting at the desk.

"Coo!" said Mrs. Groves behind her. "It's un-canny! That's what it is. Oh, there, Mrs. Fox, you look quite pale, as though you've come over queer. You need a little drop of something. Has Miss Coombe got a drop upstairs, do you know?"

"I'm quite all right," said Sybil.

She walked over to the doll, lifted her carefully, and crossed the room with her.

"Somebody's been playing a trick on you again," said Mrs. Groves.

"I don't see how they could have played a trick on me this time," said Sybil slowly. "I locked that door last night. You know yourself that no one could get in."

"Somebody's got another key, maybe," said Mrs. Groves, helpfully.

"I don't think so," said Sybil. "We've never both-ered to lock this door before. It's one of those old-fashioned keys and there's only one of them."

"Perhaps the other key fits it—the one to the door opposite."

In due course they tried all the keys in the shop, but none fitted the door of the fitting room.

"It *is* odd, Miss Coombe," said Sybil later, as they were having lunch together.

Alicia Coombe was looking rather pleased.

"My dear," she said. "I think it's simply extraor-dinary. I think we ought to write to the psychical research people about it. You know, they might send an investigator—a medium or someone—to see if there's anything peculiar about the room."

"You don't seem to mind at all," said Sybil.

"Well, I rather enjoy it in a way," said Alicia Coombe. "I mean, at my age, it's rather fun when things happen! All the same—no," she added thoughtfully, "I don't think I do quite like it. I mean, that doll's getting rather above herself, isn't she?"

On that evening Sybil and Alicia Coombe locked the door once more on the outside.

"I still think," said Sybil, "that somebody might be playing a practical joke, though really, I don't see why . . ."

"Do you think she'll be at the desk again tomorrow morning?" demanded Alicia.

"Yes," said Sybil, "I do."

But they were wrong. The doll was not at the desk. Instead, she was on the window sill, looking out into the street. And again there was an extraordinary naturalness about her position.

"It's all frightfully silly, isn't it?" said Alicia Coombe, as they were snatching a quick cup of tea that afternoon. By common consent they were not having it in the fitting room, as they usually did, but in Alicia Coombe's own room opposite.

"Silly in what way?"

"Well, I mean, there's nothing you can get hold of. Just a doll that's always in a different place."

As day followed day it seemed a more and more apt observation. It was not only at night that the doll now moved. At any moment when they came into the fitting room, after they had been absent even a few minutes, they might find the doll in a different place. They could have left her on the sofa and find her on a chair. Then she'd be on a different chair.

Sometimes she'd be in the window seat, sometimes at the desk again.

"She just moves about as she likes," said Alicia Coombe. "And I think, Sybil, I *think* it's amusing her."

The two women stood looking down at the inert sprawling figure in its limp, soft velvet, with its painted silk face.

"Some old bits of velvet and silk and a lick of paint, that's all it is," said Alicia Coombe. Her voice was strained. "I suppose, you know, we could—er— we could dispose of her."

"What do you mean, dispose of her?" asked Sybil. Her voice sounded almost shocked.

"Well," said Alicia Coombe, "we could put her in the fire, if there was a fire. Burn her, I mean, like a witch . . . Or of course," she added matter-of-factly, "we could just put her in the dustbin."

"I don't think that would do," said Sybil. "Somebody would probably take her out of the dustbin and bring her back to us."

"Or we could send her somewhere," said Alicia Coombe. "You know, to one of those societies who are always writing and asking for something—for a sale or a bazaar. I think that's the best idea."

"I don't know . . ." said Sybil. "I'd be almost afraid to do that."

"Afraid?"

"Well, I think she'd come back," said Sybil.

"You mean, she'd come back *here?*"

"Yes."

"Like a homing pigeon?"

"Yes, that's what I mean."

"I suppose we're not going off our heads, are we?" said Alicia Coombe. "Perhaps I've really gone gaga and perhaps you're just humoring me, is that it?"

"No," said Sybil. "But I've got a nasty frightened feeling—a horrid feeling that she's too strong for us."

"What? That mess of rags?"

"Yes, that horrible limp mess of rags. Because, you see, she's so determined."

"Determined?"

"To have her own way. This is *her* room now!"

"Yes," said Alicia Coombe, looking round, "it is, isn't it? Of course, it always was, when you come to think of it—the colors and everything . . . I thought she fitted in here, but it's the room that fits her. I must say," added the dressmaker, with a touch of briskness in her voice, "it's rather absurd when a doll comes and takes possession of things like this. You know, Mrs. Groves won't come in here any longer and clean."

"Does she say she's frightened of the doll?"

"No. She just makes excuses of some kind or other." Then Alicia added with a hint of panic, "What are we going to do, Sybil? It's getting me down, you know. I haven't been able to design anything for weeks."

"I can't keep my mind on cutting out properly," Sybil confessed. "I make all sorts of silly mistakes. Perhaps," she said uncertainly, "your idea of writing to the psychical research people might do some good."

"Just make us look like a couple of fools," said Alicia Coombe. "I didn't seriously mean it. No, I suppose we'll just have to go on until—"

"Until what?"

"Oh, I don't know," said Alicia, and she laughed uncertainly.

On the following day Sybil, when she arrived, found the door of the fitting room locked.

"Miss Coombe, have you got the key? Did you lock this last night?"

"Yes," said Alicia Coombe, "I locked it and it's going to stay locked."

"What do you mean?"

"I just mean I've given up the room. The doll can have it. We don't need two rooms. We can fit in here."

"But it's your own private sitting room."

"Well, I don't want it any more. I've got a very nice bedroom. I can make a bed-sitting room out of that, can't I?"

"Do you mean you're really not going into that fitting room ever again?" said Sybil incredulously.

"That's exactly what I mean."

"But—what about cleaning? It'll get in a terrible state."

"Let it!" said Alicia Coombe. "If this place is suffering from some kind of possession by a doll, all right—let her keep possession. And clean the room herself." And she added, "She hates us, you know."

"What do you mean?" said Sybil. "The doll *hates* us?"

"Yes," said Alicia. "Didn't you know? You must have known. You must have seen it when you looked at her."

"Yes," said Sybil thoughtfully, "I suppose I did. I suppose I felt like that all along—that she hated us and wanted to get us out of there."

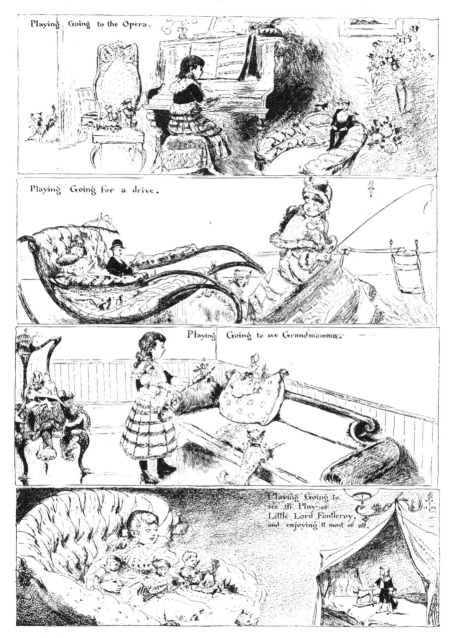

Dolls in the nineteenth century occupied the child from morning to night. It is not surprising that fantasy life extended to the creation of many memorable stories about dolls.

"She's a malicious little thing," said Alicia Coombe. "Anyway, she ought to be satisfied now."

Things went on rather more peacefully after that. Alicia Coombe announced to her staff that she was giving up the use of the fitting room for the present —it made too many rooms to dust and clean, she explained.

But it hardly helped her to overhear one of the work girls saying to another on the evening of the same day, "She really is batty, Miss Coombe is now. I always thought she was a bit queer—the way she lost things and forgot things. But it's really beyond anything now, isn't it? She's got a sort of thing about that doll downstairs."

"Ooo, you don't think she'll go really bats, do you?" said the other girl. "That she might knife us or something?"

They passed, chattering, and Alicia sat up indignantly in her chair. Going bats indeed! Then she added ruefully, to herself, "I suppose, if it wasn't for Sybil, I should think myself that I was going bats. But with me and Sybil and Mrs. Groves too, well, it does look as though there was *something* in it. But what I don't see is, how is it going to end?"

Three weeks later, Sybil said to Alicia Coombe, "We've got to go into that room *sometime*."

"Why?"

"Well, I mean, it must be in a filthy state. Moths will be getting into things, and all that. We ought just to dust and sweep it and then lock it up again."

"I'd much rather keep it shut up and not go back in there," said Alicia Coombe.

Sybil said, "Really, you know, you're even more superstitious than I am."

"I suppose I am," said Alicia Coombe. "I was much more ready to believe in all this than you were, but to begin with, you know—I—well, I found it exciting in an odd sort of way. I don't know. I'm just scared, and I'd rather not go into that room again."

"Well, I want to," said Sybil, "and I'm going to."

"You know what's the matter with you?" said Alicia Coombe. "You're simply curious, that's all."

"All right, then I'm curious. I want to see what the doll's done."

"I still think it's much better to leave her alone," said Alicia. "Now we've got out of that room, she's satisfied. You'd better leave her satisfied." She gave an exasperated sigh. "What nonsense we are talking!"

"Yes, I know we're talking nonsense, but if you tell me of any way of *not* talking nonsense—come on, now, give me that key."

"All right, all right."

"I believe you're afraid I'll let her out or something. I should think she was the kind that could pass through doors or windows."

Sybil unlocked the door and went in.

"How terribly odd," she said.

"What's odd?" said Alicia Coombe, peering over her shoulder.

"The room hardly seems dusty at all, does it? You'd think, after being shut up all this time—"

"Yes, it is odd."

"There she is," said Sybil.

The doll was on the sofa. She was not lying in her usual limp position. She was sitting upright, a cushion behind her back. She had the air of the mistress of the house, waiting to receive people.

"Well," said Alicia Coombe, "she seems at home all right, doesn't she? I almost feel I ought to apologize for coming in."

"Let's go," said Sybil.

She backed out, pulled the door to, and locked it again.

The two women gazed at each other.

"I wish I knew," said Alicia Coombe, "why it scares us so much . . ."

"My goodness, who wouldn't be scared?"

"Well, I mean, what *happens,* after all? It's nothing really—just a kind of puppet that gets moved around the room. I expect it isn't the puppet itself— it's a poltergeist."

"Now that *is* a good idea."

"Yes, but I don't really believe it. I think it's—it's that doll."

"Are you *sure* you don't know where she really came from?"

"I haven't the faintest idea," said Alicia. "And the more I think of it the more I'm perfectly certain that I didn't buy her, and that nobody gave her to me. I think she—well, she just came."

"Do you think she'll—ever go?"

"Really," said Alicia, "I don't see why she should . . . She's got all she wants."

But it seemed that the doll had not got all she wanted. The next day, when Sybil went into the showroom, she drew in her breath with a sudden gasp. Then she called up the stairs.

"Miss Coombe, Miss Coombe, come down here."

"What's the matter?"

Alicia Coombe, who had got up late, came down the stairs, hobbling a little precariously for she had rheumatism in her right knee.

"What is the matter with you, Sybil?"

"Look. Look what's happened now."

They stood in the doorway of the showroom. Sitting on a sofa, sprawled easily over the arm of it, was the doll.

"She's got out," said Sybil. *"She's got out of that room!* She wants this room as well."

Alicia Coombe sat down by the door. "In the end," she said, "I suppose she'll want the whole shop."

"She might," said Sybil.

"You nasty, sly, malicious brute," said Alicia, addressing the doll. "Why do you want to come and pester us so? We don't want you."

It seemed to her, and to Sybil too, that the doll moved very slightly. It was as though its limbs relaxed still further. A long limp arm was lying on the arm of the sofa and the half-hidden face looked as if it were peering from under the arm. And it was a sly, malicious look.

"Horrible creature," said Alicia. "I can't bear it! I can't bear it any longer."

Suddenly, taking Sybil completely by surprise, she dashed across the room, picked up the doll, ran to the window, opened it, and flung the doll out into the street. There was a gasp and a half-cry of fear from Sybil.

"Oh, Alicia, you shouldn't have done that! I'm sure you shouldn't have done that!"

"I had to do something," said Alicia Coombe. "I just couldn't stand it any more."

Sybil joined her at the window. Down below on the pavement the doll lay, loose-limbed, face down.

"You've *killed* her," said Sybil.

"Don't be absurd . . . How can I kill something that's made of velvet and silk, bits and pieces? It's not real."

"It's horribly real," said Sybil.

Alicia caught her breath.

"Good heavens. That child—"

A small ragged girl was standing over the doll on the pavement. She looked up and down the street—a street that was not unduly crowded at this time of the morning though there was some automobile traffic; then, as though satisfied, the child bent, picked up the doll, and ran across the street.

"Stop, stop!" called Alicia.

She turned to Sybil.

"That child mustn't take the doll. She *mustn't!* That doll is dangerous—it's evil. We've got to stop her."

It was not they who stopped her. It was the traffic. At that moment three taxis came down one way and two tradesmen's vans in the other direction. The child was marooned on an island in the middle of the road. Sybil rushed down the stairs, Alicia

Coombe following her. Dodging between a trades-
man's van and a private car, Sybil, with Alicia
Coombe directly behind her, arrived on the island
before the child could get through the traffic on the
opposite side.

"You can't take that doll," said Alicia Coombe.
"Give her back to me."

The child looked at her. She was a skinny little
girl about eight years old, with a slight squint. Her
face was defiant.

"Why should I give 'er to you?" she said. "Pitched
her out of the window, you did—I saw you. If you
pushed her out of the window, you don't want her,
so now she's mine."

"I'll buy you another doll," said Alicia frantically.
"We'll go to a toy shop—anywhere you like—and I'll
buy you the best doll we can find. But give me back
this one."

"Shan't," said the child.

Her arms went protectingly round the velvet doll.

"You *must* give her back," said Sybil. "She isn't
yours."

She stretched out to take the doll from the child
and at that moment the child stamped her foot,
turned, and screamed at them.

"Shan't! Shan't! Shan't! She's my very own. I love
her. *You* don't love her. You hate her. If you didn't
hate her, you wouldn't of pushed her out of the window. I love her, I tell you, and that's what she
wants. She *wants* to be loved."

And then like an eel, sliding through the vehicles,

the child ran across the street, down an alleyway, and out of sight before the two older women could decide to dodge the cars and follow.

"She's gone," said Alicia.

"She said the doll wanted to be loved," said Sybil.

"Perhaps," said Alicia, "perhaps that's what she wanted all along . . . to be loved . . ."

In the middle of the London traffic the two frightened women stared at each other.

ROSEMARY TIMPERLEY

THE PEG-DOLL

In the history of dolldom, none have been more beloved than the wooden peg-dolls. In America pioneer
parents whittled these dolls themselves for their children. In Britain and Germany, however, as well as
other spots on the Continent, a legion of doll makers
came into being for the audience of doll lovers that
covered the world.

Among the collectors of dolls, none was more
delighted with them than the young Princess Vic-
toria; a lonely child, she collected many. Indeed, she
had 132, which she knew by name, and nearly all of
them she dressed herself. Most, too, were pegged
wooden dolls from three to nine inches tall. Her dolls
had a "queer mixture of infancy and matronliness in
their little wooden faces."

Due to the combination of small, sharp noses and
bright vermilion cheeks, there was something particularly lonely, pathetic and original in the pegged doll.

Something mysterious. Something as though the spirit of the maker, the owner, and perhaps even the trees from which they were made, somehow encompassed a spirit.

It is not surprising that supernatural stories should cling around those enduring pegged dolls of the past. Nor is it surprising that a great contemporary supernatural writer such as Rosemary Timperley should find that they offer her a haunting theme.

IT ALL STARTED in such a commonplace way. Alan came home from work as usual. He'd just completed a job for the demolition contractors who employed him.

"Look what I found on the site today," he said to his wife.

She looked at the object in his hand. "What is it?"

"A very old doll."

The thing was hardly recognizable as a doll. There was a rough head and shoulders, the body tapering away to nothing, and no paintwork or features left.

"It must be at least a hundred years old," he said. "Claver Hall—that's the building we've just knocked down—used to be an orphanage in the nineteenth century. Maybe this belonged to one of the kids."

"How fascinating." Joan took the crude little doll into her hands and studied it. "Is it worth anything?"

"I doubt it. I just thought Alma might like it."

Joan laughed, for Alma, their seven-year-old daughter, was a most un-doll-loving child. Well-meaning friends and relations had given her pretty

The New Doll. *A very early
nineteenth-century wood engraving.
(Manley-Lewis collection)*

dolls at various times and she had treated them with
disdain. They sat neglected in her toy cupboard.

Now the little girl came into the room. She was
small, pale, black-haired and with beautiful brown
eyes.

"What's that?" she asked immediately, looking at
the object in her mother's hands.

"It's a very old doll, darling. Daddy found it at
work. Would you like it?"

Alma stood looking cautiously at the doll, as if it
were some strange animal. Then she put out her

hand and touched it. She passed her fingers over the rough head and shoulders.

"I like her," she said. "Can I take her to bed with me?"

"Of course, darling." Joan was pleased. Sometimes her daughter's unlovingness towards dolls had worried her. As a child herself, her dolls had been her beloved family.

So Alma took the doll to bed with her that night, and Alan and Joan laughed a little afterwards at the way their child despised her pretty, fashionable, painted dolls, yet took this funny little peg-thing straight to her heart. She named it Rosalind.

The parents were less amused as the weeks passed and Alma, who took Rosalind with her wherever she went, became quiet and nervous during the day, and sometimes had bad dreams at night. It was Joan who first connected the change in Alma with the doll. "It's uncanny the way she won't be without it," she said to Alan. "And I don't like the way she insists on taking it to bed with her."

Alan said: "Nonsense. What child hasn't taken a toy to bed at some time?"

"A teddy-bear, or a pretty doll, maybe," said Joan, "but that thing—it's beginning to give me the creeps."

And it was during this conversation that Alma screamed out in the night. Joan dashed up to the bedroom. Alma was saying, sobbingly:

"I didn't mean to be naughty. Don't hurt me any more. Stop!"

And she was talking in her sleep.

Joan didn't wake her. She put her hand on the child's hair and said: "It's all right, darling." Alma quietened but did not wake.

Alan was in the bedroom now, standing just behind Joan, who whispered: "I'm going to take that doll away from her."

Gently, cautiously, she drew back the bedclothes, saw the doll enclosed in Alma's hands, and tried to take it.

Alma screamed, then said: "No—no—I'll do anything if you let me keep her—I won't eat for a week —I promise—"

"For God's sake give it back to her," said Alan.

So Joan stopped trying to take the doll, covered her daughter up again, watched her relax into quiet sleep, then the parents crept out of the room.

"What are we going to do?" Joan asked her husband.

"A child's nightmare——"

"It has something to do with that damned doll. We must find out more about it—where it came from——"

"You know where it came from."

"We must find someone who knows about old dolls."

This was more easily said than done, but they read an article in a magazine by a certain Miss Letherington, who called herself a "plangonologist", collected dolls as a hobby, and knew a lot about them.

So Alan wrote to Miss Letherington, care of the magazine, and asked if he might have her address and come and see her. Her reply was an almost illegible scrawl, but he did get the address and went round there, taking the doll with him. This had not been easy, and he had felt guilty doing it—waiting for a moment when Alma left Rosalind for a second on a chair, turned her back—and then he had grabbed the doll and set out, leaving Joan to comfort the child.

Miss Letherington lived in a bedsitting-room full of dolls. They were of all nationalities, costumes and ages. They crowded together on her bed, her bookshelves, her chairs and on the floor. Miss Letherington was rather like a doll herself. She was neatly made and blank of face.

"Do come in," she said to Alan. "But don't disturb my darlings."

Her "darlings" gazed at him imperviously with glass eyes or empty sockets.

"Thank you for your letter," she said. "Have you brought me another darling for my collection?"

"I'm afraid not," said Alan. "It's your advice I want. Would you look at this doll and tell me what you can about it?" He held out Rosalind. The woman took it into her hands as if it were a living child, so gentle she was.

"Old," she murmured. "Full of pain. Much suffering." Then she added in a more practical voice: "These wooden peg-dolls were very popular in the nineteenth century. I have a similar one and it's 1850. It's rare to have one today, but they were cheap little toys at the time."

"You don't find it sinister?" said Alan.

"No. Only sad. It's not a witchcraft doll. Not

Nineteenth-century engravings of peg-dolls.
(*Manley-Lewis collection*)

many of them survive because they were made of wax—right for sticking pins into."

"So it's just an ordinary old peg-doll," said Alan.

"No doll is ordinary," she reproved him. "All are exciting and individual. I am never sure whether they have characters of their own, or whether they have absorbed the character of someone who has loved them. Where did you find this child?"

"In the ruins of Claver Hall. It used to be an orphanage."

"And once it was a pretty, gay, painted little doll, and someone loved it."

"My daughter loves it. That's the trouble."

"Nonsense," said Miss Letherington. "If your daughter loves this doll, it shows what a sensible girl she is. So many children nowadays fancy dolls in blonde wigs and bikinis with coy expressions."

"Alma, my daughter, has been behaving strangely ever since she had this doll."

"Perhaps she senses its suffering—or the suffering of someone who once owned it."

"But what suffering? Can't you help me?"

Miss Letherington shook her head. "When there is pain in a doll, I feel it," she said. "But the cause of the pain eludes me. Dolls are my children, and no parent ever really knows what is going on in the children's mind. The mind is a secret place." Her voice drifted off. She looked round at her "darlings." "I know which is happy and which is sad and which is unfeeling, but I never know why," she added. "Like any parent."

Alan was shivering. With the cool, businesslike

part of his mind he thought all this was a load of nonsense—and yet——

"What shall I do?" he said.

"Try to find out *why* the poor little thing was so unhappy," said Miss Letherington, quite brusquely. "Learn more about that orphanage, Claver Hall. And if your daughter could be persuaded to part with this dear little child, who has suffered so much, then I'd be delighted to have her in my collection."

Alan stuffed Rosalind back into his pocket and left. He went to the public library, which seemed beautifully sane and down-to-earth contrasted against the doll-infested claustrophobia of Miss Letherington's bedsitter. He found a book on nineteenth-century orphanages. "Claver Hall" was in the index. And as he read the relevant pages, he wondered why he hadn't had the sense to do it before—even before that demolition job in which he had organized the building's destruction.

He read. "Claver Hall was like other orphanages of the period—cold, uncomfortable, short of funds. The children's welfare depended on the personal qualities of those in charge. Often these were not suitable people—as Charles Dickens has shown us. However, Claver Hall ran smoothly enough, except for an unpleasant episode between 1857 and 1860. During this time, a widow called Grace Webb was in charge. She starved the children to line her own pockets. She terrorized them, punished them for "eating too much", and one of her punishments is said to be that she would take away the children's dolls if they were "naughty" or "ate too much". During those three years of Mrs Webb's rule, so many children escaped by either running away or dying, that even the negligent local authorities became suspicious, and Claver Hall was investigated. As a result, Mrs Webb was put in jail, where she died five years later. According to the records, she went mad before she died, believing herself to be haunted by dead children."

Alan went home, the doll heavy in his pocket.

"Have you got Rosalind?" was the first thing Joan asked him. "Alma's been wandering about all day looking for her, like a little ghost."

And Alma came in. "Daddy, did you take her?"

"Take whom?" he said.

"Rosalind, of course."

"Why should I?"

"She's gone. I can't find her."

"Perhaps she wanted to go away." And he felt the doll hard against him in his pocket.

"I wouldn't mind not eating anything ever again if she came back," said Alma, and wandered out again, to continue her search.

Alan told Joan what Miss Letherington had said, and what he'd read at the library. And he drew the peg-doll out of his pocket.

"We must get rid of her," said Joan. She took the doll out of Alan's hands. "It's nothing," she said. "Only a bit of old wood. Nothing. When I first saw it, I didn't even recognize it as a doll. Remember?" She passed her fingers over the rough head and shoulders. Pain shot through her fingers. A bright fire was burning in the grate. To get rid of the pain in her hands as much as anything else, she flung the peg-doll into the fire.

An unearthly voice cried: "You're cruel! I hate you! You're cruel! You're cruel!" And, somewhere, Alma screamed.

Alan and Joan were never to know whether Alma had spoken those words before she screamed, or whether it was some other child's voice entirely.

Alma, still screaming, ran into the room. She knelt down before the brightly blazing fire. She called: "Rosalind!"

And although the fire was burning brightly, so very brightly, the room was cold as death.

M. R. JAMES

THE HAUNTED DOLL'S HOUSE

There is a special joy in the delight of smallness; a particular affection that the peoples of the world have always had for the miniature and, in particular, for dollhouses. Dame Agatha Christie, for example, said that her principal source of indoor amusement as a child was her dollhouses. She had several of them, and the range of doll furniture in the shops in those days was cheap and "enormously enchanting" to the imagination.

The pleasure and delight in dollhouses exploded in the nineteenth century, then went underground for a while to emerge again as it is today, one of the greatest hobbies in the United States and one of the most delightful of collectors' enchantments.

Many consider M. R. James the most important supernatural writer of the twentieth century. The Haunted Doll's House has a history of its own. It

*Everything served as a dollhouse in the nineteenth
century. Dame Agatha Christie was allowed two closets.
An open shelf serves here. (Manley-Lewis collection)*

*was written for that remarkable collection, The
Queen's Doll House Library. This is probably the
smallest fine library in the world, each book bound in
swatches of small pieces of leather. The Queen in the
title was Queen Mary, the grandmother of the present Queen Elizabeth.*

*The Queen's dollhouse was presented to Queen
Mary in 1922 by her loyal subjects. It was designed
by one of Britain's foremost architects. It contains a
garage with a number of limousines, including a
Rolls-Royce; it has a garden, elaborate plumbing,
and in addition to its fascinating little library, a mu-
sical library that contained works of British com-
posers. British craftsmen made all the miniature furniture as well as the murals and paintings, and of
course the very best writers contributed to the library.*

"I SUPPOSE you get stuff of that kind through your hands pretty often?" said Mr. Dillet, as he pointed with his stick to an object which shall be described when the times comes: and when he said it, he lied in his throat, and knew that he lied. Not once in twenty years—perhaps not once in a lifetime—could Mr. Chittenden, skilled as he was in ferreting out the forgotten treasures of half-a-dozen counties, expect to handle such a specimen. It was collectors' palaver, and Mr. Chittenden recognized it as such.

"Stuff of that kind, Mr. Dillet! It's a museum piece, that is."

"Well, I suppose there are museums that'll take anything."

"I've seen one, not as good as that, years back," said Mr. Chittenden, thoughtfully. "But that's not likely to come into the market: and I'm told they 'ave some fine ones of the period over the water. No: I'm only telling you the truth, Mr. Dillet, when I say that if you was to place an unlimited order with me for the very best that could be got—and you know I 'ave facilities for getting to know of such things, and a reputation to maintain—well, all I can say is, I should lead you straight up to that one and say, 'I can't do no better for you than that, Sir.'"

"Hear, hear!" said Mr. Dillet, applauding ironically with the end of his stick on the floor of the shop. "How much are you sticking the innocent American buyer for it, eh?"

"Oh, I shan't be over hard on the buyer, American or otherwise. You see, it stands this way, Mr.

Dillet—if I knew just a bit more about the pedigree——"

"Or just a bit less," Mr. Dillet put in.

"Ha, ha! you will have your joke, Sir. No, but as I was saying, if I knew just a little more than what I do about the piece—though anyone can see for themselves it's a genuine thing, every last corner of it, and there's not been one of my men allowed to so much as touch it since it came into the shop—there'd be another figure in the price I'm asking."

"And what's that: five and twenty?"

"Multiply that by three and you've got it, Sir. Seventy-five's my price."

"And fifty's mine," said Mr. Dillet.

The point of agreement was, of course, somewhere between the two, it does not matter exactly where—I think sixty guineas. But half an hour later the object was being packed, and within an hour Mr. Dillet had called for it in his car and driven away. Mr. Chittenden, holding the cheque in his hand, saw him off from the door with smiles, and returned, still smiling, into the parlour where his wife was making the tea. He stopped at the door.

"It's gone," he said.

"Thank God for that!" said Mrs. Chittenden, putting down the teapot. "Mr. Dillet, was it?"

"Yes, it was."

"Well, I'd sooner it was him than another."

"Oh, I don't know, he ain't a bad feller, my dear."

"May be not, but in my opinion he'd be none the worse for a bit of a shake up."

"Well, if that's your opinion, it's my opinion he's

put himself into the way of getting one. Anyhow, we shan't have no more of it, and that's something to be thankful for."

And so Mr. and Mrs. Chittenden sat down to tea.

And what of Mr. Dillet and of his new acquisition? What it was, the title of this story will have told you. What it was like, I shall have to indicate as well as I can.

There was only just room enough for it in the car, and Mr. Dillet had to sit with the driver: he had also to go slow, for though the rooms of the Doll's House had all been stuffed carefully with soft cotton-wool, jolting was to be avoided, in view of the immense number of small objects which thronged them; and the ten-mile drive was an anxious time for him, in spite of all the precautions he insisted upon. At last his front door was reached, and Collins, the butler, came out.

"Look here, Collins, you must help me with this thing—it's a delicate job. We must get it out upright, see? It's full of little things that mustn't be displaced more than we can help. Let's see, where shall we have it? (After a pause for consideration.) Really, I think I shall have to put it in my own room, to begin with at any rate. On the big table—that's it."

It was conveyed—with much talking—to Mr. Dillet's spacious room on the first floor, looking out on the drive. The sheeting was unwound from it, and the front thrown open, and for the next hour or two Mr. Dillet was fully occupied in extracting the padding and setting in order the contents of the rooms.

When this thoroughly congenial task was finished,

I must say that it would have been difficult to find a more perfect and attractive specimen of a Doll's House in Strawberry Hill Gothic than that which now stood on Mr. Dillet's large kneehole table, lighted up by the evening sun which came slanting through three tall sash-windows.

It was quite six feet long, including the Chapel or Oratory which flanked the front on the left as you faced it, and the stable on the right. The main block of the house was, as I have said, in the Gothic manner; that is to say, the windows had pointed arches and were surmounted by what are called ogival hoods, with crockets and finials such as we see on the canopies of tombs built into church walls. At the angles were absurd turrets covered with arched panels. The Chapel had pinnacles and buttresses and a bell in the turret and coloured glass in the windows. When the front of the house was open you saw four large rooms, bedroom, dining-room, drawing-room and kitchen, each with its appropriate furniture in a very complete state.

The stable on the right was in two storeys, with its proper complement of horses, coaches and grooms, and with its clock and Gothic cupola for the clock bell.

Pages, of course, might be written on the outfit of the mansion—how many frying pans, how many gilt chairs, what pictures, carpets, chandeliers, four-posters, table linen, glass, crockery and plate it possessed; but all this must be left to the imagination. I will only say that the base or plinth on which the house stood (for it was fitted with one of some depth

which allowed of a flight of steps to the front door
and a terrace, partly balustraded) contained a shallow drawer or drawers in which were neatly stored
sets of embroidered curtains, changes of raiment for
the inmates, and, in short, all the materials for an
infinite series of variations and refittings of the most ab-
sorbing and delightful kind.

"Quintessence of Horace Walpole, that's what it
is: he must have had something to do with the making of it." Such was Mr. Dillet's murmured reflection
as he knelt before it in a reverent ectasy. "Simply
wonderful; this is my day and no mistake. Five hundred pounds coming in this morning for that cabinet
which I never cared about, and now this tumbling
into my hands for a tenth, at the very most, of what
it would fetch in town. Well, well! It almost makes
one afraid something'll happen to counter it. Let's
have a look at the population, anyhow."

Accordingly, he set them before him in a row.
Again, here is an opportunity, which some would
snatch at, of making an inventory of costume: I am
incapable of it.

There were a gentleman and lady, in blue satin
and brocade respectively. There were two children, a
boy and a girl. There was a cook, a nurse, a foot-
man, and there were the stable servants, two pos-
tillions, a coachman, two grooms.

"Anyone else? Yes, possibly."

The curtains of the four-poster in the bedroom
were closely drawn round four sides of it, and he
put his finger in between them and felt in the
bed. He drew the finger back hastily, for it almost

A scarred, battered, broken yesterday's doll was lovingly nursed.
(*Manley-Lewis collection*)

seemed to him as if something had—not stirred, perhaps, but yielded—in an odd live way as he pressed
it. Then he put back the curtains, which ran on rods
in the proper manner, and extracted from the bed a
white-haired old gentleman in a long linen nightdress
and cap, and laid him down by the rest. The tale
was complete.

Dinner time was now near, so Mr. Dillet spent but
five minutes in putting the lady and children into the
drawing-room, the gentleman into the dining-room,
the servants into the kitchen and stables, and the old
man back into his bed. He retired into his dressing-
room next door, and we see and hear no more of
him until something like eleven o'clock at night.

His whim was to sleep surrounded by some of the
gems of his collection. The big room in which we
have seen him contained his bed: bath, wardrobe,
and all the appliances of dressing were in a com-
modious room adjoining: but his four-poster, which
itself was a valued treasure, stood in the large room
where he sometimes wrote, and often sat, and even
received visitors. Tonight he repaired to it in a
highly complacent frame of mind.

There was no striking clock within earshot—none
on the staircase, none in the stable, none in the distant church tower. Yet it is indubitable that Mr. Dillet was startled out of a very pleasant slumber by a
bell tolling One.

He was so much startled that he did not merely lie
breathless with wide-open eyes, but actually sat up in
his bed.

He never asked himself, till the morning hours,
how it was that, though there was no light at all in

the room, the Doll's House on the kneehole table stood out with complete clearness. But it was so. The effect was that of a bright harvest moon shining full on the front of a big white stone mansion—a quarter of a mile away it might be, and yet every detail was photographically sharp. There were trees about it, too—trees rising behind the chapel and the house. He seemed to be conscious of the scent of a cool still September night. He thought he could hear an occasional stamp and clink from the stables, as of horses stirring. And with another shock he realized that, above the house, he was looking, not at the wall of his room with its pictures, but into the profound blue of a night sky.

There were lights, more than one, in the windows, and he quickly saw that this was no four-roomed house with a movable front, but one of many rooms, and staircases—a real house, but seen as if through the wrong end of a telescope. "You mean to show me something," he muttered to himself, and he gazed earnestly on the lighted windows. They would in real life have been shuttered or curtained, no doubt, he thought; but, as it was, there was nothing to intercept his view of what was being transacted inside the rooms.

Two rooms were lighted—one on the ground floor to the right of the door, one upstairs, on the left— the first brightly enough, the other rather dimly. The lower room was the dining-room: a table was laid, but the meal was over, and only wine and glasses were left on the table. The man of the blue satin and the woman of the brocade were alone in the room, and they were talking very earnestly, seated close together at the table, their elbows on it: every now and again stopping to listen, as it seemed. Once *he* rose, came to the window and opened it and put his head out and his hand to his ear. There was a lighted taper in a silver candlestick on a sideboard. When the man left the window he seemed to leave the room also; and the lady, taper in hand, remained standing and listening. The expression on her face was that of one striving her utmost to keep down a fear that threatened to master her—and succeeding. It was a hateful face, too; broad, flat and sly. Now the man came back and she took some small thing from him and hurried out of the room. He, too, disappeared, but only for a moment or two. The front door slowly opened and he stepped out and stood on the top of the *perron,* looking this way and that; then turned towards the upper window that was lighted, and shook his fist.

It was time to look at that upper window. Through it was seen a four-poster bed: a nurse or other servant in an armchair, evidently sound asleep; in the bed an old man lying: awake, and, one would say, anxious, from the way in which he shifted about and moved his fingers, beating tunes on the coverlet. Beyond the bed a door opened. Light was seen on the ceiling, and the lady came in: she set down her candle on a table, came to the fireside and roused the nurse. In her hand she had an old-fashioned wine bottle, ready uncorked. The nurse took it, poured some of the contents into a little silver saucepan, added some spice and sugar from casters on the table, and set it to warm on the fire. Meanwhile the old man in the bed beckoned feebly to the lady, who came to him, smil-

Nineteenth-century dollhouses. (Manley-Lewis collection)

ing, took his wrist as if to feel his pulse, and bit her lip as if in consternation. He looked at her anxiously, and then pointed to the window, and spoke. She nodded, and did as the man below had done; opened the casement and listened—perhaps rather ostentatiously: then drew in her head and shook it, looking at the old man, who seemed to sigh.

By this time the posset on the fire was steaming, and the nurse poured it into a small two-handled silver bowl and brought it to the bedside. The old man seemed disinclined for it and was waving it away, but the lady and the nurse together bent over him and evidently pressed it upon him. He must have yielded, for they supported him into a sitting position, and put it to his lips. He drank most of it, in several draughts, and they laid him down. The lady left the room, smiling goodnight to him, and took the bowl, the bottle and the silver saucepan with her. The nurse returned to the chair, and there was an interval of complete quiet.

Suddenly the old man started up in his bed—and he must have uttered some cry, for the nurse started out of her chair and made but one step of it to the bedside. He was a sad and terrible sight—flushed in the face, almost to blackness, the eyes glaring whitely, both hands clutching at his heart, foam at his lips.

For a moment the nurse left him, ran to the door, flung it wide open, and, one supposes, screamed aloud for help, then darted back to the bed and seemed to try feverishly to soothe him—to lay him down—anything. But as the lady, her husband, and several servants rushed into the room with horrified faces, the old man collapsed under the nurse's hands and lay back, and the features, contorted with agony and rage, relaxed slowly into calm.

A few moments later, lights showed out to the left of the house, and a coach with flambeaux drove up to the door. A white-wigged man in black got nimbly out and ran up the steps, carrying a small leather trunk-shaped box. He was met in the doorway by the man and his wife, she with her handkerchief clutched between her hands, he with a tragic face, but retaining his self-control. They led the newcomer into the dining-room, where he set his box of papers on the table, and, turning to them, listened with a face of consternation at what they had to tell. He nodded his head again and again, threw out his hands slightly, declined, it seemed, offers of refreshment and lodging for the night, and within a few minutes came slowly down the steps, entering the coach and driving off the way he had come. As the man in blue watched him from the top of the steps, a smile not pleasant to see stole slowly over his fat white face. Darkness fell over the whole scene as the lights of the coach disappeared.

But Mr. Dillet remained sitting up in the bed: he had rightly guessed that there would be a sequel. The house front glimmered out again before long. But now there was a difference. The lights were in other windows, one at the top of the house, the other illuminating the range of coloured windows of the chapel. How he saw through these is not quite obvious, but he did. The interior was as carefully furnished as the rest of the establishment, with its minute red cushions on the desks, its Gothic stall-

canopies, and its western gallery and pinnacled organ
with gold pipes. On the centre of the black and
white pavement was a bier: four tall candles burned
at the corners. On the bier was a coffin covered with
a pall of black velvet.

As he looked the folds of the pall stirred. It
seemed to rise at one end: it slid downwards: it fell
away, exposing the black coffin with its silver handles
and name-plate. One of the tall candlesticks swayed
and toppled over. Ask no more, but turn, as Mr.
Dillet hastily did, and look in at the lighted window
at the top of the house, where a boy and girl lay in
two truckle-beds, and a four-poster for the nurse rose
above them. The nurse was not visible for the moment; but the father and mother were there, dressed
now in mourning, but with very little sign of mourning in their demeanour. Indeed, they were laughing
and talking with a good deal of animation, sometimes to each other, and sometimes throwing a remark to one or other of the children, and again
laughing at the answers. Then the father was seen to
go on tiptoe out of the room, taking with him as he
went a white garment that hung on a peg near the
door. He shut the door after him. A minute or two
later it was slowly opened again, and a muffled head
poked round it. A bent form of sinister shape stepped
across to the truckle-beds, and suddenly stopped,
threw up its arms and revealed, of course, the father,
laughing. The children were in agonies of terror, the
boy with the bedclothes over his head, the girl
throwing herself out of bed into her mother's arms.
Attempts at consolation followed—the parents took

the children on their laps, patted them, picked up the white gown and showed there was no harm in it, and so forth; and at last putting the children back into bed, left the room with encouraging waves of the hand. As they left it, the nurse came in, and soon the light died down.

Still Mr. Dillet watched immovable.

A new sort of light—not of lamp or candle—a pale ugly light, began to dawn around the door-case at the back of the room. The door was opening again. The seer does not like to dwell upon what he saw entering the room: he says it might be described as a frog—the size of a man—but it had scanty white hair about its head. It was busy about the truckle-beds, but not for long. The sound of cries—faint, as if coming out of a vast distance—but, even so, infinitely appalling, reached the ear.

There were signs of a hideous commotion all over the house: lights passed along and up, and doors opened and shut, and running figures passed within the windows. The clock in the stable turret tolled one, and darkness fell again.

It was only dispelled once more, to show the house front. At the bottom of the steps dark figures were drawn up in two lines, holding flaming torches. More dark figures came down the steps, bearing, first one, then another small coffin. And the lines of torch-bearers with the coffins between them moved silently onward to the left.

The hours of night passed on—never so slowly, Mr. Dillet thought. Gradually he sank down from sitting to lying in his bed—but he did not close an eye: and early next morning he sent for the doctor.

The doctor found him in a disquieting state of nerves, and recommended sea air. To a quiet place on the East Coast he accordingly repaired by easy stages in his car.

One of the first people he met on the sea front was Mr. Chittenden, who, it appeared, had likewise been advised to take his wife away for a bit of a change.

Mr. Chittenden looked somewhat askance upon him when they met: and not without cause.

"Well, I don't wonder at you being a bit upset, Mr. Dillet. What? Yes, well, I might say 'orrible upset, to be sure, seeing what me and my poor wife went through ourselves. But I put it to you, Mr. Dillet, one of two things: was I going to scrap a lovely piece like that on the one 'and, or was I going to tell customers: 'I'm selling you a regular picture-palace-dramar in reel life of the olden time, billed to perform regular at one o'clock a.m.'? Why, what would you 'ave said yourself? And next thing you know, two Justices of the Peace in the back parlour, and pore Mr. and Mrs. Chittenden off in a spring cart to the County Asylum and everyone in the street saying, 'Ah, I thought it 'ud come to that. Look at the way the man drank'!—and me next door, or next door but one, to a total abstainer, as you know. Well, there was my position. What? Me 'ave it back in the shop? Well, what do *you* think? No, but I'll tell you what I will do. You shall have your money back, bar the ten pounds I paid for it, and you make what you can."

Later in the day, in what is offensively called the

"smoke-room" of the hotel, a murmured conversation between the two went on for some time.

"How much do you really know about that thing, and where it came from?"

"Honest, Mr. Dillet, I don't know the 'ouse. Of course, it came out of the lumber room of a country 'ouse—that anyone could guess. But I'll go as far as say this, that I believe it's not a hundred miles from this place. Which direction and how far I've no notion. I'm only judging by guesswork. The man as I actually paid the cheque to ain't one of my regular men, and I've lost sight of him; but I 'ave the idea that this part of the country was his beat, and that's every word I can tell you. But now, Mr. Dillet, there's one thing that rather physics me—that old chap—I suppose you saw him drive up to the door— I thought so: now, would he have been the medical man, do you take it? My wife would have it so, but I stuck to it that was the lawyer, because he had papers with him, and one he took out was folded up."

"I agree," said Mr. Dillet. "Thinking it over, I came to the conclusion that was the old man's will, ready to be signed."

"Just what I thought," said Mr. Chittenden, "and I took it that will would have cut out the young people, eh? Well, well! It's been a lesson to me, I know that. I shan't buy no more dolls' houses, nor waste no more money on the pictures—and as to this business of poisonin' grandpa, well, if I know myself, I never 'ad much of a turn for that. Live and let live: that's bin my motto throughout life, and I ain't found it a bad one."

Filled with these elevated sentiments, Mr. Chittenden retired to his lodgings. Mr. Dillet next day repaired to the local institute, where he hoped to find
some clue to the riddle that absorbed him. He gazed
in despair at a long file of the Canterbury and York
Society's publications of the Parish Registers of the
district. No print resembling the house of his nightmare was among those that hung on the staircase
and in the passages. Disconsolate, he found himself at
last in a derelict room, staring at a dusty model of a
church in a dusty glass case:

> *Model of St. Stephen's Church, Coxham. Pre-
> sented by J. Merewether, Esq., of Ilbridge
> House, 1877. The work of his ancestor James
> Merewether, d. 1786.*

There was something in the fashion of it that reminded him dimly of his horror. He retraced his
steps to a wall map he had noticed, and made out
that Ilbridge House was in Coxham Parish. Coxham
was, as it happened, one of the parishes of which he
had retained the name when he glanced over the file
of printed registers, and it was not long before he
found in them the record of the burial of Roger Milford, aged 76, on the 11th of September, 1757, and
of Roger and Elizabeth Merewether, aged 9 and 7,
on the 19th of the same month. It seemed worthwhile to follow up this clue, frail as it was; and in
the afternoon he drove out to Coxham. The east end
of the north aisle of the church is a Milford chapel,
and on its north wall are tablets to the same persons;
Roger, the elder, it seems, was distinguished by all

the qualities which adorn "the Father, the Magistrate, and the Man": the memorial was erected by his attached daughter Elizabeth, "who did not long survive the loss of a parent ever solicitous for her welfare, and of two amiable children." The last sentence was plainly an addition to the original inscription.

A yet later slab told of James Merewether, husband of Elizabeth, "who in the dawn of life practised, not without success, those arts which, had he continued their exercise, might in the opinion of the most competent judges have earned for him the name of the British Vitruvius: but who, overwhelmed by the visitation which deprived him of an affectionate partner and a blooming offspring, passed his Prime and Age in a secluded yet elegant Retirement: his grateful Nephew and Heir indulges a pious sorrow by this too brief recital of his excellences."

The children were more simply commemorated. Both died on the night of the 12th of September.

Mr. Dillet felt sure that in Ilbridge House he had found the scene of his drama. In some old sketch book, possibly in some old print, he may yet find convincing evidence that he is right. But the Ilbridge House of today is not that which he sought; it is an Elizabethan erection of the forties, in red brick with stone quoins and dressings. A quarter of a mile from it, in a low part of the park, backed by ancient, stag-horned, ivy-strangled trees and thick undergrowth, are marks of a terraced platform overgrown with rough grass. A few stone balusters lie here and there, and a heap or two, covered with nettles and ivy, of wrought stones with badly carved crockets. This, someone told Mr. Dillet, was the site of an older house.

As he drove out of the village, the hall clock struck four, and Mr. Dillet started up and clapped his hands to his ears. It was not the first time he had heard that bell.

Awaiting an offer from the other side of the Atlantic, the doll's house still reposes, carefully sheeted, in a loft over Mr. Dillet's stables, whither Collins conveyed it on the day when Mr. Dillet started for the sea coast.

ALGERNON BLACKWOOD

✳◇✳◇✳◇✳◇✳◇✳◇✳◇✳◇✳◇✳◇✳◇✳◇✳

THE DOLL

The doll as an image or likeness of a person (or of an animal, for that matter) is part of the history of magic and witchcraft that goes far back to the time of primitive man. When the very sophisticated, and in many ways, the very civilized Egyptians were on the throne, black magic was still very much of importance. There are manuscripts describing how images or dolls could be made to destroy the Pharaohs themselves. Such confiscated documents were actually found in the royal library.

In Britain at the time of Queen Elizabeth I, an image was once found very near the Queen's dwelling. Even in those days the people believed implicitly that such an image could cause sickness and perhaps even death. It took the royal Doctor Dee to assure the Queen that she was not menaced. He took possession of the doll, and by his own "magic" erased the doll's.

Of all the witchcraft doll stories that have ever been written, none is more eerie, indeed more downright frightening, than Algernon Blackwood's The Doll.

In many ways Algernon Blackwood led a remarkably protected childhood. His family was devoutly religious; his mother was a woman of almost no humor, and his father a very successful civil servant. He was cosseted, fortunately, by nannies and even the stout family butler, who did not share his parents' terrible agony of spirit. His family's fear of a hell was so

Do dolls have a secret life?

complete and overshadowing that this was one of the traits that were to linger in Blackwood's remarkable supernatural writing. Blackwood believed even as an adult that danger was always imminent, that the human race must always be on its guard. He acquired, with these beliefs, all sorts of interest in magic and the esoteric. He began to be fond of what he called "delicious alarm"—delicious alarm that the sky might truly fall in, that there were secret powers latent in man, latent in animals, and even, in dolls.

Of course. (Old sketches from the Manley-Lewis collection)

SOME NIGHTS are merely dark, others are dark in a suggestive way as though something ominous, mysterious, is going to happen. In certain remote outlying suburbs, at any rate, this seems true, where great spaces between the lamps go dead at night, where little happens, where a ring at the door is a summons almost, and people cry "Let's go to town!" In the villa gardens the mangy cedars sigh in the wind, but the hedges stiffen, there is a muffling of spontaneous activity.

On this particular November night a moist breeze barely stirred the silver pine in the narrow drive leading to the "Laurels" where Colonel Masters lived, Colonel Hymber Masters, late of an Indian regiment, with many distinguished letters after his name. The housemaid in the limited staff being out, it was the cook who answered the bell when it rang with a sudden, sharp clang soon after ten o'clock— and gave an audible gasp half of surprise, half of fear. The bell's sudden clangour was an unpleasant and unwelcome sound. Monica, the Colonel's adored yet rather neglected child, was asleep upstairs, but the cook was not frightened lest Monica be disturbed, nor because it seemed a bit late for the bell to ring so violently; she was frightened because when she opened the door to let the fine rain drive in she saw a dark stranger standing on the steps. There in the wind and rain he stood, a tall, slim man holding a parcel.

Wearing a stained yellow mackintosh and dirty slouch hat, and "looking like a devil, so help me,

God," he shoved the little parcel at her out of the gloom, the light from the hall flaring red into his gleaming eyes. "For Colonel Masters," he whispered rapidly, "and very special into his own personal touch and no one else." And he melted away into the night with his "strange foreign accent, his eyes of fire, and his nasty hissing voice."

He was gone, swallowed up in the wind and rain.

"But I saw his eyes," swore the cook the next morning to the housemaid, "his fiery eyes, and his nasty look, and he looked to me—if you know wot I mean—he looked like—death . . ."

Thus the cook, so far as she was intelligently articulate next day, but standing now against the closed door with the small brown-paper parcel in her hands, impressed by the orders that it was to be given into his personal touch, she was relieved by the fact that Colonel Masters never returned till after midnight and that she need not act at once. The reflection brought a certain comfort that restored her equanimity a little, though she still stood there, holding the parcel gingerly in her grimy hands, reluctant, hesitating, uneasy. A parcel, even brought by a mysterious dark stranger, was not in itself frightening, yet frightened she certainly felt. Instinct and superstition worked perhaps; the wind, the rain, the fact of being alone in the house, the unexpected visitor, these also contributed to her discomfort. A vague sense of horror touched her, her Irish blood stirred ancient dreams, so that she began to shake a little, as though the parcel contained something alive, explosive, poisonous, unholy almost, as though it moved, and, her fingers loosening their hold, the parcel—

dropped. It fell on the tiled floor with a queer, sharp clack, but it lay motionless. She eyed it closely, cautiously, but, thank God, it did not move, an inert, brown-paper parcel. Brought by an errand boy in daylight, it might have been groceries, tobacco, even a mended shirt. She peeped and tinkered, that sharp clack puzzled her. Then, after a few minutes, remembering her duty, she picked it up gingerly even while she shivered. It was to be handed into the Colonel's "personal touch." She compromised, deciding to place it on his desk and to tell him about it in the morning; only Colonel Masters, with those mysterious years in the East behind him, his temper and his tyrannical orders, was not easy of direct approach at the best of times, in the morning least of all.

The cook left it at that—that is, she left it on the desk in his study, but left out all explanations about its arrival. She had decided to be vague about such unimportant details, for Mrs. O'Reilly was afraid of Colonel Masters, and only his professed love of Monica made her believe that he was quite human. He paid her well, oh yes, and sometimes he smiled, and he was a handsome man, if a bit too dark for her fancy, yet he also paid her an occasional compliment about her curry, and that soothed her for the moment. They suited one another, at any rate, and she stayed, robbing him comfortably, if cautiously.

"It ain't no good," she assured the housemaid next day, "wot with that 'personal touch into his hands, and no one else,' and that dark man's eyes and that clack when it came away in my hands and fell on the floor. It ain't no good, not to us nor anybody. No man like him means lucky stars to anybody. A parcel indeed—with those devil's eyes—"

"What did you do with it?" enquired the housemaid.

The cook looked her up and down. "Put it in the fire o'course," she replied. "On the stove if you want to know exact."

It was the housemaid's turn to look the cook up and down.

"I don't think," she remarked.

The cook reflected, probably because she found no immediate answer.

"Well," she puffed out presently, "d'you know wot *I* think? You don't. So I'll tell you. It was something the master's afraid of, that's wot it was. He's afraid of something—ever since I been here I've known that. And that's wot it was. He done somebody wrong in India long ago and that lanky stranger brought wot's coming to him, and that's why I say I put it on the stove—see?" She dropped her voice. "It was a bloody idol," she whispered, "that's wot it was, that parcel, and he—why, he's a bloody secret worshipper." And she crossed herself. "That's why I said I put it on the stove—see?"

The housemaid stared and gasped.

"And you mark my words, young Jane!" added the cook, turning to her dough.

And there the matter rested for a period, for the cook, being Irish, had more laughter in her than tears, and beyond admitting to the scared housemaid that she had not really burnt the parcel but had left it on the study table, she almost forgot the incident.

It was not her job, in any case, to answer the front door. She had "delivered" the parcel. Her conscience was quite clear.

Thus, nobody "marked her words" apparently, for nothing untoward happened, as the way is in remote Suburbia, and Monica in her lonely play was happy, and Colonel Masters as tyrannical and grim as ever. The moist wintry wind blew through the silver pine, the rain beat against the bow window and no one called. For a week this lasted, a longish time in uneventful Suburbia.

But suddenly one morning Colonel Masters rang his study bell and, the housemaid being upstairs, it was the cook who answered. He held a brown-paper parcel in his hands, half opened, the string dangling.

"I found this on my desk. I haven't been in my room for a week. Who brought it? And when did it come?" His face, yellow as usual, held a fiery tinge.

Mrs. O'Reilly replied, post-dating the arrival vaguely.

"I asked *who* brought it?" he insisted sharply.

"A stranger," she fumbled. "Not any one," she added nervously, "from hereabouts. No one I ever seen before. It was a man."

"What did he look like?" The question came like a bullet.

Mrs. O'Reilly was rather taken by surprise. "D-darkish," she stumbled. "Very darkish," she added, "if I saw him right. Only he came and went so quick I didn't get his face proper like, and . . ."

"Any message?" the Colonel cut her short.

She hesitated. "There was no answer," she began, remembering former occasions.

"Any *message,* I asked you?" he thundered.

"No message, sir, none at all. And he was gone before I could get his name and address, sir."

In another minute she would have burst into tears or dropped to the floor in a faint, such was her terror of her employer, especially when she was lying blind. The Colonel, however, saved her both disasters by abruptly holding out the half opened parcel towards her. He neither cross-examined nor cursed her as she had expected. He spoke with the curtness that betrayed anger and anxiety, almost, it occurred to her, distress.

"Take it away and burn it," he ordered in his army voice, passing it into her outstretched hands. "Burn it," he repeated it, "or chuck the damned thing away." He almost flung it at her as though he did not want to touch it. "If the man comes back," he ordered in a voice of steel, "tell him it's been destroyed—and say *it didn't reach me,*" laying tremendous emphasis on the final words. "You understand?" He almost chucked it at her.

"Yes, sir. Exactly, sir," and she turned and stumbled out, holding the parcel gingerly in her arms rather than in her hands and fingers, as though it contained something that might bite or sting.

Yet her fear had somehow lessened, for if he, Colonel Masters, could treat the parcel so contemptuously, why should she feel afraid of it. And, once alone in her kitchen among her household gods, she opened it. Turning back the thick paper wrappings, she started, and to her rather disappointed amazement, she found herself staring at nothing but a fair, waxen-faced doll that could be bought in any toy-shop for one shilling and sixpence. A commonplace little cheap doll! Its face was pallid, white, expressionless, its flaxen hair was dirty, its tiny ill-shaped hands and fingers lay motionless by its side, its mouth was closed, though somehow grinning, no teeth visible, its eyelashes ridiculously like a worn tooth brush, its entire presentment in its flimsy skirt, contemptible, harmless, even ugly.

A doll! She giggled to herself, all fear evaporated.

"Gawd!" she thought. "The master must have a conscience like the floor of a parrot's cage! And worse than that!" She was too afraid of him to despise him, her feeling was probably more like pity. "At any rate," she reflected, "he had the wind up pretty bad. It was something else he expected—not a two penny halfpenny doll!" Her warm heart felt almost sorry for him.

Instead of "chucking the damned thing away or burning it," however,—for it was quite a nice looking doll, she presented it to Monica, and Monica, having few new toys, instantly adored it, promising faithfully, as gravely warned by Mrs. O'Reilly, that she would never *never* let her father know she had it.

Her father, Colonel Hymber Masters, was, it seems, what's called a "disappointed" man, a man whose fate forced him to live in surroundings he detested, disappointed in his career probably, possibly in love as well, Monica a love-child doubtless, and limited by his pension to face daily conditions that he loathed.

He was a silent, bitter sort of fellow, no more than that, and not so much disliked in the neighbourhood, as misunderstood. A sombre man they reckoned him,

with his dark, furrowed face and silent ways. Yet
"dark" in the suburbs meant mysterious, and "silent"
invited female fantasy to fill the vacuum. It's the
frank, corn-haired man who invites sympathy and
generous comment. He enjoyed his Bridge, however,
and was accepted as a first-class player. Thus, he
went out nightly, and rarely came back before midnight. He was welcome among the gamblers evidently, while the fact that he had an adored child at
home softened the picture of this "mysterious" man.
Monica, though rarely seen, appealed to the women
of the neighbourhood, and "whatever her origin"
said the gossips, "he loves her."

To Monica, meanwhile, in her rather play-less,
toy-less life, the doll, her new treasure, was a spot of
gold. The fact that it was a "secret" present from
her father, added to its value. Many other presents
had come to her like that; she thought nothing of it;
only, he had never given her a doll before, and it
spelt rapture. Never, never, would she betray her
pleasure and delight; it should remain her secret and
his; and that made her love it all the more. She
loved her father too, his taciturn silence was something she vaguely respected and adored. "That's just
like father," she always said, when a strange new
present came, and she knew instinctively that she
must never say *Thank you* for it, for that was part of
the lovely game between them. But this doll was ex-
ceptionally marvellous.

"It's much more real and alive than my Teddy
bears," she told the cook, after examining it crit-
ically. "What ever made him think of it? Why, it
even talks to me!" and she cuddled and fondled the

half misshapened toy. "It's my baby," she cried, taking it against her cheek.

For no Teddy bear could really be a child; cuddly bears were not offspring, whereas a doll was a potential baby. It brought sweetness, as both cook and governess realised, into a rather grim house, hope and tenderness, a maternal flavour almost, something anyhow that no young bear could possibly bring. A child, a human baby! And yet both cook and governess—for both were present at the actual delivery —recalled later that Monica opened the parcel and recognised the doll with a yell of wild delight that seemed almost a scream of pain. There was this too high note of delirious exultation as though some instinctive horror or revulsion were instantly smothered and obliterated in a whirl of overmastering joy. It was Madame Jodzka who recalled—long afterwards —this singular contradiction.

"I did think she shrieked at it a bit, now you ask me," admitted Mrs. O'Reilly later, though at the actual moment all she said was "Oh, lovely, darling, ain't it a pet!" While all Madame Jodzka said was a cautionary "If you squash its mouth like that, Monica, it won't be able to breathe!"

While Monica, paying no attention to either of them, fell to cuddling the doll with ecstasy.

A cheap little flaxen-haired, waxen-faced doll.

That so strange a case should come to us at second hand is, admittedly, a pity; that so much of the information should reach us largely through a cook and housemaid and through a foreigner of questionable validity, is equally unfortunate. Where precisely the reported facts creep across the feathery frontier into the incredible and thence into the fantastic would need the spider's thread of the big telescopes to define. With the eye to the telescope, the thread of that New Zealand spider seems thick as a rope; but with the eye examining second-hand reports the thread becomes elusive gossamer.

The Polish governess, Madame Jodzka, left the house rather abruptly. Though adored by Monica and accepted by Colonel Masters, she left not long after the arrival of the doll. She was a comely, youngish widow of birth and breeding, tactful, discreet, understanding. She adored Monica, and Monica was happy with her; she feared her employer, yet perhaps secretly admired him as the strong, silent, dominating Englishman. He gave her great freedom, she never took liberties, everything went smoothly. The pay was good and she needed it. Then, suddenly she left. In the suddenness of her departure, as in the odd reason she gave for leaving, lie doubtless the first hints of this remarkable affair, creeping across that "feathery frontier" into the incredible and fantastic. An understandable reason she gave for leaving was that she was too frightened to stay in the house another night. She left at twenty-four hours' notice. Her reason was absurd, even if understandable, because any woman might find herself so frightened in a certain building that it has become intolerable to her nerves. Foolish or otherwise, this is understandable. An *idée fixe,* an obsession, once lodged in the mind of a superstitious, therefore hysterically-favoured woman, cannot be dislodged by argument. It may be absurd, yet it is "understandable."

The story behind the reason for Madame Jodzka's sudden terror is another matter, and it is best given quite simply. It relates to the doll. She swears by all her gods that she saw the doll "walking by itself." It was walking in a disjointed, hoppity, hideous fashion across the bed in which Monica lay sleeping.

In the gleam of the night-light, Madame Jodzka swears she saw this happen. She was half inside the opened door, peeping in, as her habit, and duty decreed, to see if all was well with the child before going up to bed herself. The light, if faint, was clear. A jerky movement on the counterpane first caught her attention, for a smallish object seemed blundering awkwardly across its slippery silken surface. Something rolling, possibly, some object Monica had left outside on falling asleep rolling mechanically as the child shifted or turned over.

After staring for some seconds, she then saw that it was not merely an "object," since it had a living outline, nor was it rolling mechanically, or sliding, as she had first imagined. It was horribly taking steps, small but quite deliberate steps as though alive. It had a tiny, dreadful face, it had an expressionless tiny face, and the face had eyes—small, brightly shining eyes, and the eyes looked straight at Madame Jodzka.

She watched for a few seconds thunderstruck, and then suddenly realised with a shock of utter horror that this small, purposive monster was the doll, Monica's doll! And this doll was moving towards her across the tumbled surface of the counterpane. It was coming in her direction—straight at her.

Madame Jodzka gripped herself, physically and mentally, making a great effort, it seems, to deny the abnormal, the incredible. She denied the ice in her veins and down her spine. She prayed. She thought frantically of her priest in Warsaw. Making no audible sound, she screamed in her mind. But the doll, quickening its pace, came hobbling straight towards her, its glassy eyes fixed hard upon her own.

Then Madame Jodzka fainted.

That she was, in some ways, a remarkable woman, with a sense of values, is clear from the fact that she realised this story "wouldn't wash," for she confided it only to the cook in cautious whispers, while giving her employer some more "washable" tale about a family death that obliged her to hurry home to Warsaw. Nor was there the slightest attempt at embroidery, for on recovering consciousness she had recovered her courage, too—and done a remarkable thing: she had compelled herself to investigate. Aided and fortified by her religion, she compelled herself to make an examination. She had tiptoed further into the room, had made sure that Monica was sleeping peacefully, and that the doll lay—motionless —half way down the counterpane. She gave it a long, concentrated look. Its lidless eyes, fringed by hideously ridiculous black lashes, were fixed on space. Its expression was not so much innocent, as blankly stupid, idiotic, a mask of death that aped cheaply a pretence of life, where life could never be. Not ugly merely, it was revolting.

Madame Jodzka, however, did more than study

this visage with concentration, for with admirable
pluck she forced herself to touch the little horror.
She actually picked it up. Her faith, her deep religious conviction, denied the former evidence of her
senses. She had *not* seen movement. It was incredible, impossible. The fault lay somewhere in herself.
This persuasion, at any rate, lasted long enough to
enable her to touch the repulsive little toy, to pick it
up, to lift it. She placed it steadily on the table near
the bed between the bowl of flowers and the night-
light, where it lay on its back helpless, innocent, yet
horrible, and only then on shaking legs did she leave
the room and go up to her own bed. That her fingers
remained ice-cold until eventually she fell asleep can
be explained, of course, too easily and naturally to
claim examination.

Whether imagined or actual, it must have been, none
the less, a horrifying spectacle—a mechanical outline
from a commercial factory walking like a living thing
with a purpose. It holds the nightmare touch. To
Madame Jodzka, protected since youth within cast-
iron tenets, it came as a shock. And a shock dislo-
cates. The sight smashed everything she knew as
possible and real. The flow of her blood was interrupted, it froze, there came icy terror into her heart,
her normal mechanism failed for a moment, she
fainted. And fainting seemed a natural result. Yet it
was the shock of the incredible masquerade that gave
her the courage to act. She loved Monica, apart
from any consideration of paid duty. The sight of
this tiny monstrosity strutting across the counterpane
not far from the child's sleeping face and folded

hands—it was this that enabled her to pick it up with naked fingers and set it out of reach . . .

For hours, before falling asleep, she reviewed the incredible thing, alternately denying the facts, then accepting them, yet taking into sleep finally the assured conviction that her senses had not deceived her. There seems little, indeed, that in a court of law could have been advanced against her character for reliability, for sincerity, for the logic of her detailed account.

"I'm sorry," said Colonel Masters quietly, referring, to her bereavement. He looked searchingly at her. "And Monica will miss you," he added with one of his rare smiles. "She needs you." Then just as she turned away, he suddenly extended his hand. "If perhaps later you can come back—do let me know. Your influence is—so helpful—and good."

She mumbled some phrase with a promise in it, yet she left with a queer, deep impression that it was not merely, not chiefly perhaps, Monica who needed her. She wished he had not used quite those words. A sense of shame lay in her, almost as though she were running away from duty, or at least from a chance to help that God had put in her way. "Your influence is—so good."

Already in the train and on the boat conscience attacked her, biting, scratching, gnawing. She had deserted a child she loved, a child who needed her, because she was scared out of her wits. No, that was a one-sided statement. She had left a house because the Devil had come into it. No, that was only partially true. When a hysterical temperament, engrained since early childhood in fixed dogmas, begins to sift facts and analyse reactions, logic and common sense themselves become confused. Thought led one way, emotion another, and no honest conclusion dawned on her mind.

She hurried on to Warsaw, to a stepfather, a retired General whose gay life had no place for her and who would not welcome her return. It was a derogatory prospect for this youngish widow who had taken a job in order to escape from his vulgar activities to return now empty-handed. Yet it was easier, perhaps, to face a stepfather's selfish anger than to go and tell Colonel Masters her real reason for leaving his service. Her conscience, too, troubled her on another score as thoughts and memories travelled backwards and half-forgotten details emerged.

Those spots of blood, for instance, mentioned by Mrs. O'Reilly, the superstitious Irish cook. She had made it a rule to ignore Mrs. O'Reilly's silly fairy tales, yet now she recalled suddenly those ridiculous discussions about the laundry list and the foolish remarks that the cook and housemaid had let fall.

"But there ain't no paint in a doll, I tell you. It's all sawdust and wax and muck," from the housemaid. "I know red paint when I see it, and that ain't paint, it's blood." And from Mrs. O'Reilly later: "Mother o'God! Another red blob! She's biting her finger-nails—and that's not *my* job . . . !"

The red stains on sheets and pillow cases were puzzling certainly, but Madame Jodzka, hearing these remarks by chance as it were, had paid no particular attention to them at the moment. The laundry lists were hardly her affair. These ridiculous servants anyhow . . . ! And yet, now in the train, those spots of red, be they paint or blood, crept back to trouble her.

Another thing, oddly enough, also troubled her—the ill-defined feeling that she was deserting a man who needed help, help that she could give. It was too vague to put into words. Was it based on his remark that her influence was "good" perhaps? She could not say. It was an intuition, and few intuitions bear analysis. Supporting it, however, was a conviction she had felt since first she entered the service of Colonel Masters, the conviction, namely, that he had a past that frightened him. There was something he had done, something he regretted and was probably ashamed of, something at any rate, for which he feared retribution. A retribution, moreover, he expected; a punishment that would come like a thief in the night and seize him by the throat.

It was against this dreaded vengeance that her influence was "good," a protective influence possibly that her religion supplied, something on the side of the angels, in any case, that her personality provided.

Her mind worked thus, it seems; and whether a concealed admiration for this sombre and mysterious man, an admiration and protective instinct never admitted even to her inmost self, existed below the surface, hidden yet urgent, remains the secret of her own heart.

It was naturally and according to human nature, at any rate, that after a few weeks of her stepfather's outrageous behaviour in the house, his cruelty too, she decided to return. She prayed to her gods inces-

santly, also she found oppressive her sense of neglected duty and failure of self-respect. She returned
to the soulless suburban villa. It was understandable;
the welcome from Monica was also understandable,
the relief and pleasure of Colonel Masters still more
so. It was expressed, this latter, in a courteous message only, tactfully worded, as though she had merely
left for brief necessity, for it was some days before
she actually saw him to speak to. From cook and
housemaid the welcome was voluble and—disquieting. There were no more inexplicable "spots of red,"
but there were other unaccountable happenings even
more distressing.

"She's missed you something terrible," said Mrs.
O'Reilly, "though she's found something else to keep
her quiet—if you like to put it that way." And she
made the sign of the cross.

"The doll?" asked Madame Jodzka with a start of
shocked horror, forcing herself to come straight to
the point and forcing herself also to speak lightly,
casually.

"That's it, Madame. The bleeding doll."

The governess had heard the strange adjective
many times already, but did not know whether to
take it figuratively or not. She chose the latter.

"Blood?" she asked in a lowered voice.

The cook's body gave an odd jerk. "Well," she explained. "I meant more the way it goes on. Like a
thing of flesh and blood, if you get me. And the way
she treats it and plays with it," and her voice, while
loud, had a hush of fear in it somewhere. She held
her arms before her in a protective, shielding way, as
though to ward off aggression.

"Scratches ain't proof of nothing," interjected the housemaid scornfully.

"You mean," asked Madame Jodzka gravely, "there's a question of—of injury—to someone?" She suppressed an involuntary gasp, but paid no attention to the maid's interruption otherwise.

Mrs. O'Reilly seemed to mismanage her breath for a moment.

"It ain't Miss Monica it's after," she announced in a defiant whisper as soon as she recovered herself, "it's someone else. *That's* what I mean. And no man as dark as *he* was," she let herself go, "ever brought no good into a house, not since I was born."

"Someone else—?" repeated Madame Jodzka almost to herself, seizing the vital words.

"You and yer dark man!" interjected the housemaid. "Get along with yer! Thank God I ain't a Christian or anything like that! But I did 'ear them sort of jerky shuffling footsteps one night, I admit, and the doll did look bigger—swollen like—when I peeked in and looked—"

"Stop it!" cried Mrs. O'Reilly, "for you ain't saying what's true or what you reely know."

She turned to the governess.

"There's more talk what means nothing about this doll," she said by way of apology, "than all the fairy tales I was brought up with as a child in Mayo, and I—I wouldn't be believing anything of it."

Turning her back contemptuously on the chattering housemaid, she came close to Madame Jodzka.

"There's no harm coming to Miss Monica, Madame," she whispered vehemently, "you can be quite sure about *her*. Any trouble there may be is for someone else." And again she crossed herself.

Madame Jodzka, in the privacy of her room, reflected between her prayers. She felt a deep, a dreadful uneasiness.

A doll! A cheap, tawdry little toy made in factories by the hundred, by the thousand, a manufactured article of commerce for children to play with . . . But . . .

"The way she treats it and plays with it . . ." rang on in her disturbed mind.

A doll! But for the maternal suggestion, a doll was a pathetic, even horrible plaything, yet to watch a child busy with it involved deep reflections, since here the future mother prophesied. The child fondles and caresses her doll with passionate love, cares for it, seeks its welfare, yet stuffs it down into the perambulator, its head and neck twisted, its limbs broken and contorted, leaving it atrociously upside down so that blood and breathing cannot possibly function, while she runs to the window to see if the rain has stopped or the sun has come out. A blind and hideous automatism dictated by the race, provided nothing of more immediate interest interferes, yet a herd-instinct that overcomes all obstacles, its vitality insuperable. The maternity instinct defies, even denies death. The doll, whether left upside down on the floor with broken teeth and ruined eyes, or lovingly arranged to be overlaid in the night, squashed, tortured, mutilated, survives all cruelties and disasters, and asserts finally its immortal qualities. It is unkillable. It is beyond death.

A child with her doll, reflected Madame Jodzka, is an epitome of nature's remorseless and unconquerable passion, of her dominant purpose—the survival of the race. . . .

Such thoughts, influenced perhaps by her bitter subconscious grievance against nature for depriving her of a child of her own, were unable to hold that level for long; they soon dropped back to the concrete case that perplexed and frightened her—Monica and her flaxen-haired, sightless, idiotic doll. In the middle of her prayers, falling asleep incontinently, she did not even dream of it, and she woke refreshed and vigorous, facing the fact that sooner or later, sooner probably, she would have to speak to her employer.

She watched and listened. She watched Monica; she watched the doll. All seemed as normal as in a thousand other homes. Her mind reviewed the position, and where mind and superstition clashed, the former held its own easily. During her evening off she enjoyed the local cinema, leaving the heated building with the conviction that coloured fantasy benumbed the faculties, and that ordinary life was in itself prosaic. Yet before she had covered the half-mile to the house, her deep, unaccountable uneasiness returned with overmastering power.

Mrs. O'Reilly had seen Monica to bed for her, and it was Mrs. O'Reilly who let her in. Her face was like the dead.

"It's been talking," whispered the cook, even before she closed the door. She was white about the gills.

"Talking! *Who's* been talking? What do you mean?"

Mrs. O'Reilly closed the door softly. "Both," she

stated with dramatic emphasis, then sat down and wiped her face. She looked distraught with fear.

Madame took command, if only a command based on dreadful insecurity.

"Both?" she repeated, in a voice deliberately loud so as to counteract the other's whisper. "What are you talking about?"

"They've *both* been talking—talking together," stated the cook.

The governess kept silent for a moment, fighting to deny a shrinking heart.

"You've heard them talking together, you mean?" she asked presently in a shaking voice that tried to be ordinary.

Mrs. O'Reilly nodded, looking over her shoulder as she did so. Her nerves were, obviously, in rags. "I thought you'd *never* come back," she whimpered. "I could hardly stay in the house."

Madame looked intently into her frightened eyes.

"You *heard* . . . ?" she asked quietly.

"I listened at the door. There were two voices. Different voices."

Madame Jodzka did not insist or cross-examine, as though acute fear helped her to a greater wisdom.

"You mean, Mrs. O'Reilly," she said in flat, quiet tones, "that you heard Miss Monica talking to her doll as she always does, and herself inventing the doll's answers in a changed voice? Isn't that what you mean you heard?"

But Mrs. O'Reilly was not to be shaken. By way of answer she crossed herself and shook her head.

She spoke in a low whisper. "Come up now and listen with me, Madame, and judge for yourself."

Thus, soon after midnight, and Monica long since asleep, these two, the cook and governess in a suburban villa, took up their places in the dark corridor outside a child's bedroom door. It was a quiet windless night; Colonel Masters, whom they both feared, doubtless long since gone to his room in another corner of the ungainly villa. It must have been a long dreary wait before sounds in the child's bedroom first became audible—the low quiet sound of voices talking audibly—two voices. A hushed, secretive, unpleasant sound in the room where Monica slept peacefully with her beloved doll beside her. Yet two voices assuredly, it was.

Both women sat erect, both crossed themselves involuntarily, exchanging glances. Both were bewildered, terrified. Both sat aghast.

What lay in Mrs. O'Reilly's superstitious mind, only the gods of "ould Oireland" can tell, but what the Polish woman's contained was clear as a bell; it was not two voices talking, it was only one. Her ear was pressed against the crack in the door. She listened intently; shaking to the bone, she listened. Voices in sleep-talking, she remembered, changed oddly.

"The child's talking to herself in sleep," she whispered firmly, "and that's all it is, Mrs. O'Reilly. She's just talking in her sleep," she repeated with emphasis to the woman crowding against her shoulder as though in need of support. "Can't you hear it," she added loudly, half angrily, "isn't it the same voice always? Listen carefully and you'll see I'm right."

She listened herself more closely than before.

"Listen! Hark . . . !" she repeated in a breathless

whisper, concentrating her mind upon the curious sound, "isn't that the same voice—answering itself?"

Yet, as she listened, another sound disturbed her concentration, and this time it seemed a sound behind her—a faint, rustling, shuffling sound rather like footsteps hurrying away on tiptoe. She turned her head sharply and found that she had been whispering to no one. There was no one beside her. She was alone in the darkened corridor. Mrs. O'Reilly was gone. From the well of the house below a voice came up in a smothered cry beneath the darkened stairs: "Mother o'God and all the Saints . . ." and more besides.

A gasp of surprise and alarm escaped her, doubtless at finding herself deserted and alone, but in the same instant, exactly as in the story books, came another sound that caught her breath still more aghast —the rattle of a key in the front door below. Colonel Masters, after all, had not yet come in and gone to bed as expected: he was coming in now. Would Mrs. O'Reilly have time to slip across the hall before he caught her? More—and worse—would he come up and peep into Monica's bedroom on his way up to bed, as he rarely did? Madame Jodzka listened, her nerves in rags. She heard him fling down his coat. He was a man quick in such actions. The stick or umbrella was banged down noisily, hastily. The same instant his step sounded on the stairs. He was coming up. Another minute and he would start into the passage where she crouched against Monica's door.

He was mounting rapidly, two stairs at a time.

She, too, was quick in action and decision. She thought in a flash. To be caught crouching outside the door was ludicrous, but to be caught inside the door would be natural and explicable. She acted at once.

With a palpitating heart, she opened the bedroom door and stepped inside. A second later she heard Colonel Masters' tread, as he stumped along the corridor up to bed. He passed the door. He went on. She heard this with intense relief.

Now, inside the room, the door closed behind her, she saw the picture clearly.

Monica, sound asleep, was playing with her beloved doll, but in her sleep. She was indubitably in deep slumber. Her fingers, however, were roughing the doll this way and that, as though some dream perplexed her. The child was mumbling in her sleep, though no words were distinguishable. Muffled sighs and groans issued from her lips. Yet another sound there certainly was, though it could not have issued from the child's mouth. Whence, then, did it come?

Madame Jodzka paused, holding her breath, her heart panting. She watched and listened intently. She heard squeaks and grunts, but a moment's examination convinced her whence these noises came. They did not come from Monica's lips. They issued indubitably from the doll she clutched and twisted in her dream. The joints, as Monica twisted them emitted these odd sounds, as though the sawdust in knees and elbows wheezed and squeaked against the unnatural rubbing. Monica obviously was wholly unconscious of these noises. As the doll's neck screwed round, the material—wax, thread, sawdust—produced this curious grating sound that was almost like syllables of a word or words.

Madame Jodzka stared and listened. She felt icy cold. Seeking for a natural explanation she found none. Prayer and terror raced in her helter-skelter. Her skin began to sweat.

Then, suddenly Monica, her expression peaceful and composed, turned over in her sleep, and the dreadful doll, released from the dream-clutch, fell to one side on the bed and lay apparently lifeless and inert. In which moment, to Madame Jodzka's unbelieving yet horrified ears, it continued to squeak and utter. It went on mouthing by itself. Worse than that, the next instant it stood abruptly upright, rising on its twisted legs. It started moving. It began to move, walking crookedly, across the counterpane. Its glassy, sightless eyes, seemed to look straight at her. It presented an inhuman and appalling picture, a picture of the utterly incredible. With a queer, hoppity motion of its broken legs and joints, it came fumbling and tumbling across the rough unevenness of the slippery counterpane towards her. Its appearance was deliberate and aggressive. The sounds, as of syllables, came with it—strange, meaningless syllables that yet managed to convey anger. It stumbled towards her like a living thing. Its whole presentment conveyed attack.

Once again, this effect of a mere child's toy, aping the life of some awful monstrosity with purpose and passion in its hideous tiny outline, brought collapse to the plucky Polish governess. The rush of blood without control drained her heart, and a moment of unconsciousness supervened so that everything, as it were, turned black.

This time, however, the moment of dark unconsciousness passed instantly: it came and went, almost like a moment of forgetfulness in passion. Passionate it certainly was, for the reaction came upon her like a storm. With recovered consciousness a sudden rage rushed into her woman's heart—perhaps a coward's rage, an exaggerated fury against her own weakness? It rushed, in any case, to help her. She staggered, caught her breath, clutched violently at the cupboard near her, and—recovered her self-control. A fury of resentment blazed through her, fury against this utterly incredible exhibition of a wax doll walking and squawking as though it were something intelligently alive that could utter syllables. Syllables, she felt convinced, in a language she did not know.

If the monstrous can paralyse, it also can affront. The sight and sound of this cheap factory toy behaving with a will and heart of its own stung her into an act of violence that became imperative. For it was more than she could stand. Irresistibly, she rushed forward. She hurled herself against it, her only available weapon the high-heeled shoe her foot kicked loose on the instant, determined to smash down the frightful apparition into fragments and annihilate it. Hysterical, no doubt, she was at the moment, and yet logical: the godless horror must be blotted out of visible existence. This one thing obsessed her—to destroy beyond all possibility of survival. It must be smashed into fragments, into dust.

They stood close, face to face, the glassy eyes staring into her own, her hand held high for the destruction she craved—but the hand did not fall. A stinging pain, sharp as a serpent's bite, darted suddenly through her fingers, wrist and arm, her grip was bro-

ken, the shoe spun sideways across the room, and in
the flickering light of the candle, it seemed to her,
the whole room quivered. Paralysed and helpless, she
stood utterly aghast. What gods or saints could come
to aid her? None. Her own will alone could help her.
Some effort, at any rate, she made, trembling, on the
edge of collapse: "My God!" she heard her half
whispering, strangled voice cry out. "It is not true!
You are a lie! My God denies you! I call upon my
God . . . !"

Whereupon, to her added horror, the dreadful little doll, waving a broken arm, squawked back at her,
as though in definite answer, the strange disjointed
syllables she could not understand, syllables as though
in another tongue. The same instant it collapsed
abruptly on the counterpane like a toy balloon that
had been pricked. It shrank down in a mutilated
mess before her eyes, while Monica—added touch of
horror—stirred uneasily in her sleep, turning over
and stretching out her hands as though feeling
blindly for something that she missed. And this sight
of the innocently sleeping child fumbling instinctively
towards an incomprehensibly evil and dangerous
something that attracted her proved again too strong
for the Polish woman to control.

The blackness intervened a second time.

It was undoubtedly a blur in memory that followed, emotion and superstition proving too much for
common sense to deal with. She just remembers violent, unreasoned action on her part before she came
back to clearer consciousness in her own room, praying volubly on her knees against her own bed. The
interval of transit down the corridor and upstairs

remained a blank. Yet her shoe was with her, clutched tightly in her hand. And she remembered also having clutched an inert, waxen doll with frantic fingers, clutched and crushed and crumpled its awful little frame till the sawdust came spurting from its broken joints and its tiny body was mutilated beyond recognition, if not annihilated . . . then stuffing it down ruthlessly on a table far out of Monica's reach—Monica lying peacefully in deepest sleep. She remembered that. She also saw the clear picture of the small monster lying upside down, grossly untidy, an obscene attitude in the disorder of its flimsy dress and exposed limbs, lying motionless, its eyes crookedly aglint, motionless, yet alive still, alive moreover with intense and malignant purpose.

No duration or intensity of prayer could obliterate the picture.

She knew now that a plain, face to face talk with her employer was essential; her conscience, her peace of mind, her sanity, her sense of duty all demanded this. Deliberately, and she was sure, rightly, she had never once risked a word with the child herself. Danger lay that way, the danger of emphasising something in the child's mind that was best left ignored. But with Colonel Masters, who paid her for her services, believed in her integrity, trusted her, with him there must be an immediate explanation.

An interview was absurdly difficult; in the first place because he loathed and avoided such occasions; secondly because he was so exceedingly impervious to approach, being so rarely even visible at all. At night he came home late, in the mornings no one dared go near him. He expected the little household, its routine once established, to run itself. The only inmate who dared beard him was Mrs. O'Reilly, who periodically, once every six months, walked straight into his study, gave notice, received an addition to her wages, and then left him alone for another six months.

Madame Jodzka, knowing his habits, waylaid him in the hall next morning while Monica was lying down before lunch, as usual. He was on his way out and she had been watching from the upper landing. She had hardly set eyes on him since her return from Warsaw. His lean, upright figure, his dark, emotionless face, she thought magnificent. He was the perfect expression of the soldier. Her heart fluttered as she raced downstairs. Her carefully prepared sentences, however, evaporated when he stopped and looked at her, a jumble of wild words pouring from her in confused English instead. He cut her rigmarole short, though he listened politely enough at first.

"I'm so glad you were able to come back to us, as I told you. Monica missed you very much—"

"She has something now she plays with—"

"The very thing," he interrupted. "No doubt the kind of toy she needs . . . Your excellent judgment . . . Please tell me if there's anything else you think . . ." and he half turned as though to move away.

"But I didn't get it. It's a horrible—*horrible*—"

Colonel Masters uttered one of his rare laughs. "Of course, all children's toys are horrible, but if she's pleased with it . . . I haven't seen it, I'm no judge . . . If you can buy something better—" and he shrugged his shoulders.

"I didn't buy it," she cried desperately. "It was brought. It makes sounds by itself—syllables. I've seen it move—move by itself. It's a doll."

He turned from the front door, which he had just reached, as though he had been shot; the skin held a sudden pallor beneath the flush and something contradicted the blazing eyes, something that seemed to shrink.

"A doll," he repeated in a very quiet voice. "You said—a doll?"

But his eyes and face disconcerted her, so that she merely gave a fumbling account of a parcel that had been brought. His question about a parcel he had ordered strictly to be destroyed added to her confusion.

"Wasn't it?" he asked in a rasping whisper, as though a disobeyed order seemed incredible.

"It was thrown away, I believe," she prevaricated, unable to meet his eyes, anxious to protect the cook as well. "I think Monica—perhaps found it." She despised her lack of courage, but his intensity scattered her wits; she was conscious, moreover, of a strange desire not to give him pain, as though his safety and happiness, not Monica's, were at stake. "It —talks!—as well as *moves*," she cried desperately, forcing herself at last to look at him.

Colonel Masters seemed to stiffen; his breath caught oddly.

"You say Monica has it? Plays with it? You've seen movement and heard sounds like syllables?" He asked the questions in a low voice, almost as though talking to himself. "You've—listened?" he whispered.

Unable to find convincing words, she bowed her head, while some terror in him came across to her

like a blast of icy wind. The man was afraid in his
heart. Instead, however, of some explosive reply by
way of blame or criticism, he spoke quietly, even
calmly: "You did right to come and tell me this—
quite right," adding then in so low a tone that she
barely caught the ominous words, "for I have been
expecting something of the sort . . . sooner or later
. . . it was bound to come . . ." the voice dying
away into the handkerchief he put to his face.

And abruptly then, as though aware of an appeal
for sympathy, an emotional reaction swept her fear
away. Stepping closer, she looked her employer
straight in the eyes.

"See the child for yourself," she said with sudden
firmness. "Come and listen with me. Come into the
bedroom."

She saw him stagger. For a moment he said
nothing.

"Who," he then asked, the low voice unsteady,
"who brought that parcel? I don't seem to remember."

"A man, I believe."

There was a pause that seemed like minutes before
his next question.

"What did he look like?" he asked.

"Dark," she told him, "very dark."

He was shaking like a leaf, the skin of his face
blanched; he leaned against the door, wilted, limp;
unless she somehow took command there threatened
a collapse she did not wish to witness.

"You shall come with me tonight," she said firmly,
"and we shall listen together. Wait till I return now.
I go for brandy," and a minute later as she came
back breathless and watched him gulp down half

a tumbler full, she knew that she had done right in telling him. His obedience proved it, though it seemed strange that cowardice should borrow from its like to produce courage.

"Tonight," she repeated, "tonight after your Bridge. We meet in the corridor outside the bedroom. At half-past twelve."

He pulled himself into an upright position, staring at her fixedly, making a movement of his head, half bow, half nod.

"Twelve thirty," he muttered, "in the passage outside the bedroom door," and using his stick rather heavily, he opened the door and passed out into the drive. She watched him go, aware that her fear had changed to pity, aware also that she watched the stumbling gait of a man too conscience-stricken to know a moment's peace, too frightened even to think of God.

Madame Jodzka kept the appointment; she had eaten no supper, but had stayed in her room—praying. She had first put Monica to bed.

"My doll," the child pleaded, good as gold, after being tucked up. "I must have my doll or else I'll never get to sleep," and Madame Jodzka had brought it with reluctant fingers, placing it on the night-table beside the bed.

"She'll sleep quite comfortably here, Monica, darling. Why not leave her outside the sheets?" It had been carefully mended, she noticed, patched together with pins and stitches.

The child grabbed at it. "I want her in bed beside me, close against me," she said with a happy smile. "We tell each other stories. If she's too far away I can't hear what she says." And she seized it with a cuddling pleasure that made the woman's heart turn cold.

"Of course, darling—if it helps you to fall asleep quickly, you shall have it," and Monica did not see the trembling fingers, nor notice the horror in the face and voice. Indeed, hardly was the doll against her cheek on the pillow, her fingers half stroking the flaxen hair and pink wax cheeks, than her eyes closed, a sigh of deep content breathed out, and Monica was asleep.

Madame Jodzka, fearful of looking behind her, tiptoed to the door, and left the room. In the passage she wiped a cold sweat from her forehead. "God bless her and protect her," her heart murmured, "and may God forgive me if I've sinned."

She kept the appointment; she knew Colonel Masters would keep it, too.

It had been a long wait from eight o'clock till after midnight. With great determination she had kept away from the bedroom door, fearful lest she might hear a sound that would necessitate action on her part: she went to her room and stayed there. But praying exhausted itself, for it both excited and be-trayed her. If her God could help, a brief request alone was needed. To go on praying for help hour by hour was not only an insult to her deity, but it also wore her out physically. She stopped, therefore, and read some pages of a Polish saint which she did not understand. Later she fell into a state of horrified nervous drowse. In due course, she slept . . .

A noise awoke her—steps going softly past her door. A glance at her watch showed eleven o'clock.

The steps, though stealthy, were familiar. Mrs. O'Reilly was waddling up to bed. The sounds died away. Madame Jodzka, a trifle ashamed, though she hardly knew why, returned to her Polish saint, yet determined to keep her ears open. Then slept again . . .

What woke her a second time she could not tell. She was startled. She listened. The night was unpleasantly still, the house quiet as the grave. No casual traffic passed. No wind stirred the gloomy evergreens in the drive. The world outside was silent. And then, as she saw by her watch that it was some minutes after midnight, a sharp click became audible that acted like a pistol shot to her keyed-up nerves. It was the front door closing softly. Steps followed across the hall below, then up the stairs, unsteadily a little. Colonel Masters had come in. He was coming up slowly, unwillingly she felt, to keep the appointment. Madame Jodzka started from her chair, looked in the glass, mumbled a quick confused prayer, and opened her door into the dark passage.

She stiffened, physically and mentally. "Now, he'll hear and perhaps see—for himself," she thought. "And God help him!"

She marched along the passage and reached the door of Monica's bedroom, listening with such intentness that she seemed to hear only the confused running murmur of her own blood. Having reached the appointed spot, she stood stock still and waited while his steps approached. A moment later his bulk blocked the passage, shown up as a dark shadow by the light in the hall below. This bulk came nearer, came right up to her. She believed she said "Good evening," and that he mumbled something about "I said I'd come . . . damned nonsense . . ." or words to that effect, whereupon the couple stood side by side in the darkened silence of the corridor, remote from the rest of the house, and waited without further words. They stood shoulder to shoulder outside the door of Monica's bedroom. Her heart was knocking against her side.

She heard his breathing, there came a whiff of spirits, of stale tobacco smoke, his outline seemed to shift against the wall unsteadily, he moved his feet; and a sudden, extraordinary wave of emotion swept over her, half of protective maternal yearning, half almost of sexual desire, so that for a passing instant she burned to take him in her arms and kiss him savagely, and at the same time shield him from some appalling danger his blunt ignorance laid him open to. With revulsion, pity, and a sense of sin and passion, she acknowledged this odd sudden weakness in herself, but the face of the Warsaw priest flashed across her fuddled mind the next instant. There was evil in the air. This meant the Devil. She felt herself trembling dreadfully, shaking in her shoes, losing her balance, her whole body leaning over, but leaning in his direction. A moment more and she must have fallen towards him, dropped into his arms.

A sound broke the silence, and she drew up just in time. It came from beyond the door, from inside the bedroom.

"Hark!" she whispered, her hand upon his arm, and while he made no movement, spoke no word, she saw his head and shoulders bend down toward the panel of the closed door. There was a noise, upon the other side, there were noises, Monica's voice distinctly recognisable, another slighter, shriller sound accompanying it, breaking in upon it, answering it. Two voices.

"Listen," she repeated in a whisper scarcely audible, and felt his warm hand grip her own so fiercely that it hurt her.

No words were distinguishable at first, just these odd broken sounds of two separate voices in that dark corridor of the silent house—the voice of a child, and the other a strange, faint, hardly a human sound, while yet a voice.

"*Que le bon Dieu—*" she began, then faltered, breath failing her, for she saw Colonel Masters stoop down suddenly and do the last thing that would have occurred to her as likely: he put his eye to the keyhole and kept it there steadily, for the best part of a minute, his hand still gripping her own firmly. He knelt on one knee to keep his balance.

The sounds had ceased, no movement now stirred inside the room. The night-light, she knew, would show him clearly the pillows of the bed, Monica's head, the doll in her arms. Colonel Masters must see clearly anything there was to see, and he yet gave no sign that he saw anything. She experienced a queer sensation for a few seconds—almost as though she had perhaps imagined everything and proved herself a consummate, idiotic, hysterical fool. For a few seconds this ghastly thought flashed over her, the odd silence emphasising it. Had she been, after all, just a crazy lunatic? Had her senses all deceived her? Why

should he see nothing, make no sign? Why had the
voice, the voices, ceased? Not a murmur of any sort
was audible in the room.

Then Colonel Masters, suddenly releasing his grip
of her hand, shuffled on to both feet and stood up
straight, while in the same instant she herself
stiffened, trying to prepare for the angry scorn, the
contemptuous abuse he was about to pour upon her.
Protecting herself against this attack, expecting it,
she was the more amazed at what she did hear:

"I saw it," came in a strangled whisper. "I saw it
walk!"

She stood paralysed.

"It's watching me," he added, scarcely audible.
"*Me!*"

The revulsion of feeling at first left her speechless;
it was the sheer terror in his strangled whisper that
restored a measure of self-possession to her. Yet it
was he who found words first, awful whispered
words, words spoken to himself, it seemed, more than
to her.

"It's what I've always feared—I knew it must
come some day—yet not like this. Not this way."

Then immediately the voice in the room became
audible, and it was a sweet and gentle voice, sincere
and natural, with feeling in it—Monica's childish
voice, pleading:

"Don't go, don't leave me! Come back into bed—
please."

An incomprehensible sound followed, as though by
way of answer. There were syllables in that faint,
creaky tone Madame Jodzka recognised, but syllables
she could not comprehend. They seemed to enter her

like points of ice. She froze. And facing her stood the motionless, inanimate bulk of him, his outline, then leaned over towards her, his lips so close to her own face that, as he spoke, she felt the breath upon her cheek.

"Buth laga . . ." she heard him repeat the syllables to himself again and again. *"Revenge . . .* in Hindustani . . . !" He drew a long, anguished breath. The sounds sank into her like drops of poison, the syllables she had heard several times already but had not understood. At last she understood their meaning. Revenge!

"I must go in, go in," he was mumbling to himself. "I must go in and face it." Her intuition was justified: the danger was not for Monica but for himself. Her sudden protective maternal instinct found its explanation too. The lethal power concentrated in that hideous puppet was aimed at *him.* He began to edge impetuously past her.

"No!" she cried. "I'll go! Let me go in!" pushing him aside with all her strength. But his hand was already on the knob and the next instant the door was open and he was inside the room. On the threshold they stood still a second, side by side, though she was slightly behind, struggling to shove past him and stand protectively in front.

She stared across his shoulder, her eyes so wide open that the intense strain to note everything at once threatened to defeat its own end. Sight, none the less, worked normally; she saw all there was to see, and that was—nothing; nothing unusual, that is, nothing abnormal, nothing terrifying, so that this second time the threat of anti-climax rose to her mind.

Had she worked herself up to this peak of horror
merely to behold Monica lying sound asleep in a safe
and quiet room? The flickering night-light revealed
no more than a child in natural slumber without a
toy of any sort against her pillow. There stood the
glass of water beside the flowers in their saucer, the
picture-book on the sill of the window within reach,
the window opened a little at the bottom, and there
also lay the calm face of Monica with eyes tight shut
upon the pillow. Her breathing was deep and regular, no sign of disquiet anywhere, no hint of disturbance that might have accompanied that pleading
sentence of two minutes ago, except that the bedclothes were perhaps somewhat tumbled. The counterpane humped itself in folds towards the foot of the
bed, she noticed, as though Monica, finding it too
warm, had tossed it away in sleep. No more than
that.

In that first moment Colonel Masters and the governess took in this whole pretty picture complete.
The room was so still that the child's breathing was
distinctly audible. Their eyes roved all over. Nothing
was anywhere in movement. Yet the same instant
Madame Jodzka became aware that there *was* movement. Something stirred. The report came, perhaps,
through her skin, for no sense announced it. It was
undeniable; in that still, silent room there was movement somewhere, and with that unreported movement there was danger.

Certain, rightly or wrongly, that she herself was
safe, also that the quietly sleeping child was safe, she
was equally certain that Colonel Masters was the one
in danger. She knew that in her very bones.

"Wait here by the door," she said almost peremptorily, as she felt him pushing past her further into the quiet room. "You saw it watching you. It's somewhere?—Take care!"

She clutched at him, but he was already beyond her.

"Damned nonsense," he muttered and strode forward.

Never before in her whole life had she admired a man more than in this instant when she saw him moving towards what she knew to be physical and spiritual danger—never before, and never again, was such a hideous and dreadful sight to be repeatable in a woman's life. Pity and horror drowned her in a sea of passionate, futile longing. A man going to meet his fate, it flashed over her, was something none, without power to help, should witness. No human power can stay the course of the stars.

Her eye rested, as it were by chance, on the crumpled ridges and hollows of the discarded counterpane. These lay by the foot of the bed in shadow, confused a little in their contours and their masses. Had Monica not moved, they must have lain thus till morning. But Monica did move. At this particular moment she turned over in her sleep. She stretched her little legs before settling down in the new position, and this stretching squeezed and twisted the contours of the heavy counterpane at the foot of the bed. The tiny landscape altered thus a fraction, its immediate detail shifted. And an outline—a very small outline—emerged. Hitherto, it had lain concealed among the shadows. It emerged now with disconcerting rapidity, as though a spring released it.

Out of its nest of darkness it seemed almost to leap forward. Fast it came, supernaturally fast, its velocity actually shocking, for a shock came with it. It was exceedingly small, it was exceedingly dreadful, its head erect and venomous and the movement of its legs and arms, as of its bitter, glittering eyes, aping humanity. Malignant evil, personified and aggressive, shaped itself in this otherwise ridiculous outline.

It was the doll.

Racing with incredible security across the slippery surface of the crumpled silk counterpane, it dived and climbed and shot forward with an appearance of complete control and deliberate purpose. That it had a definite aim was overwhelmingly obvious. Its fixed, glassy eyes were concentrated upon a point beyond and behind the terrified governess, the point precisely where Colonel Masters, her employer, stood against her shoulder.

A frantic, half protective movement on her part, seemed lost in the air . . .

She turned instinctively, putting an arm about his shoulders, which he instantly flung off.

"Let the bloody thing come," he cried. "I'll deal with it . . . !" He thrust her violently aside.

The doll came at him. The hinges of its diminutive broken arms and its jointed legs emitted a thin, creaking sound as it came darting—the syllables Madame Jodzka had already heard more than once. Syllables she had heard without understanding— "*buth laga*"—but syllables now packed with awful meaning: *Revenge.*

The sounds hissed and squeaked, yet clear as a bell as the beast advanced at this miraculous speed.

Before Colonel Masters could move an inch backwards or forwards in self protection, before he could command himself to any sort of action, or contrive the smallest measure of self defence, it was off the bed and at him. It settled. Savagely, its little jaws of tiny make-believe were bitten deep into Colonel Masters' throat, fastened tightly.

In a flash this happened, in a flash it was over. In Madame Jodzka's memory it remained like the impression of a lightning flash, simultaneously etched in black and white. It had happened in the present as though it had no past. It came and was gone again. Her faculties, as after a vivid lightning, were momentarily paralysed, without past or present. She had witnessed these awful things, but had not realised them. It was this lack of realisation that struck her motionless and dumb.

Colonel Masters, on the other hand, stood beside her quietly as though nothing unusual had happened, wholly master of himself, calm, collected. At the moment of attack no sound had left his lips, there had been no gesture even of defence. Whatever had come, he had apparently accepted. The words that now fell from his lips were, thus, all the more dreadful in their appalling common-placeness.

"Hadn't you better put that counterpane straight a bit . . . perhaps?"

Common sense, as always, enables the gas of hysteria to escape. Madame Jodzka gasped, but she obeyed. Automatically she moved across to do his bidding, yet aware, even as she thus moved, that he flicked something from his neck, as though a wasp, a mosquito, or some poisonous insect, had tried to sting him. She remembered no more than that, for he, in his calmness, had contributed nothing else.

Fumbling with the folds of slippery counterpane she tried to straighten out, she was startled to find that Monica was sitting up in bed, awake.

"Oh, Doska—you here!" the child exclaimed innocently, straight out of sleep and using the affectionate nickname. "And Daddy too! Oh, my goodness . . . !"

"Sm-moothing your bed, darling," she stammered, hardly aware of what she said. "You ought to be asleep. I just looked in to see . . ." She mumbled a few other automatic words.

"And Daddy with you!" repeated the child excitedly, sleep still about her, wondering what it all meant. "Ooh! Ooh!" holding out her arms.

This brief exchange of spoken words, though it takes a minute to describe, occurred simultaneously with the action—perhaps ten seconds all told, for while the governess fumbled with the counterpane, Colonel Masters was in the act of brushing something from his neck. Nothing else was audible, nothing but his quick gasp and sudden intake of breath: but something else—she swears it on her Warsaw priest—was visible. Madame Jodzka maintains by all her gods she saw this other thing.

In moments of paralysing stress it is not the senses that act less speedily nor with less precision; their action, on the contrary, is intensified and speeded up: what takes longer is the registration of their reports. The numbed brain causes the apparent delay; realisation is slowed down.

Madame Jodzka thus only realised a fraction of

a second later what her eyes had indubitably witnessed; a dark-skinned arm slanting in through the open window by the bed and snatching at a small object that lay on the floor after dropping from Colonel Masters' throat, then withdrawing again at lightning speed into the darkness of the night outside.

No one but herself, apparently, had seen this—it was almost supernaturally swift.

"And now you'll be asleep again in two minutes, lucky Monica," Colonel Masters was whispering over by the bed. "I just peeped in to see that you were all right . . ." His voice was thin, dreadfully soundless.

Madame Jodzka, against the door, frozen, terrified, looked on and listened. "Are you quite well, Daddy? Sure? I had a dream, but it's gone now."

"Splendid. Never better in my life. But better still if I saw you sound asleep. Come now, I'll blow out this silly night-light, for that's what woke you up, I'll be bound."

He blew it out, he and the child blew it out together, the latter with sleepy laughter that then hushed. And Colonel Masters tiptoed to join Madame Jodzka at the door. "A lot of damned fuss about nothing," she heard him muttering in that same thin dreadful voice, and then, as they closed the door and stood a moment in the darkened passage, he did suddenly an unexpected thing. He took the Polish woman in his arms, held her fiercely to him for a second, kissed her vehemently, and flung her away.

"Bless you and thank you," he said in a low, angry voice. "You did your best. You made a great fight. But I got what I deserved. I've been waiting years for it." And he was off down the stairs to his own quarters. Half way down he stopped and looked up to where she stood against the rails. "Tell the doctor," he whispered hoarsely, "that I took a sleeping draught—an overdose." And he was gone.

And this was, roughly, what she did tell the doctor next morning when a hurried telephone summons brought him to the bed whereon a dead man lay with a swollen, blackened tongue. She told the same tale at the inquest too and an emptied bottle of a powerful sleeping-draught supported her . . .

And Monica, too young to realise grief beyond its trumpery meaning of a selfishly felt loss, never once —oddly enough—referred to the absence of the lovely doll that had comforted so many hours, proved such an intimate companion day and night in a life that held no other playmates. It seemed forgotten, expunged utterly from her memory, as though it had never existed at all. She stared blankly, stupidly, when a doll was mentioned: she preferred her worn-out Teddy bears. The slate of memory, in this particular, was wiped clean.

"They're so warm and comfy," she described her bears, "and they cuddle without tickling. Besides," she added innocently, "they don't squeak and try to slip away . . ."

Thus in the suburbs, where great spaces between the lamps go dead at night, where the moist wind comes whispering through the mournful branches of the silver pines, where nothing happens and people cry "Let's go to town!" there are occasional stirrings among the dead dry bones that hide behind respectable villa walls . . .

JEROME K. JEROME

❖❖*❖*❖*❖*❖*❖*❖*❖*❖*❖*❖*❖*

THE
DANCING
PARTNER

Frankenstein as a great big doll? Not really, perhaps, but giant dolls fascinated Mary Shelley and her husband, Percy Shelley, when they were in Switzerland in the time immediately before she wrote Frankenstein. *Automatons, many of which were life-size and lifelike dolls or robots being created on the Continent as precision instruments, made "thinking machines" possible.*

From the very earliest history of man there had been a great desire to fashion another living thing. But there were many of those who also thought that the cost of creating such a creature would be placing oneself in league with the devil. Mary Shelley well knew and was inspired by many of these European tales.

She visited the giant dolls, the statues of warriors and saints that struck the hours in the great clocks.

Automatic clockworks led to the construction of automatons and then the mechanical doll. This clock was constructed by Stephen D. Engle of Hazelton, Pennsylvania.

The famous clock in the Frauenkirche, Nuremberg. The clock was decorated in 1356 by an unknown locksmith. The Emperor Charles IV was represented, seated upon a throne; at the stroke of twelve, the seven Electors, large moving figures, passed and bowed before him to the sound of trumpets.

Indeed, the golden age of robots was not in our own time, but actually in the time of Mary Shelley. One life-size, handsome doll dipped his pen in an inkwell and wrote a number of limited words. He was exhibited in Paris at the very end of the eighteenth century and was capable of drawing pictures: ". . . he first sketched the essential features and then added the shading. Finally, he retouched and corrected his work; to do this he raised his hand from time to time so as to get a better view of what he was doing. The various movements of the eyes and hands faithfully imitated nature." The creator of this doll was charged with sorcery.

Jerome K. Jerome's fascinating story is based on the background of this time and this excitement. No one realized at that time that a new world was being entered—one that would propel us into the automation of our late twentieth century.

THIS STORY, commenced MacShaugnassy, comes from Furtwangen, a small town in the Black Forest. There lived there a very wonderful old fellow named Nicholau Geibel. His business was the making of mechanical toys, at which work he had acquired an almost European reputation. He made rabbits that would emerge from the heart of a cabbage, flop their ears, smooth their whiskers, and disappear again; cats that would wash their faces, and mew so naturally that dogs would mistake them for real cats and fly at them; dolls, with phonographs concealed within them, that would raise their hats and say, "Good morning; how do you do?" and some that would even sing a song.

But he was something more than a mere mechanic; he was an artist. His work was with him a hobby, almost a passion. His shop was filled with all manner of strange things that never would, or could, be sold—things he had made for the pure love of

An automaton made by Pierre Jacquet-Droz. (Courtesy of the Deutsches Museum, Munich)

making them. He had contrived a mechanical donkey that would trot for two hours by means of stored electricity, and trot, too, much faster than the live article, and with less need for exertion on the part of the driver; a bird that would shoot up into the air, fly round and round in a circle, and drop to earth at the exact spot from where it started, a skeleton that, supported by an upright iron bar, would dance a hornpipe; a life-size lady doll that could play the fiddle; and a gentleman with a hollow inside who could smoke a pipe and drink more lager beer than any three average German students put together, which is saying much.

Indeed, it was the belief of the town that old Geibel could make a man capable of doing everything that a respectable man need want to do. One day he made a man who did too much, and it came about in this way:

Young Doctor Follen had a baby, and the baby had a birthday. Its first birthday put Doctor Follen's household into somewhat of a flurry, but on the occasion of its second birthday, Mrs. Doctor Follen gave a ball in honour of the event. Old Geibel and his daughter Olga were among the guests.

During the afternoon of the next day some three or four of Olga's bosom friends, who had also been present at the ball, dropped in to have a chat about it. They naturally fell to discussing the men, and to criticizing their dancing. Old Geibel was in the room, but he appeared to be absorbed in his newspaper, and the girls took no notice of him.

"There seem to be fewer men who can dance at every ball you go to," said one of the girls.

"Yes, and don't the ones who can, give themselves airs," said another; "they make quite a favour of asking you."

"And how stupidly they talk," added a third. "They always say exactly the same things: 'How charming you are looking tonight.' 'Do you often go to Vienna? Oh, you should, it's delightful.' 'What a charming dress you have on.' 'What a warm day it has been.' 'Do you like Wagner?' I do wish they'd think of something new."

"Oh, I never mind how they talk," said a fourth. "If a man dances well he may be a fool for all I care."

"He generally is," slipped in a thin girl, rather spitefully.

"I go to a ball to dance," continued the previous speaker, not noticing the interruption. "All I ask of a partner is that he shall hold me firmly, take me round steadily, and not get tired before I do."

"A clockwork figure would be the thing for you," said the girl who had interrupted.

"Bravo!" cried one of the others, clapping her hands, "what a capital idea!"

"What's a capital idea?" they asked.

"Why, a clockwork dancer, or, better still, one that would go by electricity and never run down."

The girls took up the idea with enthusiasm.

"Oh, what a lovely partner he would make," said one; "he would never kick you, or tread on your toes."

"Or tear your dress," said another.

"Or get out of step."

"Or get giddy and lean on you."

"And he would never want to mop his face with his handkerchief. I do hate to see a man do that after every dance."

"And wouldn't want to spend the whole evening in the supper-room."

"Why, with a phonograph inside him to grind out all the stock remarks, you would not be able to tell him from a real man," said the girl who had first suggested the idea.

"Oh yes, you would," said the thin girl, "he would be so much nicer."

Old Geibel had laid down his paper, and was listening with both his ears. On one of the girls glancing in his direction, however, he hurriedly hid himself again behind it.

After the girls were gone, he went into his workshop, where Olga heard him walking up and down, and every now and then chuckling to himself; and that night he talked to her a good deal about dancing and dancing men—asked what they usually said and did—what dances were most popular—what steps were gone through, with many other questions bearing on the subject.

Then for a couple of weeks he kept much to his factory, and was very thoughtful and busy, though prone at unexpected moments to break into a quiet low laugh, as if enjoying a joke that nobody else knew of.

A month later another ball took place in Furtwangen. On this occasion it was given by old Wenzel, the wealthy timber merchant, to celebrate his niece's betrothal, and Geibel and his daughter were again among the invited.

When the hour arrived to set out, Olga sought her father. Not finding him in the house, she tapped at the door of his workshop. He appeared in his shirt-sleeves, looking hot but radiant.

"Don't wait for me," he said, "you go on. I'll follow you. I've got something to finish."

As she turned to obey he called after her, "Tell them I'm going to bring a young man with me—such a nice young man, and an excellent dancer. All the girls will like him." Then he laughed and closed the door.

Her father generally kept his doings secret from everybody, but she had a pretty shrewd suspicion of what he had been planning, and so, to a certain extent, was able to prepare the guests for what was coming. Anticipation ran high, and the arrival of the famous mechanist was eagerly awaited.

At length the sound of wheels was heard outside, followed by a great commotion in the passage, and old Wenzel himself, his jolly face red with excitement and suppressed laughter, burst into the room and announced in stentorian tones:

"Herr Geibel—and a friend."

Herr Geibel and his "friend" entered, greeted with shouts of laughter and applause, and advanced to the centre of the room.

"Allow me, ladies and gentlemen," said Herr Geibel, "to introduce you to my friend, Lieutenant Fritz. Fritz, my dear fellow, bow to the ladies and gentlemen."

Geibel placed his hand encouragingly on Fritz's shoulder, and the lieutenant bowed low, accompanying the action with a harsh clicking noise in his throat, unpleasantly suggestive of a death rattle. But that was only a detail.

"He walks a little stiffly," (old Geibel took his arm and walked him forward a few steps; he certainly did walk stiffly) "but then walking is not his forte. He is essentially a dancing man. I have only been able to teach him the waltz as yet, but at that he is faultless. Come, which of you ladies may I introduce him to as a partner. He keeps perfect time; he never gets tired; he won't kick you or tread on your dress; he will hold you as firmly as you like, and go as quickly or as slowly as you please; he never gets giddy; and he is full of conversation. Come, speak up for yourself, my boy."

The old gentleman twisted one of the buttons at the back of his coat, and immediately Fritz opened his mouth, and in thin tones that appeared to proceed from the back of his head, remarked suddenly, "May I have the pleasure?" and then shut his mouth again with a snap.

That Lieutenant Fritz had made a strong impression on the company was undoubted, yet none of the girls seemed inclined to dance with him. They looked askance at his waxen face, with its staring eyes and fixed smile, and shuddered. At last old Geibel came to the girl who had conceived the idea.

"It is your own suggestion, carried out to the letter," said Geibel, "an electric dancer. You owe it to the gentleman to give him a trial."

She was a bright, saucy little girl, fond of a frolic. Her host added his entreaties, and she consented.

Herr Geibel fixed the figure to her. Its right arm was screwed round her waist, and held her firmly; its delicately jointed left hand was made to fasten itself upon her right. The old toy-maker showed her how to regulate its speed, and how to stop it, and released her.

"It will take you round in a complete circle," he explained. "Be careful that no one knocks against you, and alters its course."

The music struck up. Old Geibel put the current in motion, and Annette and her strange partner began to dance.

For a while everyone stood watching them. The figure performed its purpose admirably. Keeping perfect time and step, and holding its little partner tightly clasped in an unyielding embrace, it revolved steadily, pouring forth at the same time a constant flow of squeaky conversation, broken by brief intervals of grinding silence.

"How charming you are looking tonight," it remarked in its thin, far away voice. "What a lovely day it has been. Do you like dancing? How well our steps agree. You will give me another, won't you? Oh, don't be so cruel. What a charming gown you have on. Isn't waltzing delightful? I could go on dancing for ever—with you. Have you had supper?"

As she grew more familiar with the uncanny creature, the girl's nervousness wore off, and she entered into the fun of the thing.

"Oh, he's just lovely," she cried, laughing, "I could go on dancing with him all my life."

Couple after couple now joined them, and soon all the dancers in the room were whirling round them. Nicholau Geibel stood looking on, beaming with childish delight at his success.

Old Wenzel approached him, and whispered something in his ear. Geibel laughed and nodded, and the two worked their way quietly towards the door.

"This is the young people's house tonight," said Wenzel, as soon as they were outside; "you and I will have a quiet pipe and a glass of hock, over in the counting-house."

Meanwhile the dancing grew more fast and furious. Little Annette loosened the screw regulating her partner's rate of progress, and the figure flew round with her, swifter and swifter. Couple after couple dropped out exhausted, but they only went the faster, till at length they remained dancing alone.

Madder and madder became the waltz. The music lagged behind: the musicians, unable to keep pace, ceased, and sat staring. The younger guests applauded, but the older faces began to grow anxious.

"Hadn't you better stop, dear?" said one of the women. "You'll make yourself so tired."

But Annette did not answer.

"I believe she's fainted," cried out a girl who had caught sight of her face as it was swept by.

One of the men sprang forward and clutched at the figure, but its impetus threw him down on to the floor, where its steel-cased feet laid bare his cheek. The thing evidently did not intend to part with its prize easily.

Had anyone retained a cool head, the figure, one cannot help thinking, might easily have been stopped. Two or three men acting in concert might have lifted it bodily off the floor, or have jabbed it into a corner. But few human heads are capable of remaining cool under excitement. Those who are not present think how stupid must have been those who were; those who are reflect afterwards how simple it would have been to do this, that, or the other, if only they had thought of it at the time.

The women grew hysterical. The men shouted contradictory directions to one another. Two of them made a bungling rush at the figure, which had the result of forcing it out of its orbit in the centre of the room, and sending it crashing against the walls and furniture. A stream of blood showed itself down the girl's white frock, and followed her along the floor. The affair was becoming horrible. The women rushed screaming from the room. The men followed them.

One sensible suggestion was made: "Find Geibel— fetch Geibel."

No one had noticed him leave the room, no one knew where he was. A party went in search of him. The others, too unnerved to go back into the ball-room, crowded outside the door and listened. They could hear the steady whir of the wheels upon the polished floor as the thing spun round and round; the dull thud as every now and again it dashed itself and its burden against some opposing object and ricocheted off in a new direction.

And everlastingly it talked in that thin ghostly voice, repeating over and over the same formula: "How charming you are looking tonight. What a lovely day it has been. . . . Oh, don't be so cruel. . . . I could go on dancing for ever—with you. Have you had supper?"

Of course they sought for Geibel everywhere but where he was. They looked in every room in the house, then they rushed off in a body to his own place, and spent precious minutes in waking up his deaf, old housekeeper. At last it occurred to one of the party that Wenzel was missing also, and then the idea of the counting-house across the yard presented itself to them, and there they found him.

He rose up, very pale, and followed them; and he and old Wenzel forced their way through the crowd of guests gathered outside, and entered the room, and locked the door behind them.

From within there came the muffled sound of low voices and quick steps, followed by a confused scuffling noise, the silence, then the low voices again.

After a time the door opened, and those near it pressed forward to enter, but old Wenzel's broad shoulders barred the way.

"I want you—and you, Bekler," he said, addressing a couple of the older men. His voice was calm, but his face was deadly white. "The rest of you, please go—get the women away as quickly as you can."

From that day old Nicholau Geibel confined himself to the making of mechanical rabbits, and cats that mewed and washed their faces.

ASPECTS OF A DOLL'S LIFE. (*Pictures from the Manley-Lewis collection*)

The bride-doll and a bee.

The traveler.

The bather.

The confidante.

The social being.

The patient.

The doll that's left behind after the child grows up.

MARY DANBY

❖❖*❖*❖*❖*❖*❖*❖*❖*❖*❖*

THE GREY LADY

It is no wonder that Mary Danby, a very fine writer in the supernatural vein as well as one of Britain's most inspired editors, should be interested in supernatural stories about dolls. Her great-great-grandfather, Charles Dickens, who had an extraordinary insight for doll life and their creators, was well ahead of his time in realizing that some toys could be terrifying to children.

He knew the doll world well, and the doll makers. His remarks about dollhouses in The Cricket on the Hearth *are classic:*

> *There were houses in it, finished and*
> *unfinished, for Dolls of all stations in life.*
> *Suburban tenements for Dolls of moderate*
> *means; kitchens and single apartments for*
> *Dolls of the lower classes; capital town*
> *residences for Dolls of high estate. Some of*
> *these establishments were already furnished*

according to estimate, with a view to the
convenience of Dolls of limited income; others,
could be fitted in the most expensive scale, at a
moment's notice, from whole shelves of chairs
and tables, sofas, bedsteads, and upholstery.

In this poignant story Mary Danby speaks of a
doll and the doll maker of the Dickensian period
with her own contemporary touch.

"PEG-DOLL? Buy a peg-doll, sir?"

Billy stood on the corner of Bond Street and Pic-cadilly, where he hoped to find customers among the rich, smartly-dressed shoppers. He was twelve years old, but very small for his age, and the tray of dolls hanging round his neck made him stoop slightly.

A man in a tall hat came by, and holding his arm was a pretty, elegant young girl. Billy stepped forward.

"Peg-doll for the lady, sir?"

The girl stopped and looked at him, at his pale, bony face and uncombed hair, the scraps of clothes that barely covered his skinny frame.

"Oh dear," she said, putting up a tiny, gloved hand to stifle a giggle. "Look, John, he's wearing odd boots!"

"Dash me, so he is!" exclaimed the man. "What peculiar ideas of fashion some people have, eh?" He tweaked at the enormous, floppy bow of orange silk which adorned his neck. "Would you like a peg-doll, precious creature?" he asked.

The girl turned on her heel and, with a dismissive wave of her hand, said: "Heavens, no! They're altogether the quaintest things I ever saw!"

Billy withdrew, as if to protect his dolls from her scorn. They were like people to him—his only friends. He liked to give them names: Princess Paula, Dancing Jenny, Wizard Wonderful, the Silver Prince . . .

A little girl came skipping towards him, followed by her mother. Both were wrapped in warm, woollen cloaks.

"Peg-doll, ma'am? Peg-doll for the little one?"

"Oh, Mama . . . here's a boy with pretty dollies. May I buy one? Please, Mama, oh, please!"

Billy smiled at her and tilted the tray so that she could inspect the dolls. He held them up for her to admire: the Fairy, the Bride, Cinderella, the Snow Queen . . . "Only twopence," he said. "Lovely peg-dolls. Only twopence."

The little girl bought the Cinderella doll, with its ragged skirt and dear little raffia broom. She skipped away down the pavement, and Billy clutched the two coins tightly in his thin and grimy hand.

"Peg-dolls! Buy a peg-doll, sir? Buy a peg-doll, missus?"

A sharp east wind blew down from Piccadilly Circus, and he moved round into Albemarle Street to escape its cold bite. He had no coat to keep him warm —just an old, frayed jacket with holes where the elbows had once been. The daylight was fading fast, and gentlemen were leaving their offices and making for the comfort of their clubs, or their firesides at home, where their lace-capped wives would pour tea

for them and hand round plates of toasted muffins
and seedcake.

A hansom cab drew up at the kerb and a man
leant out. Billy hurried forward eagerly, thinking the
man wished to buy a doll, but he was merely asking
the whereabouts of the nearest flower-seller. Billy told
him, then had to step back quickly to avoid being hit
by the cab's wheel as the horse bounded forward,
stung by the driver's whip. Billy's foot slipped in the
gutter, and two of the dolls fell out of the tray. He
picked them up and gave them a brief wipe on his
sleeve.

"Peg-dolls! Peg-dolls!"

But though he waited until the street-lamps were
lit and the home-going crowds all departed, he could
sell no more that day. He packed the remaining dolls
into a drawstring calico bag and lifted the strap of
the tray over his head. Then, with the tray in one
hand, the bag in the other, and six pennies—his
day's takings—tied up in an old handkerchief, he
trudged to a stall at Oxford Circus where he could
get a cup of soup and a slice of pudding for twopence.

Mrs. Gibbins was talking to her friend Mrs. Fraser
on the steps of number 42 as Billy edged past them,
making for his room at the back of the house.

"'Evening, Mrs. Gibbins," Billy greeted his land-
lady.

"'Evenin', Billy."

Mrs. Fraser cast a knowing eye over the hunched,
shuffling figure, the threadbare clothes. "'E's lookin'
sorry for 'isself," she remarked.

Mrs. Gibbins folded her arms and leant against the doorframe.

"Didn't you 'ear?"

"'Ear? 'Ear what?"

"'E's on 'is own, now, Billy is. 'Is sister went and died on 'im last week. Took very sudden. It were that cold spell, y'see. 'E comes 'ome one day and finds 'er gone. Well *gone*, I mean, she was *there*, but she weren't, if you understand my meaning, Mrs. Fraser. They buried 'er Friday mornin'."

"There now." Mrs. Fraser sucked at a gap in her teeth.

"She was a good girl, was Sarah. Paid me the rent regular and made no noise to speak of. But, then, they came from a very respectable 'ome, y'know. Their father was a clerk or some such."

"Parents dead, eh?"

Mrs. Gibbins nodded. "'S far as I know. Not that they ever used to talk much to me. Kept themselves very private. She used to sit in that back room all day, makin' 'er dolls, and 'e'd be out sellin' 'em . . ."

"What now, then? If she's gone, who's to make the dolls?"

"'Oo indeed?" said Mrs. Gibbins, peering down the gas-lit hallway to see if Billy might be listening. She turned back to Mrs. Fraser and said under her breath: "And what bothers me is, no dolls to sell, no rent money, see? Unless 'e can get work somewhere, o' course, but 'e's none too strong in the body—nor the 'ead, for that matter."

"Weak in the 'ead?" asked Mrs. Fraser.

Mrs. Gibbins shrugged. "'E's not an idiot, I don't mean. Not *wanting*, you understand. But 'e can't read, nor write neither, even though 'is sister could, and she must 'ave tried teachin' 'im. And when I asked 'im what 'is plans was now 'e's on 'is own, 'e gave me this funny look, sort of blank, as if I'd gone and asked 'im the name of the man in the moon."

"You'll 'ave to turn 'im out, I s'pose," said Mrs. Fraser. "That's a nice back room you've got. Someone would be glad to pay as much as two shillin's a week for that, I dare say."

"Do you think so?" asked Mrs. Gibbins, brightening. "I only gets one and sixpence from *'im.*"

"One and sixpence?" echoed Mrs. Fraser. "My 'usband's young nephew 'Orace would pay much more than *that.* And it 'appens 'e's lookin' for a room this very moment . . ."

"Oh?" Mrs. Gibbins sounded most interested. "Well . . . if you think 'e'd be comfortable . . . if you think it might suit . . . Of course," she continued, "I couldn't tell young Billy to go right away, not just like that. But if 'e's not able to pay . . . Mind you, I dare say it'd be the work'ouse for 'im, 'im being only twelve-ish and no parents."

"It'd keep 'im off the streets, though," said Mrs. Fraser. "Otherwise 'e'd turn to thievin', like as not."

"Yes, that's the truth of it," agreed Mrs. Gibbins. "I dare say it would be a kindness to the boy. Poor motherless lamb."

Billy tipped his four remaining pennies into the tobacco tin he kept under his pillow. There was a shilling in there already. Tomorrow was Friday, when he had to pay the rent money to Mrs. Gibbins. That meant he would have to sell at least two dolls, if he was to eat as well. He opened the calico bag and laid the dolls out on the thin blanket that covered his bed. He should have had Sarah's blanket too, now that she was no longer in need of it, but Mrs. Gibbins had removed both bed and blanket. There was, however, no reduction in the rent.

The Princess, the Wizard, Fairy Bluebell, Greta the Gypsy, the Snow Queen, the Dancer, the Peasant Girl, the Soldier, the Silver Prince, the Spanish Bride. Ten dolls left. If he sold them all, that would be ten times twopence, which was . . . Billy counted on his fingers, then rearranged the dolls into sets of three. "Three dolls is sixpence, Sarah said, and two sixpences is one shilling. One and sixpence . . . and a bit . . ." That was enough for the moment, but what would happen when all the dolls were sold? Perhaps he could get work in a factory. Jobs were difficult to find, but so long as he could earn enough to keep his room, he would be able to manage somehow. The main thing was to have somewhere to come home to at night.

He packed the dolls carefully away, then, without washing or removing his clothes, he climbed under the motheaten blanket and tried to sleep.

But sleep wasn't easy, when you were used to being lulled by the even breathing of someone in the next bed. To lie awake listening only to the sounds of Mrs. Gibbins' husband cursing at someone or something in the front room made Billy feel very lonely. He thought of the kind, soft face of his sister, her gentle smile, the way she never complained, even when her hands were red-raw from the cold, and her fingers torn by sewing needles, and the cold had gnawed through to her bones, so that she used to press her hand to her back when she rose from her chair in the window. "But Billy," she would say to him, "we have each other, which is more than all the money in the Bank of England."

Now, though, he had no Sarah—and very little money either. Just a cold, damp room, a bed hard as the pavement outside, and one and fourpence in a tin beneath his ear. A tear slid from Billy's eye to wet the hard little pillow. From the next room came a bellow of laughter. Mrs. Gibbins, at least, could find something to laugh at.

The next day it was raining, and no one wanted to stop and look at Billy's dolls as he sheltered beneath a shop blind. But, at last, just as he was about to turn and head for home, an old lady came and bought the Spanish Bride for her granddaughter.

"Who made these?" she enquired. "Not you, for sure," she added, inspecting his unwashed appearance.

"No, ma'am. My sister, ma'am. She's dead."

"Oh . . . indeed . . ." The old lady backed off, as if she thought he might have something catching. "What the Lord giveth, the Lord taketh away."

"Yes, ma'am," said Billy meekly.

He went straight home. There was enough for the rent, now, but nothing to spare for food. He would have to go hungry. Perhaps tomorrow the sun would shine and everyone would want peg-dolls; then he would have enough for a meat pie and perhaps a pickled onion as well.

Mrs. Gibbins and Mrs. Fraser were at their usual

post when he arrived home. They seemed to be looking at him with great interest as he went past them into the house.

"Rent day today, Billy," Mrs. Gibbins called after him. She turned to her friend and said smugly: "Not that I think for a moment 'e can pay. Not now 'e's by 'isself, I mean. Well, Mrs. Fraser, about your 'usband's nephew . . ."

Billy took the old lady's twopence out of his handkerchief, then felt under his pillow for the tobacco tin. One and fourpence, and twopence, that made . . . let's see now . . .

He picked up the pillow and shook it. His poor, pinched face, already pallid from lack of nourishing food, went as white as paper. The tin was not there.

Feverishly, he tore back the bedclothes, and, still not finding the tin, he searched the whole room. But he was sure he had left the money under the pillow, and it couldn't have just vanished. Had it been stolen? The only other person who ever went into his room was Mrs. Gibbins, who occasionally waved her mop around the bare floorboards. And surely *she* wouldn't have taken the money. After all, it was her rent.

Gulping back his sobs, Billy ran out to her.

"I had it, Mrs. Gibbins," he said tearfully. "I had the one and fourpence in a tin under my pillow. And, look, here's the other twopence." He held out the money.

Mrs. Gibbins, smiling indulgently, took the coins and said: "Twopence rent, for a lovely room like yours? No, no, Billy. It's one shillin' and sixpence.

And *that* hardly pays me for the trouble." She turned to Mrs. Fraser and gave a coy little laugh. "Dear me!" she exclaimed. "Whatever next?"

"But I *did* have the money," Billy insisted. "It's been taken."

"Taken? Taken?" Mrs. Gibbins said in a high affronted voice. "And who by, pray? I hope you're not goin' to suggest . . . No, you wouldn't be so evil, I dare say." She looked hard at him for a moment, then gave him what she meant to be a smile, but which was more of a leer. "Never mind," she said. "I'll tell you what we'll do. As one with a 'eart of gold, I'd never want it said that Mrs. Gibbins turned anyone out on the cold streets. So you can have until Monday to find the money. All right?"

Billy, crestfallen, nodded and turned to go back inside.

"And if you can't pay," added Mrs. Gibbins, "I'm sure I can find a nice kind constable to escort you to the work'ouse. We wouldn't want a young man like you to get lost on the way. Now then—" She addressed Mrs. Fraser. "I think we could say Tuesday for the new lodger, don't you?"

Saturday was another wet day, and Billy's cry of "Peg-dolls!" went unheeded as people hurried through the rain. He did manage to sell one doll, though—the Snow Queen—to a young gentleman waiting for a cab.

By the evening, it was beginning to look a little brighter, and Billy decided to move to the Edgware Road, in the hope that he might be able to sell to people coming out of the music hall. There were puddles everywhere, and he had to jump over them, as his ill-matched, worn-out boots let in so much water. Yesterday's rain seemed to have seeped right through his skin, and he felt very shivery.

As he stood outside the music hall, a commissionaire came and waved him away. "Not there, boy. The customers don't want to be a-falling over you. Move along, now. Move on."

Billy retreated, but as soon as the show was over and the people came rolling happily out, singing snatches of the songs they had just been entertained with inside, he stepped boldly up to them.

"Peg-doll for your lady, sir?" he invited, interrupting himself with a fit of painful coughing. "Peg-doll for the lady? Twopence each . . . only twopence . . ."

The Gypsy and the Dancer were soon sold, and then the merry-makers were gone. Still, that was— Billy counted out the coins—sixpence in all, which was better than yesterday. He ached inside with hunger, not having eaten for forty-eight hours, and when a baker's man passed, with a tray of warm bread balanced on his head, Billy decided it would be all right to spend just one penny on a floury roll.

That night, he slept with his money clutched in his fist, and in the morning, when he awoke, he found his hand still tightly closed over the seven pennies.

Not being well versed in sums, he was not sure how much more he needed for the rent, but he thought it must be something under one shilling. Tomorrow, Sunday, should be a good day for him, if the weather was fine, for people would come with their children for walks in the parks, and young men would be out courting, and anxious to buy presents for their lady loves. "God's favourite day," Sarah used to call it, making Billy spruce himself up.

True to her, still, he went out to the yard at the back of the house and washed himself at the pump before setting off for Hyde Park, where the gentry rode in open carriages in the hope of being admired by their friends. It was not the gentry, however, that Billy was seeking, so much as the young working men —the tradesmen and suchlike—who were easily persuaded to part with a few pence if by so doing they could impress their lady friends.

As expected, it was a good day. Of the six remaining dolls on his tray, Billy sold five: the Soldier, the Peasant Girl, the Fairy, the Princess and the Wizard. The Silver Prince was beginning to look a little grubby, having been held up for inspection by so many hands, and nobody seemed to want him. However, delighted by his success, Billy spent twopence on a hot potato and a cup of milk, then he bought a pennyworth of cough drops, which burnt his throat with their healing fire.

"One and sixpence by tomorrow," reminded Mrs. Gibbins when he returned home.

She thinks I can't pay, thought Billy, counting coins on the floor. Fourteen pennies . . . twelve was one shilling . . . and two. That meant . . . he needed four more, which was two dolls.

Two dolls? But he only had one! And the Silver Prince was looking very shabby indeed. Billy sat on his bed with his head in his hands. "Sarah," he whispered. "Oh, Sarah, *help me.*"

As if in some kind of answer, his eyes were directed to the wooden box in the corner of the room. Sarah's workbox. He had never looked inside it—at least, not since her death—feeling that he had no right to do so. After all, they were Sarah's things, not his . . . He walked over to it and undid the catch. Inside was a wonderful assortment of ribbons, and braid, and scraps of this and that—velvet, linen, satin, lace—little pots of paint, and brushes, and glue, scissors, pins and pegs.

Billy had often watched Sarah making her dolls. She would decide on a character, paint the face and hair on the round knob at the top of the peg, stuff tubes of pink ribbon for the arms, then glue and sew on the costume. The shoes would be painted on to the ends of the legs. It was surely not all that difficult. And if he could even make just one, he might manage to pay the rent tomorrow and avoid being marched to the workhouse. He was afraid of the workhouse. Boys were made to work terribly hard there, and were beaten if they were lazy—sometimes, even if they were not, he'd heard. The food was mostly a kind of thin porridge, and he believed the beds to be little more than wooden boxes. Worst of all, he would be a prisoner, unable to move freely around the city.

"I *won't* go to the workhouse," he said under his breath. "*No.*" With his mouth set in a determined line, he began to sort through the workbox. He would make a Fine Lady, with rich red lips and light brown hair, just like Sarah.

Painting the face was not as easy as he had

thought it would be. Sarah's touch had been so deft and delicate, and his was much too rough. He tried to wipe off the features with his sleeve, but he simply made a nasty blur around the eyes. Choosing a piece of grey silk for the dress, he wrapped this around the peg and fastened it at the back with large, clumsy stitches. Then he made a hooded cloak out of grey crêpe. He pulled the hood well down over the face, so that the smudged paint was less noticeable. That done, he painted grey splodges on her feet and hoped they looked like elegant boots.

The daylight was fading, and he lit a candle. By its shifting glow, he thought the doll looked quite attractive. Not as nice as any of Sarah's, of course, but he thought he would be able to sell it. That left just the Silver Prince. He found that by brightening up the crown here and there with silver paint, and dabbing at the clothes with a wet cloth, he could make it look a great deal better. Perhaps he would be able to sell both of them, then Mrs. Gibbins would get her rent. Everything would be all right.

Poor Billy could not think further ahead than one day. That he would have to find another one and sixpence by the following Friday had not yet become clear in his mind. If it had, it is doubtful whether he would have spent that night in such calm and dreamless sleep.

It must have been some lucky star that guided Billy to Piccadilly the next day, for he was approached by the same little girl and her mother who had bought the Cinderella doll from him only four days earlier.

"Mama! Here is Cinderella's Prince Charming!"

Painting a Peg-doll. (*Nineteenth-century illustration from Chatterbox*)

exclaimed the little girl, looking eagerly over the edge of the tray. "Oh, may we buy him? Cinderella *must* have her prince. Please, please Mama!"

The girl's mother smiled fondly down. "You are right," she said. "They would certainly make a most agreeable pair. Very well, then." She sniffed. "At least he's a better buy than this other doll, this strange-looking lady, here. Why, I do believe her clothes were stitched by someone with paws instead of hands!" With a tinkling laugh she handed Billy twopence, then the little girl took the Silver Prince and they were gone.

Billy was a little cast down by her remark. However, there were many hours left before he need return to his room with the rent money, and surely someone would take a fancy to his Fine Lady. No, "Fine" was perhaps the wrong word. She would be the Grey Lady, instead.

He wandered down towards Hyde Park Corner, then up Park Lane. Nobody here wanted a peg-doll. Perhaps in Oxford Street, if he stood alongside some of the other pedlars there . . .

"Off with you!" said a man selling matches. "This ain't where you belong."

"Look at 'im," cried a girl with a basket of artificial flowers. "All 'e's got is one doll to sell, and that's not worth a halfpenny. See—'er eyes is all funny!"

Billy ran from their laughter, and the running made him cough, so that he was forced to stop for a while. His chest ached, and he found himself blinking back tears. It was no good. No one would buy the doll. Mrs. Gibbins would turn him out and he would have

nowhere to go but the workhouse. He was glad
Sarah was gone, and couldn't see him in his plight.
She had once said to him: "I'd rather die than go to
that place." He'd said: "Me, too," at the time, but
now all he could think was that he would, at least,
get something to eat there, even if it was just a bowl
of gruel. He was so very hungry.

He was in one of the small streets to the north of
Marble Arch, now, and a carriage was approaching
over the cobbles. It was a smart, four-wheeled conveyance, drawn by a perfectly matched pair of dap-
ple greys. Their oiled hooves clattered to a stop on
the cobbles right by where Billy was standing, and he
looked up at the black-liveried coachman, sitting
stiffly upright on his seat at the front, his legs covered by a heavy-looking weather-sheet.

The coachman kept his eyes straight ahead and
moved not a muscle. He was thin and grey-faced,
and he sat in his place as if he never left it.

After a moment, the door of the carriage opened,
and a lady appeared. She was cloaked and hooded,
and Billy couldn't see her face properly. He thought
she must be visiting a nearby house, but she came
straight over to him.

"P-peg-doll, ma'am? Will you buy a peg-doll?" he
asked in a quivering voice.

When she answered, her voice was as sweet as
sugar and as soft as swansdown.

"Is this the only one you have left, Billy?"

Billy took a step backwards. How did she know his
name? He gulped anxiously and replied: "Yes,
ma'am. It's twopence, ma'am."

The lady looked at it, at the smudged paint and

the badly-stitched dress. "I'll have it," she said.

Billy gave a weak smile, then began again to cough. His thin shoulders shook with the effort.

"Please," said the lady, holding open the door of the carriage, "won't you ride with me?"

Billy shook his head nervously. Sarah had said never to go with strangers, however nice they might seem.

"I have food inside," the lady went on. "Cheese patties and gammon rolls—oranges bigger than your fists . . ."

Billy bit his lip. He was so hungry that nothing else seemed to matter.

"Come along . . ." invited the lady.

Billy unhitched his now empty tray and climbed into the carriage.

The lady kept her hood up even in the carriage, and he still couldn't see her face properly. Perhaps she had some disfiguring skin disease which she didn't want him to see. Or perhaps she was someone famous. On the stage . . . or royalty, even.

"Help yourself, Billy."

She had pulled out a hamper from under the seat and was spreading out the contents. There was food such as Billy had never tasted before: partridge pie, apple turnovers, rich fruit cake, cold pork sausages. As he ate, they were both silent, and Billy, intent on eating all he could, scarcely noticed that the carriage was moving.

When he finally looked up, they were on the out-skirts of London, and seemed to be heading east. The River Thames lay over to their right, and Billy could hear the hooting of the barges as they brought their wares up the river.

The broken doll was once a horror of childhood. Brothers were invaluable in the making of dollhouses and the repair of innumerable dolls. (Manley-Lewis collection)

"How do you feel?" asked the lady, when Billy sat back, unable to eat another morsel.

Billy smiled. "Wonderful, thank you, ma'am."

"Good." She, too, sat back, and Billy felt the grey crêpe cloak brush against his arm. Grey crêpe. Like the peg-doll. The Grey Lady. Yes, of course, she was so like the Grey Lady. He began to feel a little frightened. Who *was* she and, even more important, where was she taking him? This wasn't the way to where Billy lived. The light was beginning to fade, and if he wasn't home with the rent money soon, Mrs. Gibbins wouldn't let him keep his room.

"Excuse me," he said, "but could you tell me where we are going?"

The lady seemed not to hear.

"Excuse me." He tugged at her cloak. "Can we go back, now? I have to go home."

The Grey Lady turned, and he saw her face.

It wasn't the strange, crooked mouth, bright ruby red in a pale face, nor the flat, round nose . . . It was the eyes, blurred and expressionless, which really terrified him. The dreadful, painted face of the Grey Lady had come to life, to torment him with its horror.

He screamed and clutched at the door of the carriage. "Let me out!" he shrieked. "Oh, for love of pity, let me out!"

They were quite close to the river, now, and there was a thick mist which muffled the sound of the horses' hooves as they slowed to a walk. The door would not open. Billy pushed with all his meagre strength, but it would not move.

"Please!" he begged. But the Grey Lady only turned on him those smudgy eyes, with their horrible blankness.

"*Please* let me go home . . ." moaned Billy.

Then the red mouth smiled a crooked smile, and the sweet voice said: "But we are going home, Billy. That's what I've come for. To take you home."

They were going down a slope, now, and Billy saw to his horror that it was a slipway, and that nothing but the cold, black, churning river lay ahead. As the horses stepped silently into the water, they were swallowed by the haze, and Billy turned despairingly to the lady.

"Home, Billy, I'm taking you home . . ." echoed her voice. It seemed to be both inside and outside the carriage, carried here and there by the mist.

He huddled in his seat as the water began to seep under the carriage doors. "Sarah?" he asked pitifully. "Sarah, is it you? Please let it be you . . ."

The Grey Lady stretched out a hand to him. He took it. It was soft and pink, like the hand of a stuffed toy, but it comforted him on the short, dark journey home.

HANS CHRISTIAN ANDERSEN

❋✧❋✧❋✧❋✧❋✧❋✧❋✧❋✧❋✧❋✧❋

THE STEADFAST TIN SOLDIER

Tin soldiers have played a gallant role on the battlefields of literature. Such soldiers were once the boys' special dolls—but they were often taken over by sisters. The most famous collection of such soldiers were the twelve brought home to his children by an eccentric clergyman in the north of England in the early nineteenth century. It was a memorable gift because the soldiers inspired the four children—Charlotte, Branwell, Anne and Emily Brontë—to begin their adventures into literature as they wrote the stories of the soldiers in miniature books.

A near contemporary, Hans Christian Andersen was also playing with bedraggled toy soldiers in Denmark. His father died when he was eleven, and Hans abandoned school and devoted himself to his toy theater. In time, he wrote out his fantasies, including the charming, poignant, The Steadfast Tin Soldier.

THERE WERE ONCE five and twenty tin soldiers, all brothers, for they were the offspring of the same old tin spoon. Each man shouldered his gun, kept his eyes well to the front, and wore the smartest red and blue uniform imaginable. The first thing they heard in their new world, when the lid was taken off the box, was a little boy clapping his hands and crying, "Soldiers, soldiers!" It was his birthday and they had just been given to him; so he lost no time in setting them up on the table. All the soldiers were exactly alike, with one exception, and he differed from the rest in having only one leg. For he was made last, and there was not quite enough tin left to finish him.

All of the tin soldiers were made from the same old tin spoon. (One of the original illustrations for "The Steadfast Tin Soldier")

However, he stood just as well on his one leg as the others on two; in fact, he is the very one who is to become famous. On the table where they were being set up were many other toys; but the chief thing which caught the eye was a delightful paper castle. You could see through the tiny windows, right into the rooms. Outside there were some little trees surrounding a small mirror, representing a lake, whose surface reflected the waxen swans which were swimming about on it. It was altogether charming, but the prettiest thing of all was a little maiden standing at the open door of the castle. She, too, was cut out of paper, but she wore a dress of the lightest gauze, with a dainty little blue ribbon over her shoulders, by way of a scarf, set off by a brilliant spangle as big as her whole face. The little maid was stretching out both arms, for she was a dancer, and in the dance one of her legs was raised so high into the air that the tin soldier could see absolutely nothing of it, and supposed that she, like himself, had but one leg.

"That would be the very wife for me!" he thought; "but she is much too grand; she lives in a palace, while I only have a box, and then there are five and twenty of us to share it. No, that would be no place for her! but I must try to make her acquaintance!" Then he lay down full length behind a snuffbox, which stood on the table. From that point he could have a good look at the lady, who continued to stand on one leg without losing her balance.

Late in the evening the other soldiers were put into their box, and the people of the house went to bed. Now was the time for the toys to play; they amused themselves with paying visits, fighting battles,

The tin soldier sees the dancing doll. (One of the original illustrations for "The Steadfast Tin Soldier")

and giving balls. The tin soldiers rustled about in their box, for they wanted to join the games, but they could not get the lid off. The nut-crackers turned somersaults, and the pencil scribbled nonsense on the slate. There was such a noise that the canary woke up and joined in, but his remarks were in verse. The only two who did not move were the tin soldier and the little dancer. She stood as stiff as ever on tiptoe, with her arms spread out; he was equally firm on his one leg, and he did not take his eyes off her for a moment.

Then the clock struck twelve, when pop! up flew the lid of the snuffbox, but there was no snuff in it, no! There was a little black goblin, a sort of Jack-in-the-box.

"Tin soldier!" said the goblin, "have the goodness to keep your eyes to yourself."

But the tin soldier feigned not to hear.

"Ah! you just wait till tomorrow," said the goblin.

In the morning when the children got up they put the tin soldier on the window frame, and, whether it was caused by the goblin or by a puff of wind, I do not know, but all at once the window burst open, and the soldier fell head foremost from the third story.

It was a terrific descent, and he landed at last, with his leg in the air, and rested on his cap, with his bayonet fixed between two paving stones. The maidservant and the little boy ran down at once to look for him; but although they almost trod on him, they could not see him. Had the soldier only called out, "Here I am," they would easily have found him, but he did not think it proper to shout when he was in uniform.

Presently it began to rain, and the drops fell faster and faster, till there was a regular torrent. When it was over two street boys came along.

"Look out!" said one; "there is a tin soldier! He shall go for a sail."

So they made a boat out of a newspaper and put the soldier into the middle of it, and he sailed away down the gutter; both boys ran alongside, clapping their hands. Good heavens! what waves there were in the gutter, and what a current, but then it certainly had rained cats and dogs. The paper boat danced up and down, and now and then whirled round and round. A shudder ran through the tin soldier, but he remained undaunted, and did not move a muscle, only looked straight before him with his gun shouldered. All at once the boat drifted under a long wooden tunnel, and it became as dark as it was in his box.

"Where on earth am I going now!" thought he. "Well, well, it is all the fault of that goblin! Oh, if only the little maiden were with me in the boat it might be twice as dark for all I should care!"

At this moment a big water rat, who lived in the tunnel, came up.

"Have you a pass?" asked the rat. "Hand up your pass!"

The tin soldier did not speak, but clung still tighter to his gun. The boat rushed on, the rat close behind. Phew, how he gnashed his teeth and shouted to the bits of stick and straw, "Stop him, stop him,

he hasn't paid his toll; he hasn't shown his pass!"
But the current grew stronger and stronger, the tin
soldier could already see daylight before him at the
end of the tunnel; but he also heard a roaring sound,
fit to strike terror to the bravest heart. Just imagine!
Where the tunnel ended the stream rushed straight
into the big canal. That would be just as dangerous
for him as it would be for us to shoot a great rapid.

He was so near the end now that it was impossible
to stop. The boat dashed out; the poor tin soldier
held himself as stiff as he could; no one should say of
him that he even winced.

The boat swirled round three or four times, and
filled with water to the edge; it must sink. The tin
soldier stood up to his neck in water, and the boat
sank deeper and deeper. The paper became limper
and limper, and at last the water went over his head
—then he thought of the pretty little dancer, whom
he was never to see again, and this refrain rang in
his ears:

> *Onward! Onward! Soldier!*
> *For death thou canst not shun.*

At last the paper gave way entirely and the soldier
fell through—but at the same moment he was swallowed by a big fish.

Oh, how dark it was inside the fish, it was worse
than being in the tunnel even; and then it was so
narrow! But the tin soldier was as dauntless as ever,
and lay full length, shouldering his gun.

The fish rushed about and made the most frantic
movements. At last it became quite quiet, and after a
time, a flash like lightning pierced it. The soldier was

once more in the broad daylight, and someone called out loudly, "A tin soldier!" The fish had been caught, taken to market, sold, and brought into the kitchen, where the cook cut it open with a large knife. She took the soldier up by the waist, with two fingers, and carried him into the parlor, where everyone wanted to see the wonderful man who had traveled about in the stomach of a fish; but the tin soldier was not at all proud. They set him up on the table, and, wonder of wonders! he found himself in the very same room that he had been in before. He saw the very same children, and the toys were still standing on the table, as well as the beautiful castle with the pretty little dancer.

She still stood on one leg, and held the other up in the air. You see she also was unbending. The soldier was so much moved that he was ready to shed tears of tin, but that would not have been fitting. He looked at her, and she looked at him, but they said never a word. At this moment one of the little boys took up the tin soldier, and without rhyme or reason, threw him into the fire. No doubt the little goblin in the snuffbox was to blame for that. The tin soldier stood there, lighted up by the flame, and in the most horrible heat; but whether it was the heat of the real fire, or the warmth of his feelings, he did not know. He had lost all his gay color; it might have been from his perilous journey, or it might have been from grief, who can tell?

He looked at the little maiden, and she looked at him; and he felt that he was melting away, but he still managed to keep himself erect, shouldering his gun bravely.

A door was suddenly opened, the draft caught the little dancer, and she fluttered like a sylph, straight into the fire, to the soldier, blazed up, and was gone!

By this time the soldier was reduced to a mere lump, and when the maid took away the ashes next morning she found him, in the shape of a small tin heart. All that was left of the dancer was her spangle, and that was burned as black as coal.

THE DOLLS' BALL

from *Frank Leslie's Magazine*

The famous Christmas magazines of the mid-nine-teenth century were particularly cherished by those generations for whom the printed word was the form of entertainment. As each member of the family opened its pages, he or she was assailed by the smell of fresh ink accompanying Christmas greetings. Each year, too, it contained a doll story, many of them by unknown contributors.

Dolls literally haunted the families of that period; they were kept from generation to generation. Their stories were told and retold. Many highly imaginative tales resulted. Nannies were remarkably willing to go along with childhood fantasies; they dressed dolls to order, planned balls and parties for these inanimate beings at the request of their charges. Indeed, imagination was so heated at times that children often dreamed about their dolls coming alive, and many stories were written about this phenomenon. This story is one of that genre; the very pages are ghosts from the past, because it has never been reprinted since the day when the annual was printed. The ink is no longer fresh, the original pages are yellow and crumpled—but it is a sweet story of a type once very common, and evokes a childhood long since past.

ROSA AND FANNY had a sister who was quite a young lady, for she was sixteen. Her name was Clara, and the very day she was sixteen she was asked to a ball. She had never been at a ball before. She had a beautiful dress made to go in, and when the evening came she went to the hairdresser's to have her hair made as beautiful as her dress.

Rosa went with her; and while the hairdresser was brushing and plaiting and working away very busily, she walked about his shop, looking at everything. There was a delightful scent in it, and there were several pretty heads of ladies, with faces made of wax, with pink cheeks, and sweet blue or black eyes, and such shining hair, dressed with flowers or feathers! One of them, with a wreath of roses round her head, seemed to Rosa the loveliest creature she had ever seen.

Clara called her away from gazing at this lovely lady, and then she saw that Clara had a wreath round her head, and looked almost as lovely as the lady. When they got home, Clara had to dress, and she let Fanny and Rosa stay in her room all the time. How pretty she looked in her thin white dress, looped up with bows, and with that wreath in her hair! They ran to the top of the stairs to see her go down with her cloak on, and heard the carriage drive away with her.

It seemed very dull when they went back into her room. Nurse wanted them to go to the nursery, but they would not. They wandered about, touching things they ought not. Rosa took the stopper out of a bottle and spilt some of the scent, and Fanny spoiled the clasp of a bracelet in trying to put it on her arm.

Nurse did not know what to do. At last she thought of a plan.

"Suppose you give a ball," she said, "and ask your dolls to it?"

"How nice! So we will!" cried Rosa.

"But we ought to dress up," said Fanny.

Nurse said she would dress them up. They had on their white frocks, for they had been in to dessert with their papa and mamma; so when she had found some pink bows for Rosa, and blue for Fanny, and looped up the skirts and sleeves, she thought they looked quite fine; but they said they must have on their cornelian necklaces; and when she had brought the necklaces, they wanted wreaths in their hair—it was impossible to do without wreaths. Nurse could not think what was to be done. In the country she could have found plenty of flowers, but how was she to get any in London?

While she went down-stairs to try and get some flowers, they began to prepare the dolls. Fanny's doll was much the tallest. Her real name was Matilda, but she was always called Meg. Fanny did not like it, but it was her papa that gave the name. The moment he saw Matilda, he said she looked like Meg, so every one called her so. Rosa had two dolls—

Amelia and Sally. None of them were properly dressed for a ball; indeed, Amelia had her bonnet on; so there was a great deal to do still. Rosa stood them up in a row against the sofa, to look at them and think what frocks they had better put on.

At that moment Nurse came in with a little basketful of small red and white roses. Mamma had let her have them out of the flower-glasses in the drawing-room. How kind it was of her! They helped to make the roses into wreaths, Nurse fixed them in their hair, and now they were complete.

Rosa then began to give the dolls a dancing lesson, that they might not disgrace themselves at the ball, but Fanny had not done looking at herself in the glass yet. Rosa could be partner to Amelia, and if Fanny made haste she could dance with Meg; but who was there for Sally? A pair of boots must be her partner, and another must be Meg's till Fanny came.

At last Fanny came, and they played at dancing lesson for some time, and they now thought the dolls quite perfect and ready to be dressed. Meg was to have her frock on first. It was a pink gauze one.

"Oh, Fanny," said Rosa, "how nice it will be when we come to the real ball. I will lend you Sally for a partner, and Matilda must have the boots. We will call the boots Charley."

But at this minute Nurse opened the door, to say it was bedtime.

"Oh, no, no!" cried Rosa. "We haven't got to it yet."

"Let us stay a little longer," said Fanny.

Dreaming of the Ball. (*Manley-Lewis collection*)

But Nurse shook her head. Fanny slowly gathered up the dolls' frocks, and carrying Meg, followed Nurse. Poor little Rosa could not help crying bitterly. She tore off her wreath, pulled at her necklace-clasp so tight, to get it off, that she broke it, and the beads rolled round the floor, and then seized up her two dolls, one in each hand, and went sobbing off after Fanny. Long after Fanny had fallen asleep in the little bed opposite to hers, she lay awake and thought how happy Clara must be now, and thought of Fanny's bows and wreath that she had helped to put on all for nothing, and of Sally's pretty frock, that had never even been put on, and of her own wreath and broken necklace that were lying there. Then she began to be less sad, and she thought she was at the hairdresser's again, where she had been with Clara, and the lovely lady with the wreath of roses put out her hand and asked her to a ball.

Rosa did not see, when she was at the hairdresser's before, that the lady had hands, but now she had. On her hands she wore pretty white gloves, and she held in one some beautiful flowers, just as mamma did when she went to a party.

It would be very nice to go to a ball with this lady. Rosa said she should like it, and would go if she might have her hair dressed. She looked round to see if Clara's was done, and if she might go now and be seated in the chair, and let the hairdresser begin to brush and plait hers. She wanted it done exactly like the lady's.

But when she looked round, Clara was gone. There was a lady with very long black hair there, but not Clara, and the hairdresser seemed changed.

He looked so very odd! She remembered she had thought he was very ugly before, but now he was still uglier, and he had a very long nose, and peered into the lady's hair very strangely. Then he pulled it so hard, that Rosa was sure he must hurt the lady. She was really afraid to let him do hers.

Then she was troubled about her wreath. She knew that it was broken, and even if she could have got at it again the roses were too small, and not at all like the lady's.

She began wandering about the shop, to try to find some roses, and to see if any of the wax ladies would lend her some. They all smiled at her, and talked to her, and began walking about with her. It did not seem at all strange that the wax ladies should talk and move; but none of them gave her any roses, so she tried to find the lovely lady again, to ask her what she should do. She could not find her anywhere. She went walking round and round, but nowhere could she see the lady. At last she got to the very place where the lady was, but instead of her, there was Meg, so she supposed that Meg was going to the ball too.

Meg had on her pink gauze frock, but her hair was very rough; it would never do for a ball. So Rosa thought she must take her to the hairdresser to have it made pretty.

"I don't think he will pull her hair so as to hurt her," said Rosa to herself, "because she is made of china."

Rosa took her up and carried her to the hairdresser, and he looked down at her from a great height, for he had grown twice as tall now. Then,

when Rosa tried to make Meg sit down in the chair
she could not make her sit still. Meg tumbled down
first on one side, then on the other.

Suddenly she seemed to be at home again, and
there was Meg with her pink gauze frock on, and
her hair most beautifully curled, all in long ringlets,
that stuck up from her head, and nice party-shoes.
She was dancing and capering about the floor by
herself. Rosa wanted to go and dance too, but she
could not, because she was in her night-gown.

She went to look for her wreath, for it seemed to
her that if she only had it on she should be fit for
the ball; but she could not find it. When she came
back into the nursery there was Meg still dancing
about the floor, and she had got Fanny for a partner.
But Fanny was not dancing. Meg was carrying her
about and dancing. She did not seem too heavy for
Meg to carry. Indeed, Fanny looked quite babyish
and little. It was very strange. Nurse did not seem to
think it strange at all. There she sat at work, as if
she thought it was quite natural that Meg should
dance about with Fanny in her arms.

Out came a little mouse and began to dance with
them. Then a hole came in the floor on the other
side, and out came another little mouse and danced
too.

Fanny sat down and began to sing to the dancers;
at least she opened her mouth and tried to sing; but
no sound came. She did not seem to care, but sat there
quite contented; and there sat Nurse at work, as if
nothing was the matter.

The mice began to race round and round, and

The Dolls' Ball. *Original illustration for "The Dolls' Ball."* (*Manley-Lewis collection*)

Meg took Fanny up again and twirled and twisted about with her, and jumped very high, and tossed Fanny up and caught her again. At last Fanny went up so high that she never came down again. Where she went to Rosa could not think. Perhaps she was on the top of the bed, perhaps she had flown out at the window.

There was a noise at the window that sounded like Fanny crying. It frightened Rosa very much. Was anything the matter with Fanny? Perhaps she had been hurt when Meg tossed her up so high. Rosa tried to get to the window, but she could only look at it, she could not go to it. She saw, however, that Fanny was not out there, but there was a cat mewing and looking in.

Rosa tried to call out to the mice, "Oh, you poor little mice, do run away for fear of the cat!" but her voice would not come; she could only whisper. The mice had heard the mew, however, for they ran down the holes in the floor as fast as they could go. It was lucky, for the tail of the last had scarcely gone out of sight when in ran the two nursery cats and began to dance with Meg.

Now the door opened, and in came Amelia and Sally. The ball was going to begin at last.

Sally was dressed in white, and her frock was looped up with pink roses, and round her head she wore a wreath of pink roses. She looked lovely. Rosa was proud of her. Amelia was not so well dressed. Her frock was plain and too long, but it was a pretty blue color, and she had a scarlet cap on her head. She looked pretty well on the whole, but not near so well as Sally.

Meg danced with the old cat, whose name was Vevvy. It was short for Velvet, and this name was given to her because her coat was soft. Sally danced with little Kittums. Now, if Fanny would only come back and dance with Amelia. Where was Fanny?

If Rosa could have put on her pretty ball-dress, and had her hair done at the hairdresser's, she could have danced with Amelia herself; but she had not been able to find her wreath, and here she was in her night-gown!

Since Fanny never came back, the ball went on without her. Meg and Vevvy danced a polka. Sally and Kittums came after them. Amelia skipped about by herself. It was a beautiful ball.

All the time they danced the cat at the window kept singing, and there seemed to be several more cats there, for there was a great deal of music. It was all lovely.

Just as Meg and Vevvy were twirling round very fast in the polka, and Meg's ringlets were flying up in the air, a very strange thing happened. Amelia and Kittums were close behind at the time, but Sally had skipped quite out of sight. The strange thing that happened was, that Fanny peeped out of the bed curtains to see what was going on.

When she peeped out she frightened Meg and Vevvy. Vevvy tried to carry Meg off to the window, and Meg tried to call out and to run away. But something much worse happened. Kittums gave such a start that she dropped Amelia down on the floor, and began crying and looking up at Vevvy. Poor Amelia lay there looking miserable, for her face was smashed to pieces.

"Oh, Amelia, Amelia!" cried Rosa, starting up and opening her eyes wide.

Rosa looked round quite surprised. She was in her own little bed. It was morning. Fanny was asleep in the opposite bed. The fire was lighted, and Vevvy and Kittums were lying curled up on the rug. How comfortable it all looked!

But what did she see opposite to her, standing against Fanny's bed? She saw Meg, Sally, and Amelia in full dresses; Meg in her pink gauze; Sally in her white with pink roses; and Amelia in the prettiest blue, not long and plain, but looped up with bows, and her hair very nice and smooth, and no scarlet cap on, and her face was *not* smashed!

Rosa lay down again, smiling to herself. It was all a dream about the ball with the cats, and Nurse had dressed the dolls ready for a real ball, and perhaps they should have one that very day? She awoke Fanny to make her look at the dolls, now they were so pretty, and to tell her the wonderful dream.

In the evening Nurse dressed her and Fanny again, and made fresh wreaths for them, and mended the necklace; and they had the ball, and enjoyed it very much indeed.

NATHANIEL HAWTHORNE

FEATHERTOP

They called them harvest dollies; they were fashioned regularly every fall from the last grain cut,
which was brought home in a wagon, and that
wagon itself had a name—the Hock Cart. In it the
harvest dolly was escorted home from the fields.
Originally such a doll was made to represent the ancient goddess Ceres. The Harvest Doll was accompanied by music and dancers, and by the harvesters
themselves, men, women and children, tripping hand
in hand, and singing the song "Harvest Home,
Harvest Home."

Agriculture has long been associated with the
figure of the Roman goddess Ceres; her spirit is
found in figures of straw, hay, grain and corn. These
crop dolls were made to propitiate the harvest, and
everyone had a hand in the making of them.
Whether they are scarecrows or harvest figures or
even snowmen, these dolls of the changing season are

Bringing in the harvest from which the corn doll was made.

ephemeral. *Magic has always been attached to them.*

Nathaniel Hawthorne, who once worked on a utopian farm as a young man, knew rural folklore well. With laughter and more than a touch of satire, he combined the witch and the harvest doll in an enchanting story.

An Eskimo doll and three North American Indian dolls.
(Manley-Lewis collection)

"DICKON," cried Mother Rigby, "a coal for my pipe!"

The pipe was in the old dame's mouth when she said these words. She had thrust it there after filling it with tobacco, but without stooping to light it at the hearth, where indeed there was no appearance of a fire having been kindled that morning. Forthwith, however, as soon as the order was given, there was an intense red glow out of the bowl of the pipe, and a whiff of smoke came from Mother Rigby's lips. Whence the coal came, and how brought thither by an invisible hand, I have never been able to discover.

"Good!" quoth Mother Rigby, with a nod of her head. "Thank ye, Dickon! And now for making this scarecrow. Be within call, Dickon, in case I need you again."

The good woman had risen thus early (for as yet it was scarcely sunrise) in order to set about making a scarecrow, which she intended to put in the middle of her corn-patch. It was now the latter week of May, and the crows and blackbirds had already discovered the little, green, rolled-up leaf of the Indian corn just peeping out of the soil. She was determined, therefore, to contrive as lifelike a scarecrow as ever was seen, and to finish it immediately, from top to toe, so that it should begin its sentinel's duty that very morning. Now Mother Rigby (as everybody must have heard) was one of the most cunning and potent witches in New England, and might, with very little trouble, have made a scarecrow ugly enough to frighten the minister himself. But on this occasion, as she had awakened in an uncommonly pleasant humor, and was further dulcified by her pipe tobacco, she resolved to produce something fine, beautiful, and splendid, rather than hideous and horrible.

"I don't want to set up a hobgoblin in my own corn-patch, and almost at my own doorstep," said Mother Rigby to herself, puffing out a whiff of smoke; "I could do it if I pleased, but I'm tired of doing marvellous things, and so I'll keep within the bounds of every-day business just for variety's sake. Besides, there is no use in scaring the little children for a mile roundabout, though 'tis true I'm a witch."

It was settled, therefore, in her own mind, that the scarecrow should represent a fine gentleman of the period, so far as the materials at hand would allow. Perhaps it may be as well to enumerate the chief of the articles that went to the composition of this figure.

The most important item of all, probably, although it made so little show, was a certain broomstick, on which Mother Rigby had taken many an airy gallop at midnight, and which now served the scarecrow by way of a spinal column, or, as the unlearned phrase it, a backbone. One of its arms was a disabled flail which used to be wielded by Goodman Rigby, before his spouse worried him out of this troublesome world; the other, if I mistake not, was composed of the pudding stick and a broken rung of a chair, tied loosely together at the elbow. As for its legs, the right was a hoe handle, and the left an undistinguished and miscellaneous stick from the woodpile. Its lungs, stomach, and other affairs of that kind were nothing better than a meal bag stuffed

with straw. Thus we have made out the skeleton and
entire corporosity of the scarecrow, with the exception of its head; and this was admirably supplied by
a somewhat withered and shrivelled pumpkin, in
which Mother Rigby cut two holes for the eyes, and
a slit for the mouth, leaving a bluish-colored knob in
the middle to pass for a nose. It was really quite a
respectable face.

"I've seen worse ones on human shoulders, at any
rate," said Mother Rigby. "And many a fine gentleman has a pumpkin head, as well as my scarecrow."

But the clothes, in this case, were to be the making
of the man. So the good old woman took down from
a peg an ancient plum-colored coat of London make,
and with relics of embroidery on its seams, cuffs,
pocket-flaps, and button-holes, but lamentably worn
and faded, patched at the elbows, tattered at the
skirts, and threadbare all over. On the left breast was
a round hole, whence either a star of nobility had
been rent away, or else the hot heart of some former
wearer had scorched it through and through. The
neighbors said that this rich garment belonged to the
Black Man's wardrobe, and that he kept it at
Mother Rigby's cottage for the convenience of slip-
ping it on whenever he wished to make a grand appearance at the governor's table. To match the coat
there was a velvet waistcoat of very ample size, and
formerly embroidered with foliage that had been as
brightly golden as the maple leaves in October, but
which had now quite vanished out of the substance
of the velvet. Next came a pair of scarlet breeches,
once worn by the French governor of Louisbourg,
and the knees of which had touched the lower step

of the throne of Louis le Grand. The Frenchman had given these small-clothes to an Indian powwow, who parted with them to the old witch for a gill of strong waters, at one of their dances in the forest. Furthermore, Mother Rigby produced a pair of silk stockings and put them on the figure's legs, where they showed as unsubstantial as a dream, with the wooden reality of the two sticks making itself miserably apparent through the holes. Lastly, she put her dead husband's wig on the bare scalp of the pumpkin, and surmounted the whole with a dusty three-cornered hat, in which was stuck the longest tail feather of a rooster.

Then the old dame stood the figure up in a corner of her cottage and chuckled to behold its yellow semblance of a visage, with its nobby little nose thrust into the air. It had a strangely self-satisfied aspect, and seemed to say, "Come look at me!"

"And you are well worth looking at, that's a fact!" quoth Mother Rigby, in admiration at her own handiwork. "I've made many a puppet since I've been a witch, but methinks this is the finest of them all. 'Tis almost too good for a scarecrow. And, by the by, I'll just fill a fresh pipe of tobacco and then take him out to the corn-patch."

While filling her pipe the old woman continued to gaze with almost motherly affection at the figure in the corner. To say the truth, whether it were chance, or skill, or downright witchcraft, there was something wonderfully human in this ridiculous shape, bedizened with its tattered finery; and as for the countenance, it appeared to shrivel its yellow surface into a grin—a funny kind of expression betwixt scorn and merriment, as if it understood itself to be a jest at mankind. The more Mother Rigby looked the better she was pleased.

"Dickon," cried she sharply, "another coal for my pipe!"

Hardly had she spoken, than, just as before, there was a red-glowing coal on the top of the tobacco. She drew in a long whiff and puffed it forth again into the bar of morning sunshine which struggled through the one dusty pane of her cottage window. Mother Rigby always liked to flavor her pipe with a coal of fire from the particular chimney corner whence this had been brought. But where that chimney corner might be, or who brought the coal from it —further than that the invisible messenger seemed to respond to the name of Dickon—I cannot tell.

"That puppet yonder," thought Mother Rigby, still with her eyes fixed on the scarecrow, "is too good a piece of work to stand all summer in a corn-patch, frightening away the crows and blackbirds. He's capable of better things. Why, I've danced with a worse one, when partners happened to be scarce, at our witch meetings in the forest! What if I should let him take his chance among the other men of straw and empty fellows who go bustling about the world?"

The old witch took three or four more whiffs of her pipe and smiled.

"He'll meet plenty of his brethren at every street corner!" continued she. "Well; I didn't mean to dabble in witchcraft today, further than the lighting of my pipe, but a witch I am, and a witch I'm likely to be, and there's no use trying to shirk it. I'll make a man of my scarecrow, were it only for the joke's sake!"

While muttering these words, Mother Rigby took the pipe from her own mouth and thrust it into the crevice which represented the same feature in the pumpkin visage of the scarecrow.

"Puff, darling, puff!" said she. "Puff away, my fine fellow! Your life depends on it!"

This was a strange exhortation, undoubtedly, to be addressed to a mere thing of sticks, straw, and old clothes, with nothing better than a shrivelled pumpkin for a head—as we know to have been the scarecrow's case. Nevertheless, as we must carefully hold in remembrance, Mother Rigby was a witch of singular power and dexterity; and, keeping this fact duly before our minds, we shall see nothing beyond credibility in the remarkable incidents of our story. Indeed, the great difficulty will be at once got over, if we can only bring ourselves to believe that, as soon as the old dame bade him puff, there came a whiff of smoke from the scarecrow's mouth. It was the very feeblest of whiffs, to be sure; but it was followed by another and another, each more decided than the preceding one.

"Puff away, my pet! Puff away, my pretty one!" Mother Rigby kept repeating, with her pleasantest smile. "It is the breath of life to ye; and that you may take my word for."

Beyond all question the pipe was bewitched. There must have been a spell either in the tobacco or in the fiercely glowing coal that so mysteriously burned on top of it, or in the pungently aromatic smoke which exhaled from the kindled weed. The figure, after a few doubtful attempts, at length blew forth a volley of smoke extending all the way from the obscure corner into the bar of sunshine. There it eddied and melted away among the motes of dust. It seemed a convulsive effort; for the two or three next whiffs were fainter, although the coal still glowed and threw a gleam over the scarecrow's visage. The old witch clapped her skinny hands together, and smiled encouragingly upon her handiwork. She saw that the charm worked well. The shrivelled, yellow face, which heretofore had been no face at all, had already a thin, fantastic haze, as it were of human likeness, shifting to and fro across it; sometimes vanishing entirely, but growing more perceptible than ever with the next whiff from the pipe. The whole figure, in like manner, assumed a show of life, such as we impart to ill-defined shapes among the clouds, and half deceive ourselves with the pastime of our own fancy.

If we must needs pry closely into the matter, it may be doubted whether there was any real change, after all, in the sordid, wornout, worthless, and ill-jointed substance of the scarecrow; but merely a spectral illusion, and a cunning effect of light and shade so colored and contrived as to delude the eyes of most men. The miracles of witchcraft seem always to have had a very shallow subtlety; and, at least, if the above explanation does not hit the truth of the process, I can suggest no better.

"Well puffed, my pretty lad!" still cried old Mother Rigby. "Come, another good stout whiff, and let it be with might and main. Puff for thy life, I tell thee! Puff out of the very bottom of thy heart, if any heart thou hast, or any bottom to it! Well done, again! Thou didst suck in that mouthful as if for the pure love of it."

And then the witch beckoned to the scarecrow, throwing so much magnetic potency into her gesture that it seemed as if it must inevitably be obeyed, like the mystic call of the lodestone when it summons the iron.

"Why lurkest thou in the corner, lazy one?" said she. "Step forth! Thou hast the world before thee!"

Upon my word, if the legend were not one which I heard on my grandmother's knee, and which had established its place among things credible before my childish judgment could analyze its probability, I question whether I should have the face to tell it now.

In obedience to Mother Rigby's word, and extending its arm as if to reach her outstretched hand, the figure made a step forward—a kind of hitch and jerk, however, rather than a step then tottered and almost lost its balance. What could the witch expect? It was nothing, after all, but a scarecrow stuck upon two sticks. But the strong-willed old beldam scowled, and beckoned, and flung the energy of her purpose so forcibly at this poor combination of rotten wood, and musty straw, and ragged garments, that it was compelled to show itself a man, in spite of the reality of things. So it stepped into the bar of sunshine. There it stood—poor devil of a contrivance that it was!— with only the thinnest vesture of human similitude about it, through which was evident the stiff, rickety, incongruous, faded, tattered, good-for-nothing patchwork of its substance, ready to sink in a heap upon the floor, as conscious of its own unworthiness to be erect. Shall I confess the truth? At its present point of vivification, the scarecrow reminds me of some of the lukewarm and abortive characters, composed of heterogeneous materials, used for the thousandth time, and never worth using, with which romance writers (and myself, no doubt, among the rest) have so overpeopled the world of fiction.

But the fierce old hag began to get angry and show a glimpse of her diabolic nature (like a snake's head, peeping with a hiss out of her bosom), at this pusillanimous behavior of the thing which she had taken the trouble to put together.

"Puff away, wretch!" cried she, wrathfully. "Puff, puff, puff, thou thing of straw and emptiness! thou rag or two! thou meal bag! thou pumpkin head! thou nothing! Where shall I find a name vile enough to call thee by? Puff, I say, and suck in thy fantastic life with the smoke! Else I snatch the pipe from thy mouth and hurl thee where that red coal came from."

Thus threatened, the unhappy scarecrow had nothing for it but to puff away for dear life. As need was, therefore, it applied itself lustily to the pipe, and sent forth such abundant volleys of tobacco smoke that the small cottage kitchen became all vaporous. The one sunbeam struggled mistily through, and could but imperfectly define the image of the cracked and dusty window pane on the opposite wall. Mother Rigby meanwhile, with one brown arm akimbo and the other stretched towards the figure, loomed grimly amid the obscurity with such port and expression as when she was wont to heave a ponderous nightmare on her victims and stand at the bedside to enjoy their agony. In fear and trembling did this poor scarecrow puff. But its efforts, it must be acknowledged, served an excellent purpose; for, with each successive whiff, the figure lost more and more of its dizzy and perplexing tenuity and seemed to take denser substance. Its very garments, moreover, partook of the magical change, and shone with the gloss of novelty and glistened with the skilfully embroidered gold that had long ago been rent away. And, half revealed among the smoke, a yellow visage bent its lustreless eyes on Mother Rigby.

At last the old witch clinched her fist and shook it at the figure. Not that she was positively angry, but merely acting on the principle—perhaps untrue, or not the only truth, though as high a one as Mother Rigby could be expected to attain—that feeble and torpid natures, being incapable of better inspiration, must be stirred up by fear. But here was the crisis. Should she fail in what she now sought to effect, it was her ruthless purpose to scatter the miserable simulacre into its original elements.

"Thou hast a man's aspect," said she, sternly. "Have also the echo and mockery of a voice! I bid thee speak!"

The scarecrow gasped, struggled, and at length emitted a murmur, which was so incorporated with its smoky breath that you could scarcely tell whether it were indeed a voice or only a whiff of tobacco. Some narrators of this legend hold the opinion that Mother Rigby's conjurations and the fierceness of her will had compelled a familiar spirit into the figure, and that the voice was his.

"Mother," mumbled the poor stifled voice, "be not

so awful with me! I would fain speak; but being without wits, what can I say?"

"Thou canst speak, darling, canst thou?" cried Mother Rigby, relaxing her grim countenance into a smile. "And what shalt thou say, quotha! Say, indeed! Art thou of the brotherhood of the empty skull, and demandest of me what thou shalt say? Thou shalt say a thousand things, and saying them a thousand times over, thou shalt still have said nothing! Be not afraid, I tell thee! When thou comest into the world (whither I purpose sending thee forthwith) thou shalt not lack the wherewithal to talk. Talk! Why, thou shall babble like a millstream, if thou wilt. Thou hast brains enough for that, I trow!"

"At your service, mother," responded the figure.

"And that was well said, my pretty one," answered Mother Rigby. "Then thou speakest like thyself, and meant nothing. Thou shalt have a hundred such set phrases, and five hundred to the boot of them. And now, darling, I have taken so much pains with thee and thou art so beautiful, that, by my troth, I love thee better than any witch's puppet in the world; and I've made them of all sorts—clay, wax, straw, sticks, night fog, morning mist, sea foam, and chimney smoke. But thou art the very best. So give heed to what I say."

"Yes, kind mother," said the figure, "with all my heart!"

"With all thy heart!" cried the old witch, setting her hands to her sides and laughing loudly. "Thou hast such a pretty way of speaking. With all thy heart! And thou didst put thy hand to the left side of thy waistcoat as if thou really hadst one!"

So now, in high good humor with this fantastic contrivance of hers, Mother Rigby told the scarecrow that it must go and play its part in the great world, where not one man in a hundred, she affirmed, was gifted with more real substance than itself. And, that he might hold up his head with the best of them, she endowed him, on the spot, with an unreckonable amount of wealth. It consisted partly of a gold mine in Eldorado, and of ten thousand shares in a broken bubble, and of half a million acres of vineyard at the North Pole, and of a castle in the air, and a chateau in Spain, together with all the rents and income therefrom accruing. She further made over to him the cargo of a certain ship, laden with salt of Cadiz, which she herself, by her necromantic arts, had caused to founder, ten years before, in the deepest part of mid-ocean. If the salt were not dissolved, and could be brought to market, it would fetch a pretty penny among the fishermen. That he might not lack ready money, she gave him a copper farthing of Birmingham manufacture, being all the coin she had about her, and likewise a great deal of brass, which she applied to his forehead, thus making it yellower than ever.

"With that brass alone," quoth Mother Rigby, "thou canst pay thy way all over the earth. Kiss me, pretty darling! I have done my best for thee."

Furthermore, that the adventurer might lack no possible advantage towards a fair start in life, this excellent old dame gave him a token by which he was to introduce himself to a certain magistrate, member of the council, merchant, and elder of the church (the four capacities constituting but one man), who stood at the head of society in the neighboring metropolis. The token was neither more nor less than a single word, which Mother Rigby whispered to the scarecrow, and which the scarecrow was to whisper to the merchant.

"Gouty as the old fellow is, he'll run thy errands for thee, when once thou hast given him that word in his ear," said the old witch. "Mother Rigby knows the worshipful Justice Gookin, and the worshipful Justice knows Mother Rigby!"

Here the witch thrust her wrinkled face close to the puppet's, chuckling irrepressibly, and fidgeting all through her system, with delight at the idea which she meant to communicate.

"The worshipful Master Gookin," whispered she, "hath a comely maiden to his daughter. And hark ye, my pet! Thou hast a fair outside, and a pretty wit enough of thine own. Yea, a pretty wit enough! Thou wilt think better of it when thou hast seen more of other people's wits. Now, with thy outside and thy inside, thou art the very man to win a young girl's heart. Never doubt it! I tell thee it shall be so. Put but a bold face on the matter, sigh, smile, flourish thy hat, thrust forth thy leg like a dancing-master, put thy right hand to the left side of thy waistcoat, and pretty Polly Gookin is thine own!"

All this while the new creature had been sucking in and exhaling the vapory fragrance of his pipe, and seemed now to continue this occupation as much for the enjoyment it afforded as because it was an essential condition of his existence. It was wonderful to see how exceedingly like a human being it behaved. Its eyes (for it appeared to possess a pair) were bent on Mother Rigby, and at suitable junctures it nodded or shook its head. Neither did it lack words proper for the occasion: "Really! Indeed! Pray tell me! Is it possible! Upon my word! By no means! Oh! Ah! Hem!" and other such weighty utterances as imply attention, inquiry, acquiescence, or dissent on the part of the auditor. Even had you stood by and seen the scarecrow made, you could scarcely have resisted the conviction that it perfectly understood the cunning counsels which the old witch poured into its counterfeit of an ear. The more earnestly it applied its lips to the pipe, the more distinctly was its human likeness stamped among visible realities, the more sagacious grew its expression, the more lifelike its gestures and movements, and the more intelligibly audible its voice. Its garments, too, glistened so much the brighter with an illusory magnificence. The very pipe, in which burned the spell of all this wonder-work, ceased to appear as a smoke-blackened earthen stump, and became a meerschaum, with painted bowl and amber mouthpiece.

It might be apprehended, however, that as the life of the illusion seemed identical with the vapor of the pipe, it would terminate simultaneously with the reduction of the tobacco to ashes. But the beldam foresaw the difficulty.

"Hold thou the pipe, my precious one," said she, "while I fill it for thee again."

It was sorrowful to behold how the fine gentleman began to fade back into a scarecrow while Mother Rigby shook the ashes out of the pipe and proceeded to replenish it from her tobacco-box.

"Dickon," cried she, in her high, sharp tone, "another coal for this pipe!"

No sooner said than the intensely red speck of fire was glowing within the pipe bowl; and the scarecrow, without waiting for the witch's bidding, applied the tube to his lips and drew in a few short, convulsive whiffs, which soon, however, became regular and equable.

"Now, mine own heart's darling," quoth Mother Rigby, "whatever may happen to thee, thou must stick to thy pipe. Thy life is in it; and that, at least, thou knowest well, if thou knowest nought besides. Stick to thy pipe, I say! Smoke, puff, blow thy cloud; and tell the people, if any question be made, that it is for thy health, and that so the physician orders thee to do. And, sweet one, when thou shalt find thy pipe getting low, go apart into some corner, and (first filling thyself with smoke) cry sharply, 'Dickon, a fresh pipe of tobacco!' and, 'Dickon, another coal for my pipe!' and have it into thy pretty mouth as speedily as may be. Else, instead of a gallant gentleman in a gold-laced coat, thou wilt be but a jumble of sticks and tattered clothes, and a bag of straw, and a withered pumpkin! Now depart, my treasure, and good luck go with thee!"

"Never fear, mother!" said the figure, in a stout voice, and sending forth a courageous whiff of smoke, "I will thrive, if an honest man and a gentleman may!"

"Oh, thou wilt be the death of me!" cried the old witch, convulsed with laughter. "That was well said. If an honest man and a gentleman may! Thou playest thy part to perfection. Get along with thee for a smart fellow; and I will wager on thy head, as a man of pith and substance, with a brain and what they call a heart, and all else that a man should have, against any other thing on two legs. I hold myself a better witch than yesterday, for thy sake. Did not I make thee? And I defy any witch in New England to make such another! Here; take my staff along with thee!"

The staff, though it was but a plain oaken stick, immediately took the aspect of a gold-headed cane.

"That gold head has as much sense in it as thine own," said Mother Rigby, "and it will guide thee straight to worshipful Master Gookin's door. Get thee gone, my pretty pet, my darling, my precious one, my treasure; and if any ask thy name, it is Feathertop. For thou hast a feather in thy hat, and I have thrust a handful of feathers into the hollow of thy head, and thy wig, too, is of the fashion they call Feathertop—so be Feathertop thy name!"

And, issuing from the cottage, Feathertop strode manfully towards town. Mother Rigby stood at the threshold, well pleased to see how the sunbeams glistened on him, as if all his magnificence were real, and how diligently and lovingly he smoked his pipe, and how handsomely he walked, in spite of a little stiffness of his legs. She watched him until out of sight, and threw a witch benediction after her darling, when a turn of the road snatched him from her view.

Betimes in the forenoon, when the principal street of the neighboring town was just at its acme of life and bustle, a stranger of very distinguished figure was seen on the sidewalk. His port as well as his garments betokened nothing short of nobility. He wore a richly embroidered plum-colored coat, a waistcoat of costly velvet, magnificently adorned with golden foliage, a pair of splendid scarlet breeches, and the finest and glossiest of white silk stockings. His head was covered with a peruke, so daintily powdered and adjusted that it would have been sacrilege to disorder it with a hat; which, therefore (and it was a gold-laced hat, set off with a snowy feather), he carried beneath his arm. On the breast of his coat glistened a star. He managed his gold-headed cane with an airy grace, peculiar to the fine gentlemen of the period; and, to give the highest possible finish to his equipment, he had lace ruffles at his wrist, of a most ethereal delicacy, sufficiently avouching how idle and aristocratic must be the hands which they half concealed.

It was a remarkable point in the accoutrement of this brilliant personage that he held in his left hand a fantastic kind of a pipe, with an exquisitely painted bowl and an amber mouthpiece. This he applied to his lips as often as every five or six paces, and inhaled a deep whiff of smoke, which, after being retained a moment in his lungs, might be seen to eddy gracefully from his mouth and nostrils.

As may well be supposed, the street was all astir to find out the stranger's name.

"It is some great nobleman, beyond question," said

one of the townspeople. "Do you see the star at his breast?"

"Nay; it is too bright to be seen," said another. "Yes; he must needs be a nobleman, as you say. But by what conveyance, think you, can his lordship have voyaged or travelled hither? There has been no vessel from the old country for a month past; and if he have arrived overland from the southward, pray where are his attendants and equipage?"

"He needs no equipage to set off his rank," remarked a third. "If he came among us in rags, nobility would shine through a hole in his elbow. I never saw such dignity of aspect. He has the old Norman blood in his veins, I warrant him."

"I rather take him to be a Dutchman, or one of your high Germans," said another citizen. "The men of those countries have always the pipe at their mouths."

"And so has a Turk," answered his companion. "But, in my judgment, this stranger hath been bred at the French court, and hath there learned politeness and grace of manner, which none understand so well as the nobility of France. That gait, now! A vulgar spectator might deem it stiff—he might call it a hitch and jerk—but, to my eye, it hath an unspeakable majesty, and must have been acquired by constant observation of the deportment of the Grand Monarque. The stranger's character and office are evident enough. He is a French ambassador, come to treat with our rulers about the cession of Canada."

"More probably a Spaniard," said another, "and hence his yellow complexion; or, most likely, he is from the Havana, or from some port on the Spanish main, and comes to make investigation about the piracies which our government is thought to connive at. Those settlers in Peru and Mexico have skins as yellow as the gold which they dig out of their mines."

"Yellow or not," cried a lady, "he is a beautiful man!—so tall, so slender! such a fine, noble face, with so well-shaped a nose, and all that delicacy of expression about the mouth! And, bless me, how bright his star is! It positively shoots out flames!"

"So do your eyes, fair lady," said the stranger, with a bow and a flourish of his pipe; for he was just passing at the instant. "Upon my honor, they have quite dazzled me."

"Was ever so original and exquisite a compliment?" murmured the lady, in an ecstasy of delight.

Amid the general admiration excited by the stranger's appearance, there were only two dissenting voices. One was that of an impertinent cur, which, after snuffing at the heels of the glistening figure, put its tail between its legs and skulked into its master's back yard, vociferating an execrable howl. The other dissentient was a young child, who squalled at the fullest stretch of his lungs, and babbled some unintelligible nonsense about a pumpkin.

Feathertop meanwhile pursued his way along the street. Except for the few complimentary words to the lady, and now and then a slight inclination of the head in requital of the profound reverences of the bystanders, he seemed wholly absorbed in his pipe. There needed no other proof of his rank and consequence than the perfect equanimity with which he comported himself, while the curiosity and admiration of the town swelled almost into clamor around him. With a crowd gathering behind his footsteps, he finally reached the mansion-house of the worshipful Justice Gookin, entered the gate, ascended the steps of the front door, and knocked. In the interim, before his summons was answered, the stranger was observed to shake the ashes out of his pipe.

"What did he say in that sharp voice?" inquired one of the spectators.

"Nay, I know not," answered his friend. "But the sun dazzles my eyes strangely. How dim and faded his lordship looks all of a sudden! Bless my wits, what is the matter with me?"

"The wonder is," said the other, "that his pipe, which was out only an instant ago, should be all alight again, and with the reddest coal I ever saw. There is something mysterious about this stranger. What a whiff of smoke was that! Dim and faded did you call him? Why, as he turns about the star on his breast is all ablaze."

"It is, indeed," said his companion; "and it will go near to dazzle pretty Polly Gookin, whom I see peeping at it out of the chamber window."

The door being now opened, Feathertop turned to the crowd, made a stately bend of his body like a great man acknowledging the reverence of the meaner sort, and vanished into the house. There was a mysterious kind of a smile, if it might not better be called a grin or grimace, upon his visage; but, of all the throng that beheld him, not an individual appears to have possessed insight enough to detect the illusive character of the stranger except a little child and a cur dog.

Our legend here loses somewhat of its continuity, and, passing over the preliminary explanation between Feathertop and the merchant, goes in quest of the pretty Polly Gookin. She was a damsel of a soft, round figure, with light hair and blue eyes, and a fair, rosy face, which seemed neither very shrewd nor very simple. This young lady had caught a glimpse of the glistening stranger while standing on the threshold, and had forthwith put on a laced cap, a string of beads, her finest kerchief, and her stiffest damask petticoat in preparation for the interview. Hurrying from her chamber to the parlor, she had ever since been viewing herself in the large looking-glass and practising pretty airs—now a smile, now a ceremonious dignity of aspect, and now a softer smile than the former, kissing her hand likewise, tossing her head, and managing her fan; while within the mirror an unsubstantial little maid repeated every gesture and did all the foolish things that Polly did, but without making her ashamed of them. In short, it was the fault of pretty Polly's ability rather than her will if she failed to be as complete an artifice as the illustrious Feathertop himself; and, when she thus tampered with her own simplicity, the witch's phantom might well hope to win her.

No sooner did Polly hear her father's gouty footsteps approaching the parlor door, accompanied with the stiff clatter of Feathertop's high-heeled shoes, than she seated herself bolt upright and innocently began warbling a song.

"Polly! daughter Polly!" cried the old merchant. "Come hither, child."

Master Gookin's aspect, as he opened the door, was doubtful and troubled.

"This gentleman," continued he, presenting the stranger, "is the Chevalier Feathertop—nay, I beg his pardon, my Lord Feathertop—who hath brought me a token of remembrance from an ancient friend of mine. Pay your duty to his lordship, child, and honor him as his quality deserves."

After these few words of introduction, the worshipful magistrate immediately quitted the room. But, even in that brief moment, had the fair Polly glanced aside at her father instead of devoting herself wholly to the brilliant guest, she might have taken warning of some mischief nigh at hand. The old man was nervous, fidgety, and very pale. Purposing a smile of courtesy, he had deformed his face with a sort of galvanic grin, which, when Feathertop's back was turned, he exchanged for a scowl, at the same time shaking his fist and stamping his gouty foot—an incivility which brought its retribution along with it. The truth appears to have been that Mother Rigby's word of introduction, whatever it might be, had operated far more on the rich merchant's fears than on his good will. Moreover, being a man of wonderfully acute observation, he had noticed that these painted figures on the bowl of Feathertop's pipe were in motion. Looking more closely, he became convinced that these figures were a party of little demons, each duly provided with horns and a tail, and dancing hand in hand, with gestures of diabolical merriment, round the circumference of the pipe

bowl. As if to confirm his suspicions, while Master
Gookin ushered his guest along a dusky passage from
his private room to the parlor, the star on Feathertop's breast had scintillated actual flames, and threw
a flickering gleam upon the wall, the ceiling, and the
floor.

With such sinister prognostics manifesting themselves on all hands, it is not to be marvelled at that
the merchant should have felt that he was commit-
ting his daughter to a very questionable acquaintance. He cursed, in his secret soul, the in-
sinuating elegance of Feathertop's manners, as this
brilliant personage bowed, smiled, put his hand on
his heart, inhaled a long whiff from his pipe, and
enriched the atmosphere with the smoky vapor of a
fragrant and visible sigh. Gladly would poor Master
Gookin have thrust his dangerous guest into the
street; but there was a constraint and terror within
him. This respectable old gentleman, we fear, at an
earlier period of life, had given some pledge or other
to the evil principle, and perhaps was now to redeem
it by the sacrifice of his daughter.

It so happened that the parlor door was partly of
glass, shaded by a silken curtain, the folds of which
hung a little awry. So strong was the merchant's interest in witnessing what was to ensue between the
fair Polly and the gallant Feathertop that, after quit-
ting the room, he could by no means refrain from
peeping through the crevice of the curtain.

But there was nothing very miraculous to be seen;
nothing—except the trifles previously noticed—to
confirm the idea of a supernatural peril environing
the pretty Polly. The stranger it is true was evidently

a thorough and practised man of the world, systematic and self-possessed, and therefore the sort of a person to whom a parent ought not to confide a simple, young girl without due watchfulness for the result. The worthy magistrate, who had been conversant with all degrees and qualities of mankind, could not but perceive every motion and gesture of the distinguished Feathertop came in its proper place; nothing had been left rude or native in him; a well-digested conventionalism had incorporated itself thoroughly with his substance and transformed him into a work of art. Perhaps it was this peculiarity that invested him with a species of ghastliness and awe. It is the effect of anything completely and consummately artificial, in human shape, that the person impresses us as an unreality and as having hardly pith enough to cast a shadow upon the floor. As regarded Feathertop, all this resulted in a wild, extravagant, and fantastical impression, as if his life and being were akin to the smoke that curled upward from his pipe.

But pretty Polly Gookin felt not thus. The pair were now promenading the room: Feathertop with his dainty stride and no less dainty grimace; the girl with a native maidenly grace, just touched, not spoiled, by a slightly affected manner, which seemed caught from the perfect artifice of her companion. The longer the interview continued, the more charmed was pretty Polly, until, within the first quarter of an hour (as the old magistrate noted by his watch), she was evidently beginning to be in love. Nor need it have been witchcraft that subdued her in such a hurry; the poor child's heart, it may be, was

so very fervent that it melted her with its own
warmth as reflected from the hollow semblance of
a lover. No matter what Feathertop said, his words
found depth and reverberation in her ear; no matter
what he did, his action was heroic to her eye. And
by this time it is to be supposed there was a blush on
Polly's cheek, a tender smile about her mouth, and a
liquid softness in her glance; while the star kept
coruscating on Feathertop's breast, and the little demons careered with more frantic merriment than
ever about the circumference of his pipe bowl. O
pretty Polly Gookin, why should these imps rejoice so
madly that a silly maiden's heart was about to be
given to a shadow! Is it so unusual a misfortune, so
rare a triumph?

By and by Feathertop paused, and throwing himself into an imposing attitude, seemed to summon the
fair girl to survey his figure and resist him longer if
she could. His star, his embroidery, his buckles
glowed at that instant with unutterable splendor; the
picturesque hues of his attire took a richer depth of
coloring; there was a gleam and polish over his
whole presence betokening the perfect witchery of
well-ordered manners. The maiden raised her eyes
and suffered them to linger upon her companion
with a bashful and admiring gaze. Then, as if de-
sirous of judging what value her own simple come-
liness might have side by side with so much brilliancy, she cast a glance towards the full-length
looking-glass in front of which they happened to be
standing. It was one of the truest plates in the world
and incapable of flattery. No sooner did the images
therein reflected meet Polly's eye than she shrieked,

shrank from the stranger's side, gazed at him for a moment in the wildest dismay, and sank insensible upon the floor. Feathertop likewise had looked towards the mirror, and there beheld, not the glittering mockery of his outside show, but a picture of the sordid patchwork of his real composition, stripped of all witchcraft.

The wretched simulacrum! We almost pity him. He threw up his arms with an expression of despair that went further than any of his previous manifestations towards vindicating his claims to be reckoned human; for, perchance the only time since this so often empty and deceptive life of mortals began its course, an illusion had seen and fully recognized itself.

Mother Rigby was seated by her kitchen hearth in the twilight of this eventful day, and had just shaken the ashes out of a new pipe, when she heard a hurried tramp along the road. Yet it did not seem so much the tramp of human footsteps as the clatter of sticks or the rattling of dry bones.

"Ha!" thought the old witch, "what step is that? Whose skeleton is out of its grave now, I wonder?"

A figure burst headlong into the cottage door. It was Feathertop! His pipe was still alight; the star still flamed upon his breast; the embroidery still glowed upon his garments; nor had he lost, in any degree or manner that could be estimated, the aspect that assimilated him with our mortal brotherhood. But yet, in some indescribable way (as is the case with all that has deluded us when once found out), the poor reality was felt beneath the cunning artifice.

"What has gone wrong?" demanded the witch.

"Did yonder sniffling hypocrite thrust my darling from his door? The villain! I'll set twenty fiends to torment him till he offer thee his daughter on his bended knees!"

"No, mother," said Feathertop despondingly; "it was not that."

"Did the girl scorn my precious one?" asked Mother Rigby, her fierce eyes glowing like two coals of Tophet. "I'll cover her face with pimples! Her nose shall be as red as the coal in thy pipe! Her front teeth shall drop out! In a week hence she shall not be worth thy having!"

"Let her alone, mother," answered poor Feathertop; "the girl was half won; and methinks a kiss from her sweet lips might have made me altogether human. But," he added, after a brief pause and then a howl of self-contempt, "I've seen myself, mother! I've seen myself for the wretched, ragged, empty thing I am! I'll exist no longer!"

Snatching the pipe from his mouth, he flung it with all his might against the chimney, and at the same instant sank upon the floor, a medley of straw and tattered garments, with some sticks protruding from the heap, and a shrivelled pumpkin in the midst. The eyeholes were now lustreless; but the rudely carved gap, that just before had been a mouth, still seemed to twist itself into a despairing grin, and was so far human.

"Poor fellow!" quoth Mother Rigby, with a rueful glance at the relics of her ill-fated contrivance. "My poor, dear, pretty Feathertop! There are thousands upon thousands of coxcombs and charlatans in the world, made up of just such a jumble of wornout, forgotten, and good-for-nothing trash as he was! Yet they live in fair repute, and never see themselves for what they are. And why should my poor puppet be the only one to know himself and perish for it?"

While thus muttering, the witch had filled a fresh pipe of tobacco, and held the stem between her fingers, as doubtful whether to thrust it into her own mouth or Feathertop's.

"Poor Feathertop!" she continued. "I could easily give him another chance and send him forth again tomorrow. But no; his feelings are too tender, his sensibilities too deep. He seems to have too much heart to bustle for his own advantage in such an empty and heartless world. Well! Well! I'll make a scarecrow of him after all. 'Tis an innocent and useful vocation, and will suit my darling well; and, if each of his human brethren had as fit a one, 'twould be the better for mankind; and as for this pipe of tobacco, I need it more than he."

So saying, Mother Rigby put the stem between her lips. "Dickon!" cried she, in her high, sharp tone, "another coal for my pipe!"

Friend.

Enemy.

(Manley-Lewis collection

TERRY TAPP

THE DOLL

The toy and doll makers of nineteenth-century London were divided markedly into two groups: those who catered to the rich, and those, who, in a small way, eased the discomfort of the poor. Because everyone, rich or poor, had to have a doll.

Some doll makers were even barometers of the economy. Some left us personal records. "Trade is very bad at present, for when the laboring people are out of employ, I feel it in my business. They cannot buy dolls for the children; unless they have decent earnings, children must go without—poor things. As all my goods go to the poor, and are a sort of luxury to the children, I can tell what's up with working and poor people by the state of my trade. A curious test, isn't it, but a sure one."

This nineteenth-century obsession with dolls has made those particular dolls have almost a mystique about them. Some would say they are just too mysterious; certainly The Doll *in Terry Tapp's story is memorable.*

ABOUT a hundred years ago, such a doll would have been quite commonplace; it would have been held in loving arms, cuddled and cherished. But Anna simply turned her nose up at it as she cautiously pulled back the faded dress between forefinger and thumb to examine the limbs and torso. The doll was filthy.

She decided to throw it away. After all, what was the use of a doll whose eyes had fallen back into her hollow, china head? The hair had been raggedly hacked short and the face of the doll was deathly waxen.

Yes, she would throw the doll away.

Rubbing her hands on her jeans, Anna delved into the cardboard box to see what other things were in there. When her father had bought the wardrobe at the house auction, he had not realized that the shabby cardboard box was inside it, and Anna was having a splendid time exploring the contents and sorting them out.

There were some lead soldiers, a book entitled "Nature's Window", and a carefully folded Union Jack. Some seed catalogues, a bundle of papers and letters and some faded, sepia photographs. One of the photographs was of a young girl, about Anna's age, holding a very pretty doll. Anna looked from the photograph to the twisted, broken doll which lay face down on the carpet beside her. There was no doubt about it, the girl was holding the same doll.

"One would never think that you used to look like that," Anna said to the doll, holding the photograph closer to try to distinguish if the doll was still wearing the same dress. When she looked down at the doll again, it was lying on its back.

With a shrug, Anna turned her attention to the bundle of letters. Many of them were business letters, written on thick paper in a black, powdered ink which had long since faded. The writing was, on most of the letters, beautiful copperplate hand, and Anna resolved that she would pay more attention to her own writing in future. One of the letters had been torn into small pieces. Anna, who was very fond of jigsaw puzzles, idly pieced it together.

It proved to be an easy task and, before she realized it, she was reading the letter, her lips moving with each word.

> *Fairlea Boarding School,*
> *Copper Beech Drive,*
> *Abbotsteignton,*
> *Devonshire.*
> *27th February, 1898.*

Dearest Mama,
I hate this place and live only for the day when I am allowed to return to you again.

Why did you send me away? I did nothing wrong, and it is not true what you say about the doll. Dearest Bess was my greatest companion, and I am so sad to be separated from her.

Mama, will you wrap her carefully for me and put her on the next coach to Abbotsteignton? I miss her so when I am alone at night, in my darkling bed. I cry for her.

Bess is not—could not possibly be—an evil doll, as you suggest. She did not set fire to my

*bedroom that night and neither did I. She is
not an evil doll. How could she be?*

*This is a cruel and cold place to which you
have sent me, and the teachers rule us by terror.
They have been told that I purposely set fire
to my own bedroom and they watch me day
and night.*

*We are made to scrub the rough flagstones
until our knuckles are raw, and the Matron
beats us at breakfast without favour, even when
our behaviour has been exemplary.*

*I will write again before the week is out.
Please, if you have any affection left for me,
believe me when I tell you that I would not do
such a thing. I love my home, my dearest Bess,
and, above all, you, Mama.*

Ever your obedient and loving daughter,

Anna

"Same name as mine," Anna said aloud. "How strange."

She read the letter again and glanced over at the perpetual calendar which hung on her bedroom wall. It was February 27th.

"Same name and same date," she mused. "Curiouser and curiouser."

The girl in the photograph, although smiling, had a sad, rather resigned look about her, and she was holding the doll, examining the nape of the neck. Luxuriant hair fell around the shoulders of the doll.

"Why did she cut your hair, I wonder?" Anna said, gathering up the loose-jointed doll. "Maybe there was a squeaker, or something in the head."

Mending clothes for the nineteenth-century doll was one of the few pleasant aspects of the terrible tyranny of the needle suffered by young girls. (Manley-Lewis collection)

She examined the nape of the doll's neck.

"Heubach. Koppelsdorf. Three-twenty. Germany," Anna read aloud. There was no sign of a squeaker.

If Anna had sent that letter, she reasoned, her mother would have received it. And as the letter and the doll were in the same cardboard box, obviously her mother had not sent Bess. How sad. Why, anyway, would Anna's mother have blamed a doll for setting light to a room? It sounded very much as if it were the mother, and not the daughter, who deserved punishment.

"Anna? What are you doing up there?" Anna's mother called. The voice cut through the stillness of the bedroom, making Anna jump.

"Nothing, Mum," she called back, relieved that she, at least, did not have such a cruel parent as the other Anna.

"Then come downstairs and do nothing," her mother replied. "It's cold up there without the heating on."

"I'm not cold," Anna said.

"Well come down anyway. I'm just making a hot drink."

"Coming," Anna called, snatching up the photograph and the doll. Mother was right—it was getting a bit chilly, and Anna certainly didn't want to catch a cold. Besides, she could show the letter and photograph to her mother.

Perhaps, she thought, Bess could be made to look pretty again. It seemed rather heartless to throw the doll away after reading that letter. Bess had meant a lot to the other Anna. She pushed the loose-limbed doll on to her toyshelf and stood back to look at it. A new wig, some pretty clothes and a lick of paint would make all the difference. And the eyes could be put back again. That would certainly improve her appearance. Anna did not like the way the dark, lifeless sockets seemed to stare at her. It gave the doll a menacing air . . .

She turned to leave the bedroom and, just as she was closing the door, she heard a loud thump. Something had fallen down.

"Oh, bother!" she sighed, going back into the room to see what it was that had fallen.

Lying in the firegrate, its head at a peculiar angle, the doll looked quite pathetic. Anna picked it up and noticed that the third finger on the left hand had snapped off. She picked up the plaster stump of finger and placed it beside the doll.

"Never mind, Bess," she said, grinning. "That's the least of your troubles. We can soon glue the finger on."

Making sure that, this time, Bess would not fall again, Anna carefully closed the bedroom door and ran downstairs to the kitchen.

It certainly was much warmer in the cosy kitchen, and on the table there was a steaming mug of hot chocolate.

"Thanks, Mum." Anna took the drink, sipped it and felt the warmth in her hands. How nice it was to live in modern times—not like the other Anna.

"Did you find anything interesting in the box?" Anna's mother asked as she expertly peeled some apples.

"Nothing much," Anna replied, helping herself to a custard cream biscuit from the tin. "I haven't finished exploring it yet."

"You shouldn't be eating so near to dinnertime," her mother said. "Mind you just have the one biscuit, or you'll be leaving your dinner."

Anna laughed. "I won't, you know. I'm famished."

The smell of peeled apples, spices and roasting meat filled the kitchen, making Anna feel almost guilty that she was enjoying herself. It didn't seem right, somehow, when one thought of the other Anna.

"What have you got there?" Anna's mother asked as she placed the slices of apple in a baking dish.

"Just an old photograph," Anna said, picking it up and casually looking at it.

"Oh, let me see. I love looking at old pictures."

Just as Anna was about to hand over the photograph, she noticed something very peculiar. The doll in the photograph had a finger missing. The third finger on the left hand . . .

"Let me see it, then." Anna's mother held out her hand impatiently.

Still Anna stared at the picture.

"Whatever is the matter with you, child? You've gone as pale as a sheet."

"The doll," Anna said weakly. "The doll in the picture has a finger missing."

"Much-loved dolls often do have bits missing," Anna's mother replied absently.

"But you don't understand, Mum!" Anna cried. "The doll in the picture is the same one I found in the cardboard box."

"There is nothing surprising about that," came the reply. "The doll and the photograph could well have been kept together, just like all the odds and ends we keep in our souvenirs case in the attic."

Anna's mother took the photograph and smiled. "My, she is a pretty girl. Not unlike you, Anna."

"You still don't understand!" said Anna impatiently. "I've just broken the finger off that doll. I did it just now, after you had called me. How could it be shown as broken in the photograph if I've only just broken it this minute?"

"Probably a different finger," her mother suggested. "Or, maybe it had been broken off before and was just held on by glue."

"No, it was a fresh break," Anna insisted. "The plaster was pure white and powdery."

"It stands to reason," Anna's mother said patiently, "that no matter what happens to the doll, the photograph will always remain the same. And if the finger was broken in the photograph, it certainly must have been broken before you did it."

Anna thought, perhaps, her mother must be right. She had not closely examined the photograph the first time, and it was possible that she had not noticed the fingers. Yes, that must be the answer.

"Is that all there is wrong with the doll?" Anna's mother asked. "Just a broken finger?"

"Good gracious no. The hair has been cut short, the legs and arms are all floppy and the eyes have fallen back into the head."

"Euk!" Anna's mother exclaimed.

"Do you think Dad could repair her?"

"If she's got all those things wrong with her, I doubt if it would be worthwhile, Anna. And talking about your father, look at the time. He'll be home soon and the dinner is way behind. Drink your chocolate up, dear, and then go and wash your hands."

"Do you think Dad could stick a new wig on Bess?"

"Bess?"

"The doll. She's called Bess. Do you think Dad could do it?"

"I expect he could, dear. Now do hurry up with that drink. When you've washed your hands, come down quickly and help me lay the table for dinner."

Sipping back the last frothy remains of her chocolate, Anna rinsed the mug under the tap and left it on the draining board.

"Take the photograph with you and bring down a fresh tea towel when you come," Anna's mother said as she placed the thin layer of pastry over the apple pie and sliced around the edges.

"Right," Anna said. "Can I pinch the pastry around the edge of the pie when I come down?"

"There won't be time for that. I'm late enough as it is." Anna's mother used a fork to decorate the edges of the pie and quickly glazed the top with her pastry brush. "Don't stand there dreaming, now. Hurry up."

Taking the stairs two at a time, Anna dashed quickly into her bedroom and threw the photograph on to her bed. She was just about to leave again when something made her stop. Puzzled at first, she couldn't think what it was . . .

The room was colder, but maybe it was because she had just come from the warm kitchen. The doll was still on the shelf where Anna had left her. The finger was broken, and the plaster stump . . . the plaster stump of finger had a red tinge to it. Anna examined the doll's left hand.

It was bleeding!

Thinking, perhaps, she might have nicked her finger while handling the doll, she examined her own hands to see if there was any blood on them. Dolls don't bleed, she thought.

There was no blood, or marks of any kind, on Anna's hands.

She shivered as she stared at the doll and the thick, red liquid which had oozed from the stump of finger. And suddenly she was afraid.

Was it imagination, or had the hair grown an inch or two longer? She stepped closer to examine the curling locks of hair that now just touched the shoulders of the doll.

Bess sat on the shelf, her lifeless, cavernous sockets staring intensely at Anna. Almost hypnotized, Anna stared back at the horrific sight. An evil smile curled around the doll's mouth, and Anna felt that she was on the brink . . . the very brink . . .

"Anna! Do hurry up, child. I need your help down here."

"Coming, Mum!" Anna yelled back, almost in relief. Somehow, her mother's voice had cut through the menacing atmosphere and dragged her back to reality. Imagination. Of course it was imagination. Dad had always told her that she had too vivid an imagination, and he was right. The letter had started it all and she had frightened herself. After dinner, she would come back to the bedroom and try to work out how the end of Bess's finger had become red. There must be a sensible, logical answer.

One thing was certain. It wasn't blood. Dolls don't bleed. Anna grinned at the thought, thinking how silly she had been. But, all the same, she did make a mental note of the exact length of Bess's hair before she left the bedroom. It wouldn't be any longer, or shorter when she returned to the room, and she would laugh at her fears.

"Did you remember to wash your hands?" her mother asked as she burst into the kitchen.

"They're not dirty," Anna replied.

"Of course they're dirty after you've been handling all that rubbish from the auction," Anna's mother said. "What have you been doing up there? Now, for goodness' sake go up and wash your hands at once so that you can help me serve the dinner. I've had to lay the table by myself as it is."

"Sorry, Mum," Anna said.

"And don't forget the tea cloth."

"I won't," Anna called back. "What's for dinner?"

"Beef."

"Super!" Anna said, dashing from the kitchen.

The dinner was, indeed, 'super', and Anna hardly spoke a word to her father until her plate was clean.

"What's for sweet?" she asked eagerly. "Are we having that apple pie?"

"Yes, we are," Anna's mother replied. "And you can wait until we have all finished our meal. I don't know how you manage to wolf your food down so quickly. It isn't ladylike, you know."

"What have you been up to this morning?" Anna's father asked as he tackled the last potato on his plate.

"I've been sorting out that box of junk that came with the wardrobe."

"Find any fivers?"

"No, but there were some lead soldiers, an old-fashioned doll called Bess and some books," Anna told him.

"Keep the lead soldiers," her father advised. "They're becoming collectors' pieces now. What condition are they in?"

"I'll show you," Anna said.

"After dinner," her mother called.

But she was too late. Anna had jumped up from the table and was already halfway up the stairs. It had not been the thought of showing her father the lead soldiers which had made her run so eagerly to her room. It was the doll. All through dinner, the thought of the doll had intruded on her and, now that her father was home, she felt secure and confident. She would have another look at the doll and all her silly notions would disappear.

The room was still very cold, and Anna could not, at first, bring herself to look at the doll. She cast her eyes towards the bed, saw the photograph and picked it up. Slowly, she lifted her eyes to meet the black, mysterious holes in the doll's head.

Bess was staring at her . . . a blind, penetrating stare.

How could the doll stare when it had no eyes? Anna went over slowly. The lips were curled in a leer, and the eyes were filled with black, deep malevolence. Suddenly, Anna wondered why she had picked up the photograph. She had come to her room to collect the lead soldiers, and somehow . . . somehow she had, instead, picked up the photograph. Bess seemed to be holding out her hand—her blood-stained left hand—as if reaching for the photograph.

How ridiculous, Anna thought. Then, as she turned away, she noticed something out of the corner of her eye. A faint whisp of smoke was curling up from her bed. Instantly, she ran over to the bed and picked up the pile of letters. The fragments of the pieced-together letter fell out. And they were on fire!

Without thinking, Anna instantly dropped them on to the carpet and stamped out the flames. As she frantically stamped at the tongues of licking fire, the room seemed to fill with a bubbling laughter. She looked across at Bess.

Eyes! Bess had eyes! Laughing, leering eyes. An evil smile stretched across the doll's face, the lips stretched back over bared teeth. Chuckling and laughing . . . laughing . . . The room resonated with the sounds of hysterical laughter.

Smoke filled the tiny room and Anna choked as she ran to the window.

"Ha-ha-ha-ha!"

"You did it!" Anna screamed at the doll. "You set the letter on fire. You probably set the other Anna's bedroom on fire, too. It was you all the time!"

"Ha-ha-ha-ha!"

"Stop it!"

"Ha-ha-ha!" the doll roared with laughter.

"Stop it! Stop it!" Anna screamed helplessly.

"Hurry up, Anna. Your sweet is on the table and it's getting cold," Anna's father called up the stairs.

"Ha-ha-ha-ha!"

"Stop it. Daddy! Come up here quickly!"

"Anna?"

She could hear his footsteps pounding up the stairs.

"Anna? What's the matter? What's wrong?"

Jerkily, the doll raised its hands to reveal that all the fingers were now intact again. The room vibrated with the dreadful sound of echoing laughter, and the eyes fell back into the hollow china head with a dull "clunk" just as the bedroom door burst open.

Anna screamed and screamed.

Her screams sliced through the air like the raw edge of sharp steel, freezing Anna with their intensity.

"Whatever is it?" Anna's father gripped her by the shoulders and shook her.

And Bess sat on the shelf.

"What is it, Anna?"

The doll sat on the shelf.

Innocently.

"Oh . . . Daddy," Anna choked.

"What on earth was all the screaming for?" Anna's mother came into the room.

"I don't know," her father said. "She hasn't told me yet."

"Look at her face. She's petrified."

"The . . . the doll . . ." Anna blurted out.

"The doll made you scream?" her father asked.

"Well, I don't wonder at it. I must say, it looks pretty terrifying, just sitting there without any eyes. Gives me the shivers."

"It set light to the letter," Anna sobbed.

"Where?"

"There . . . on the carpet by the bed."

"Where? I can't see anything."

It was true. The carpet was quite clean, and there were no ash marks on it at all. When Anna looked around the room, she saw that the smoke had disappeared.

"What are you doing with your window wide open?" her mother asked. "No wonder it feels so cold in here."

Desperately, Anna wanted to tell them about Bess . . . how the doll had set light to the other Anna's bedroom all those years ago and how she had tried the same thing in her own room. But she realized that it would all sound too silly. They would think she was making it up. The finger was back on the doll. The ashes of the letter had disappeared and the room was no longer filled with smoke.

But the hair! The hair had grown even longer!

"Look at her hair," Anna said excitedly. At last she had positive proof that she could show. "The doll's hair has grown since I went down to dinner!"

"What is she saying?" her father asked.

"She says that the doll's hair has grown." Her mother smiled at the thought.

"Codswallop!" her father said, laughing. "You're trying to frighten yourself, child."

"I'm not!" Anna stamped her foot angrily. "The hair *has* grown longer, hasn't it, Mum?"

This picture, called The Nightmare, *shows how mistreatment of dolls could backfire into a night of fright. (Manley-Lewis collection)*

"How would I know?" Anna's mother replied pointedly. "This is the first time I've seen the doll."

Anna hadn't thought of that. Of course, her mother had only seen the photograph of Bess.

"The photograph!" Anna cried. "You do, at least, remember that the doll in the photograph had a finger broken off?"

"Yes."

"Then let's have a look at the photograph now," Anna said. She was certain that the photograph would have changed, to show a mended hand, and maybe that would convince everyone that she was telling the truth.

"Where is the photograph?" Anna's father said.

"On my bed. No . . . I picked it up when I came to get the toy soldiers. I picked it up and went over to Bess, and . . ." She paused. What had she done then? "I must have dropped it on the floor," she said desperately. "It must be somewhere around here."

"Look for it after dinner," Anna's mother said impatiently. "Our sweets are on the table and they must be stone cold by now."

"But it was right here, Mum." Anna was almost in tears.

"After dinner," her father said firmly. "And you can have a jolly good sort out in here. Your bedroom is an absolute tip. I'm having a bonfire in the garden this afternoon, and you can bring down all your rubbish to burn."

"Nobody believes me," Anna said miserably. "I was telling the truth, Mum—honestly."

"I find that very hard to believe," her mother answered coldly. "You told me that the doll's hair had been hacked short, but look at her."

Long, flowing hair curled around Bess's shoulders, sweeping down, down, down to her waist.

"But I . . ."

"Now don't make things worse by arguing, Anna," her mother said. "You told me that a finger had broken off and it has not. You said that her hair had been cut and it certainly has not. And now you make up some story about the photograph."

"When I was your age," Anna's father said sternly, "I would have had my mouth washed out with soap and water if I told lies. Now let's go downstairs and finish our dinner."

There was nothing Anna could say. She could see that Bess had trapped her, and she knew exactly how exasperated the other Anna must have felt all those years ago.

Somehow, the apple pie did not taste very nice, and Anna had great difficulty in swallowing it. Her mother ate in silence, and she knew that the best thing she could do was remain absolutely quiet until after the meal was finished.

She finished the pie, refused a second helping and waited until she was given permission to leave the table.

"Straight up to your bedroom, young lady," her father said. "Your cupboards are full of rubbish. I don't know why you keep it all."

Dutifully, Anna made her way up to her room.

"And don't make another mess while you're doing it," her mother called after her. "I know your tidy-ups, and they sometimes make a worse mess than before you started."

"I'll take care of it," she called back, her mouth set in a grim line. She now knew what she must do.

The hair, the cardboard body, the faded dress . . . they would all burn very nicely. She would burn Bess.

As her father had said, Anna's room was in a mess. Cupboards were crammed tight with things which "might come in useful one day"—but never seemed to. There were boxes, pretty pieces of wrapping paper which she had not the heart to throw away, comics and old magazines. Averting her eyes from the doll, she worked around the room, piling all the rubbish into the centre to be taken down to the bonfire. She did not want to look at Bess again, for she was afraid of what she might see. The fire in her room must have been an illusion, and the finger had not really fallen off. Anna kept telling herself that she had been very silly. Yes, it was all an illusion, brought on by reading that sad letter.

First thing would be to find a box big enough to stack all the rubbish in. The box from the auction filled that bill very nicely.

Comics, some magazines and layers of wrapping paper. She lined the box carefully.

A coffin. That's what she was making. A coffin for a doll.

Outside, she could hear the crackling of the newly-lit bonfire, and the sounds of snapping twigs and hissing leaves made her work faster. Already the blue-grey smoke was curling up from the bonfire, and her heart pounded as she frantically stuffed more and more paper into the cardboard box.

Layer upon layer, she was almost afraid to stop. She wanted this box to burn . . . really burn. She wanted it to glow white hot and dissolve everything to a black, harmless ash.

Still not daring to look at Bess, she made her way over to the shelf and reached out her hand. Groping fingers felt the edge of the faded dress . . . a leg . . . body . . . shoulders . . . head.

"Ow!" Anna screamed, withdrawing her hand. "She bit me!"

Bess sat on the shelf, her red, stained teeth bared. Her eyes were back again, and she was almost restored to the condition she was in when new. Rosy cheeks, laughing eyes, ruby lips—and even the dress was no longer faded and shabby. Anna stared at the doll.

How could she have thought of burning it? My! It was so pretty.

Bess grinned her frozen grin as Anna walked woodenly towards her.

"You're not such a bad thing after all," Anna said, reaching out her hands to take the doll. "Maybe your teeth are a bit sharp, but it was my fault for not looking what I was doing. I'll have to be careful not to put my fingers near those teeth, though. Nowadays, they wouldn't allow such sharp cutting edges on toys—and that is what you are, Bess . . . a toy."

Bess was in her arms, an innocent expression on her rosy face. She was beautiful, and Anna could not help but hug the doll tightly. Had anyone else been in the room at that time, they would have seen a much different picture. They would have seen a girl holding a ragged doll with shorn hair and cavernous sockets for eyes. They would have wondered why such a revolting doll was treated with love and affection.

But Anna could only see the rosy-cheeked doll laughing up at her and she bent over to kiss it.

"I'm sorry," she said, "to have treated you like I did. It must have been my imagination. I really don't know what was wrong with me. Do you forgive me, Bess? Say you do."

Bringing the doll up to her face, Anna placed an affectionate kiss on the rosy cheek and hugged Bess tight.

Bess raised her arms jerkily and put them around Anna's neck . . . squeezing.

"You moved!" Anna cried.

Bess squeezed.

"You moved!"

Her mouth next to Anna's ear, the doll let out a low chuckle, squeezing tighter and tighter.

Frantically, Anna struggled to pull the doll away . . . but Bess was powerful.

Tighter . . . tighter . . . tighter!

"Let go!" Anna cried, her breath almost taken away with fear. The chuckling filled her ears, and Bess wriggled to get a better grip.

"Ha-ha-ha-ha!"

With all her strength, Anna wrenched the doll from her neck and threw her into the cardboard box. Paper! More and more paper was thrust into the box. Cardboard, comics, books and more paper. Anna was heedless as to what she was throwing into the box to cover the chuckling, evil doll.

Stamp it down! Stamp, stamp, stamp!

Quick as a flash, she scooped up the box and ran helter-skelter down the stairs.

"You shouldn't be carrying so much at a time, dear," her mother said, opening the back kitchen door to let Anna out into the yard.

Out . . . out into the garden where the bonfire crackled and roared. Over to the greedy, licking flames. Her eyes filled with tears and smoke, Anna hurled the box on to the fire, and the flames leaped upon it and started to devour it instantly.

"Burn! Burn! Burn!" Anna screamed.

"It will burn quite nicely without being shouted at," her father said, laughing as he watched her.

White-faced, she watched the orange flames slither

over the cardboard coffin, seeking out the thinner paper first.

Page by page, the comics and magazines burned through and peeled back. Page after page, until Anna could see Bess's face through the roaring inferno.

One last scream of defiance, and the doll was engulfed in white hot fire.

"Don't scream so loud, Anna," her father called from the bottom of the garden. "You're not a child and you've seen a bonfire before."

"Sorry, Dad," Anna called back as she watched the black ashes of the fire soar up high into the sky. She couldn't tell him that it was Bess, not her, screaming. He wouldn't believe it anyway.

Up into the sky the black ashes flew . . . like birds.

"Free . . . like the birds," Anna breathed.

The new doll. "Chorus: should old acquaintance be forgot?" (Nineteenth-century illustration from the Manley-Lewis collection)

"THE LIFE OF AUNT SALLY, ALIAS BLACKMORE, ALIAS ROSABELLA, ALIAS AMELIA, AS RELATED BY HERSELF"

by a Contributor to *The Christmas Box*

The doll who spoke for herself in print emerged like a doll suffragette in the mid-nineteenth century. (She is still going strong as the twenty-first century approaches.) One such famous doll, Victoria-Bess (created by Mrs. Castle Smith more than a century ago), was obsessed, as many dolls were, by her past and her future. "Do not," she said, "throw us dolls away but send us where we shall be well received and welcomed."

This rare find, a doll story that appeared in a Christmas annual published well over a hundred years ago, seems like such a doll's cry from the distant past. The author is that famous Anonymous—a Ms Anonymous, we would suspect. The doll who speaks, however, is remarkably forceful even if she is reduced to being an Aunt Sally—a figure in a then-popular game in which children pitched stones at such a doll. We felt this admirable doll needed better treatment and have edited some of her voluminous asides and rescued her from the crumbled pages of the last century.

"IT IS a fine thing to be fifty years old, and not only to be of use still, but able to make oneself positively agreeable. Don't you think so, my young friends?"

"Well, my dears, I cannot hear what answer you make to my question; but whatever you may think, I can assure you positively that it is a very nice thing to be able to please other people as one grows old; it proves that one is still of use. So I am glad to find myself turned to such good account as to be made an Aunt Sally of, and played with. It's a roguish sort of game, I admit, and not the kind of thing I was accustomed to in my best days; but I am well seasoned by this time, and can bear more rubs with a quiet temper than I could have done then. One lives and learns, you know, and there's nothing one learns plainer as one grows old, than the folly of making a fuss about trifles. If I was crusty and cross, now, think how easily I could vex myself and everybody else, by grumbling at young folks' impertinence, and making out that I was ill-treated. But as I take it quite easy, and am glad to be of use, both they and I are pleased, and all goes smooth. Now, I did meet with some real impertinence a few days ago. A little girl came up to me on the lawn, stared a bit, and then said, 'You hideous old creature, I wonder where you were born? In some dusty out-of-the-way shop where everything was ugly, I'm sure.'

"Wasn't that silly? If I had been able to speak, I should have called out, 'You ignorant little goose, go home and find out where wood comes from.' That would have made the saucy young lady look rather foolish, I suspect.

"Then, too, as to my being hideous; hideousness is really a matter of taste, and tastes vary according to the fashion of the day and country. I was thought lovely once, before the new varieties of dolls came up. So I sit quite easy at being called hideous now. People have changed their tastes, that's all. I have not changed in any material point. It is true I am a little altered outwardly from what I once was, but nothing to what the young lady will be at my age. Wood wears out less than flesh, I suspect.

"How different the attitude of that young lady and my first little mistress. Think of her now, a jaunty little girl with dimpled cheeks and a sweet smile. Many a day we played together—I was all things to her (and she to me) but that was a long time ago. I have forgotten much.

"I do know she became ill, carried me listlessly. Then one day she looked at me with such a sad, sweet smile as I had never seen before, and kissed

me, and in a weak, thin voice bade me be good and
go to sleep, for she could not play till she was better
—a time which never came.

"Well! After a few more days everybody was crying, and people seemed to have forgotten I was in
the bed at all, I had been so hid away in the farthest
corner. But presently I was thrown on the floor
roughly by strange women, who evidently knew nothing about me, and were only vexed because I made a
noise in my fall. After which I was picked up and
put once more into the wicker-cradle. And then I
found out what had happened, and that the little
girl had really died, for a coffin was brought into the
room and she laid in it. And I wondered whether she
had guessed right, and it was part of my tree, and
whether I should be put in, too. For I didn't know
then, any more than she did, what I have learnt
since—namely, that dolls are made of apple-tree
wood and coffins of elm. So I kept hoping to be
taken to my dear little friend from hour to hour, and
stared at everybody who came near me, to remind
them that there I was, quite ready. But nobody even
looked into the cradle; and, oh, dear! how vexed I
was; for, thought I, everybody forgets me; how hard
it is!

"They didn't forget me, though, so I was wrong
again; but one is so hasty when one is young! Still,
though they did remember me, it was not in the way
I should have liked best; for they popped me, cradle
and all, into a large dark closet, covered me up, and
left me there for—oh! How shall I measure the
time? I cannot, but it seemed very, very long. Per-

haps because at first I could not rest, from vexation at being where I was. That was wise, wasn't it? Did one so much good, eh, to be cross about what one couldn't help? This makes you laugh, I see. Well, I am glad it does, if thinking of what I did wrong ever comes in of use. If, I mean, you are wiser than I was, and learn patience without going through the mistakes I did, first. Do, there's dears! Don't be impatient, for instance, and think yourselves ill-used every time your wishes are thwarted. Don't fancy people dislike you because they don't do everything you wish. And, above all, be contented to be wherever you are put. In nine cases out of ten, whoever put you there knows better than you do the best place for you. And every place is a good place if you can be of use in it. There! When you are as old as I am, you will know what good advice this is.

"But now you shall hear what became of me afterward. I suppose I got tired even of being cross at last; for after settling that everybody was heartless and cruel, and that nobody had cared for my little mistress, or they would have made a pet of me, I fell asleep. At all events, I knew nothing more till one day, a long time afterward, the closet door was opened, and nurse herself came in, took me up out of my cradle, and uncovered my face. Oh, dear, how she cried, to be sure! And she carried me down-stairs in her arms just as if I had been a baby, and after stopping outside the drawing-room door to wipe her eyes, she took me in; and there sat the mother of my dear little mistress, and some children in black, who turned out to be her nieces, and who had lately lost their mother. She wished to be a second mother to

them, as far as she could, she said, and they must try
and make up to her for the little girl she had lost. So
I was given them to be theirs. But when it came to
actually putting me into their hands, the poor lady
broke down. I think the merely touching me upset
her; and then it struck me, all at once, that she was
thinking of the other little hands which had handled
me last. And then, for the first time, I understood
why I had been laid by out of sight for so long; and
once more had to be ashamed for having been unjust
and selfish.

"I think the children felt sorry for their aunt when
she gave me to them, though very likely they could
not have told why. Certainly they seemed half afraid
to touch me; the second girl especially, who turned
her back and began to cry. On which her aunt kissed
her, and bade her not do so; for, said she, 'It will
make me happier to be of use to you all; and the
poor doll will be of use again, too, you see, so I really like you to have her. To be of use to other people is the only thing worth living for.'

"*There* was a new idea for me, who hitherto had
thought so little of anything but my own amusements
and comforts. Oh, I assure you what the poor lady
said quite startled me. And yet it made me very
happy, too. '*The poor doll will be of use again, too.*'
I actually *had* been of use, then, once; I was going
to be so again; and being of use to other people was
the only thing worth living for. Those words became
the text-book of my life!

"But I didn't grow wise at once. The new home
put all my wisdom out of my head at first, it was so
bewildering. The very chatter of three or four young

voices kept my head in a whirl. Then they changed
my dress, and the style of my wig, and even my
name; but this last, I believe, nurse told them they
must do. I had been *Amelia* before, now I was to be
Rosabella; and the children gave a nursery tea-
party to celebrate the event, and I was handed round
and admired as the new baby.

"This was all very well, and rather amusing to me,
who had seen nothing of the sort before; but presently I found out that the change in my life was not
for the better in the main. I had been petted before
by one mistress with one will; now I had three, and
sometimes all the three pulling different ways. Just
think of that! I tried to remind myself about being
of use, as the lady had said, but what I had to bear
was too much for me.

"Oh, dear! How sick I was of being tossed about
from one lap to another, everybody clawing hold of
me, and wanting to 'have me,' as they called it, at
once.

"It was very affectionate, I dare say, but I don't
like affection when it goes worry, worry, worry, without stopping to think whether it can be pleasant or
not. I actually, every now and then, wished myself
back in the dark closet again. Indeed, I am obliged
to own that I got very impatient, and was always
saying to myself how inferior these children were to
the one I had known before; what hopeless young
bears, etc.; which made me more irritable than I
should have been if I had tried to take things quietly
and submit.

"Nevertheless, there was *some* reason for finding
fault, for the children did tease each other amazingly

"The History of Aunt Sally"—A Squabble for
Rosabella. (*Original illustration*)

at times, actually as if they had no sense or manners
either. For instance, if one wanted to take me up for
lessons, another would very likely want to play at my
being sick in bed, and the third would insist on car-

rying me into the garden to make me swing. And each would defend her proposal with so many arguments, I used to wonder they did not talk one another deaf, especially when they were all chattering together, which was by no means an uncommon case.

"Yet they were fine, intelligent, clever children all the time, poor things, and I lived to owe them a great deal, as you shall hear. We had gone on some time in this confused way, when, one day, their aunt paid them a visit in the nursery. And as she happened to come in in the middle of a squabble, when my head was on one little girl's knees, my legs on those of another, while the third was standing by crying, she understood the whole affair at once.

"And that very evening there arrived a huge parcel for the children, which proved to contain two new dolls, one a large one exactly like myself, only that her complexion was sallower than mine—indeed, I think we must have been purchased at the same shop; the other a neat, jointed foreigner—a new invention, then, which was thought to be a model of ingenuity.

"Of course, these dolls came from that kind aunt; who wrote a letter with them, saying that the eldest girl was to have the big one, the youngest the jointed foreigner, and that I was to be the property of the second. This offended me much. I thought I ought to have had the place of honor, and belonged to the eldest. And in my vexation I got hold of a new trouble, viz., that as the new dolls looked so smart and bright, the child who had me would hate me, and so I should never be happy again; and, I added, *of no further use*. Yes, I believe I tried to persuade myself that I was fretting because I should be of use no longer; but conscience obliges me to own that this was not my real trouble, but a jealous feeling about my position in life, and the supposed superiority of others. So I wished the new dolls out of the house, felt very angry with the kind aunt, and would have given anything in the world to find myself once more an only doll, even if I had had a dozen mistresses to toss and tumble me about; for, said I to myself then, 'I was certainly too hasty in finding so much fault; the children meant kindly, and so I ought to have taken it.'

"It was my misfortune, you see, in those days, to be wise just too late. But never mind, I learnt better at last! My fright was soon over this time, for even before night I found out that I had not done my particular little girl justice. When she put me to bed, she whispered to me as she bent over my cradle, 'Dolly, dear! the new dolls are very gay and pretty, but I like you a great deal better than either of them. I used to like your face so much when you were my cousin's *Amelia*, and now I like you for having been hers, because she was my darling; and I shall teach you all manner of things, for aunt says we ought to keep a school now that we have so many young people to bring up, and I mean you to be very clever some day. Now you are my very own, I shall love you as much as my cousin did.'

"This was pleasant, was it not? Besides, it made me recollect that this was the little girl who had cried when she first saw me, and now I knew why. She and her cousin had been darling friends, and she loved me for her sake. And this, then, was the reason of the kind aunt wishing her to have me for her very own! And I ought to have been glad, instead of thinking myself ill-used! How unjust this made me feel myself! I even wondered if I should ever be cured! Well! I had had lessons enough, and I think this last made me try to turn over a new leaf: to take nothing amiss which came from a friend; to think more of being of use than of pleasing myself; and to bear little vexations easily. Vexations did come at times, of course, for who is not liable to be irritable and unreasonable now and then? My queer leathern fingers would sometimes stick in the sleeve of my frock, and it wouldn't come on; or my curls wouldn't lie smooth; or the string of my petticoat broke, just when I was going to be taken out for an airing; or my shoes dropped off those horrid flat-sided feet of mine; and my little mistress got angry; but I stuck to my resolutions, and kept calm. She was my friend, and that was enough. 'It's partly my fault, I know,' said I, to myself. 'I'm an awkward creature, and can't help being tiresome. We must forgive and forget trifles.' And so we did, for the pet was soon over, and we were as happy as ever.

"And then the learning! It was really wonderful what the children tucked into us, when they once set about it with a good heart. They had a table to themselves in a corner of the drawing-room, and round this we used to be seated every evening to be taught. I am an old creature now, but I recollect a good many of those lessons yet. One of us learnt the geography of Spain, and traced the Duke of Wellington's battles on the map. Another took to Ireland; and I at one time learnt all the Greek declensions, and part of the first verb; but there, alas! I and my mistress stuck fast. My sallow-faced sister even worked the Hebrew characters on a sampler; for you see we did not confine ourselves to commonplaces, such as French, arithmetic, etc., but rushed boldly at all sorts of difficulties. The pity was, that we did not go on far enough, for then we should have been qualified to pass a Government Inspector's examination; but, somehow or other, whenever anything very hard came, we were always whipped and sent to bed —a sign, of course, that we were supposed not to be paying proper attention, therefore couldn't be taught any further then.

"Once or twice it did come into my head on those occasions to wonder whether our mistresses themselves knew any further; but I was ashamed of the suspicion, and always repelled it. Afterward, however, I found out that this was the secret of the whole affair, and that the whipping was performed merely as a matter of course, to make a proper ending to the lesson.

"Teachers can seldom afford to acknowledge their own ignorance, you know. It wouldn't do. Nevertheless, it was droll, wasn't it, for *us* to be whipped because *they* knew no more; but we didn't mind. I told my companions my former history; and being more experienced than they were, had the pleasure of delivering a little lecture to them on the folly of impatience, and the value of being of use in the world. So we all agreed to take things as they came, and make no complaints. Anyhow, we could congratulate ourselves on being the three best educated dolls in all the countryside; and let me tell you, this source of consolation has saved me grief and mortification on more occasions than one! Look how people's tastes are constantly changing. Wood gives way to wax, no matter how brittle it may be, or how liable to melt. Leather is preferred to both, no matter how dark the paint tints look upon it. Rags are cried up by some people as best of all for babies; and gutta-percha suddenly supersedes everything else. And I might have broken my heart with vexation, as each of these new vagaries threatened to put my poor old three-cornered wooden nose out of joint, but that I had my Greek declensions and my Irish geography, and all sorts of knowledge, to support me, to say nothing of good downright bodily solidity; learning and strength, in fact. And if learning, strength, and being of use to other people, won't make one happy, I don't know what will, eh? And have I not had good reason to be satisfied, when here I am as you see, dears, at the end of a dozen common doll generations, as good an Aunt Sally as the best of them?

"Everything has an end, however; and so had my school-time. One Summer our mistresses, now biggish girls, went from home, and when they came back, the governess told them they were too old to play with dolls any longer, even though they did learn fractions and Greek. Now, had this happened a few years sooner, when I was in the hey-day of impatience and self-will, I believe I should have felt as fierce as possible, called the governess names, and abused my young mistress for submitting. But as it was, I concluded there was some good reason for the decision, though I couldn't possibly find it out. And it was no small comfort to know that the blow did not fall on me only. My young lady often came to take a peep at me in my wicker-cradle in the garret, and she would lift the coverlet as nicely as ever, and ask the poor old Dolly how she did, and say how sorry she was; nay, once or twice she brought up a friend to see me, and on one of these occasions she paid me the high compliment of saying she believed she should learn German twice as well, if she had me down-stairs to teach it to!

"What I felt when I heard these words, I can give you no notion of. I never before knew of *how much* use I had actually been, and the knowledge of it made me feel that I had nothing more left to wish for; so after she had covered me up and was gone away again, I fell into a sort of peaceful unconscious doze, which must have lasted many years.

"For the very next event I recollect happened when my young mistress was a grown-up woman and married, and had a baby of her own.

"I was roused by a great fuss and disturbance in the house, and then by her coming up to the garret and calling out, 'Whatever you do, pray find the old doll. I must have my old doll for little Gretchen. There's the wicker-cradle, I declare, behind all those boxes! Fetch it out, and let me see the dear old creature's face again.'

"And when she did see me, she laughed heartily, and took me out, and tried to put my stumpy old wig straight, but in vain. At which she laughed again, and said, 'This will never do; but I can have a new wig nailed on, which is more than can be said to a doll of modern days. It's a good hard head this, that's one comfort, and as full of solid wood and hodge-podge learning as it can hold. Eh, Rosabella, do you remember your Greek and your Dante and fractions?'

"Why, my dears, when I heard that I felt quite young again! It was as if the old jovial schooldays had come back, to hear that cheerful voice, and the fun sounding in my ears. And then the thought of the new wig—I confess I was not quite insensible to that! I knew the old one was worn almost bare, and half loose besides. Certainly a new wig is an event in life to those who wear them, and not to be talked of lightly. In fact, I spent much of my time now in wondering what color it would be—for I must own to a weakness. I had a secret wish that it should be flaxen, having once in my life seen a flaxen-haired wax doll, and thought it a sort of angel of beauty. So a flaxen-haired doll I must needs be myself; goose that I was for forgetting how little it would suit my hard, wooden face and bright, coarse coloring. When I was taken to the shop, however, the woman asked my mistress, 'Dark or flaxen, ma'am?' and my heart was in my mouth, so to speak, for a moment. But the answer sobered me at once: 'Oh, dark, certainly! With those black eyes, flaxen curls would be perfectly ridiculous. Besides, I particularly wish the doll to be as it has always been.'

"This was enough; I submitted, and my vanity subsided. I never troubled my head about flaxen wigs again, and the new dark one was made and nailed on before many days were over, to say nothing of fresh arms and legs, both of which were sadly needed. Luckily, however, I did not require repainting, which I was heartily glad of, for having undergone the operation once (just before my schooldays began), I knew how disagreeable it was to be smeared all over with oily colors, and then, when you think your troubles are over, have two or three coats of strong-smelling varnish laid on besides.

"And now, behold—Rosabella in her new wig, laid in the wicker-cradle for little Gretchen to look at. But, oh dear! The wicker-cradle was by this time nearly in pieces, for it had been sadly battered about; and as for little Gretchen, she could not lift Rosabella, and did not like her staring black eyes half as well as those of the pretty little wax thing somebody had given her, with eyes that opened and shut by pulling a wire. Oh, those eyes that opened and shut! What a trial they have been to me more than once! No matter what a doll is made of or like, if she has only eyes that open and shut, children rave about her. I confess I never could see the great advantage of it; indeed, I persuaded myself it was a much greater merit to have one's eyes always open, but that was a stupid idea of mine, I suppose. Anyhow, my only resource was to take things easy and be contented. And so I did, though I was turned out of the wicker-cradle to make way for little Waxy, and had to accommodate myself with a box for a bed.

"But I didn't grumble. I only said to myself, 'My day of being of use is over. It's what we must all come to. But why *did* she buy me that new wig?' That was all. I really abused nobody.

"It makes me smile now, however, to think of my settling so coolly that my day was over. Why, my dears, I scarcely knew then what life was at all, for I had never been among boys. Talk of troublesome girls! A dozen of them can't do as much mischief in a day as a boy does in five minutes. *Five* minutes, do I say? I might say one! As years went on, little Gretchen had brothers and sisters, till the house was full, and a new nursery had to be built; and by that time I had become a rather important fact, if not an established pet, in the nursery. But in rather a peculiar way. I was never No. 1 with anybody. Each child had a doll or a plaything preferred before me. But then I was everybody's No. 2, and therefore always of use, a universal necessity, a refuge in distress, when No. 1 pets were wearisome, or had come to grief.

"Let me not forget one exception, though. For nearly a year I was at one time the one undivided object of love to a little thing, the youngest daughter of the house, who, being herself the exact image of the flaxen doll of my vain ambition, was perhaps fond of me from the striking contrast we were to each other. Dear me! It touches my old heart now to think how we used to sleep together, both underneath the sheets, and with our heads on the same pillow; hers with the bright curls clustered close all over it like a doll's, and her rosy cheeks close to my poor old faded face, (age was telling on my colors then), and her arm across my neck as if to hold me safe. My dear mistress often came to see us as we lay so, and always smiled and said it pleased her very much, for we made such a pretty variety—my eyes always open, and the little girl's always shut in sleep. And this was the way I knew how we looked, and it used to please me to find I still pleased *her* as well as the child, for I never forgot old friends in new ones, remember!

"But with this exception, I was now always No. 2. But then No. 2's is a sort of favoritism which never dies, and I was soon satisfied that not a doll that ever came into the house could rival me in general favor; no, not even the Waxys with eyes that opened and shut! They might be very elegant, but wanted solidity, you see; and only let anything wanting solidity come near a boy, and you'll soon see how long it lasts. What do they care for *elegance,* the rough young rogues? And when once the elegant creatures' eyes are poked in, and their noses pinched off, and their necks have been melted white at the fire, the miserable remains of their bran-filled bodies are cared for by nobody.

"With me, on the contrary, it was quite different. In the first place, I was an historical character— their mother's doll. 'Mother's old doll' had a value attached to her as such, to which no modern one could ever attain. Secondly, her solidity was a match even for the boys. They might cut off her wig, scratch her cheeks, break her legs, and poke holes in her arms; but, armless, legless, wigless, and scratched, she could always be repaired. New legs, new arms, new wigs, new paint, and the old stump came out as fresh as ever: 'mother's old doll' in all her glory.

"And when once I found this out, it not only gave me a comfortable feeling of superiority over other dolls, but enabled me to bear any amount of rude treatment those *in*-elegant creatures, the boys of the family, chose to inflict.

"I wonder whether you would like to hear some of the strange things they did? I suspect you would, for every now and then they thought of something very droll, I must own. Only fancy, for instance, their taking it into their heads to burn that new wig I told you about, before it was a quarter worn out; and what for, do you suppose? Come, do try and guess! You can't? Well, I must tell you, then! Merely to smell how nasty it smelt. So like boys, wasn't it? A reason with no sense in it, and only funny because of its foolishness! One of the young rascals had singed his hair by an accident, and so discovered how disagreeable burnt hair was; and *therefore* (here comes the reason without sense) they decided 'what fun it would be' to fill the whole nursery with it, so as to stifle the nurse if she happened to come up, and perhaps, too, make her fancy something was on fire. But the difficulty was, where to get hold of any hair. I saw their faces as they sat over their candle puzzling, and then the gleam of delight when the bright idea struck them. Mother's old doll's wig—such a lot of curls—hair enough, and no mistake—and what a row the girls would make!

"'My poor mistress,' thought I, as they seized me in my cradle, forced out the nails with an old knife, tore off the wig, and held it over the flame of the candle to burn. 'My poor mistress—there goes seven-and-sixpence in smoke and smell.'

"Well, as soon as the wig was frizzled to a cinder, and the room full of the stench, off ran the young hopefuls to hide behind the door in the passage and watch the result. And there I heard them exploding with laughter, as poor old nurse toddled up-stairs,

"The History of Aunt Sally"—The Frizzled Wig.
(*Original illustration*)

and hunted every hole and corner of the nursery to
find the cause of such a terrible smell of burning.

"I, meanwhile, had been carefully replaced in bed,

only with one of the baby's caps on my head; so no disturbance took place till next day, when poor, dear, unconscious Gretchen, looking into my cradle, called out in delight, 'Oh, nurse, how nice mother's old doll looks in the cap! Thank you so much for giving it to her! She looks quite pretty!'

"You can just fancy the rest, I'm sure! It was baby's best cap, with three frillings of Valenciennes lace all round it, and a blue rosette on one side. It might have been becoming—I don't say it wasn't— but nurse tore it indignantly off my poor bald head, as if all the fault had been mine.

"I suppose it's the same with everybody's memory, but certainly mine is clearer upon startling events of life like this, than upon the little particulars of what happened every day. Indeed, of these I can give you no connected account, for there was always such a racket going on with such a large party of children, that I never knew what to expect from day to day, and nothing did happen two days alike. So you must be contented to hear the chief points of interest which remain impressed upon my mind. Generally, however, I may say that Gretchen and her sister were very nice little girls, and though I was, as I said before, only pet No. 2 with them, I had nothing to complain of but the general wear and tear of life.

"Yet, in justice to the boys, I must admit that I cannot say the same about the next sister—the one who came between the boys, like a slice of meat in a sandwich—for she was, at times, as great a Tomboy as either of them; but then, it *was* only at times; now and then, that is, not always. At other times she could be as reasonable as anybody; quite motherly, indeed, as she got a little sense into her head. But what a roguish face she had, grave as she looked to strangers; and the most comfortable fat cheeks that ever were seen. Her mamma used to kiss each at night, and call one the apple and the other the rose. My own were not more rosy in my young days, so I don't wonder people were pleased when they looked at her.

"But her mother didn't know half her odd ways. For instance, she never heard, till years afterward, who it was that had cut the long hair off the front which I wore after the wig was burnt, and so made it look like that of a shorn workhouse girl. But *I* knew! *I* could have told her of Tom-boy miss taking me on her knee as quietly as possible, and snip, snip, snipping the front quite close, that she might stuff a hole in her brother's fur donkey with the hair. But, poor dear! she meant it out of good-nature to him, and I consoled myself by thinking my very wig was of use to somebody. Certainly, I was left a very wild-looking creature, with the bristles that remained; so much so, that Gretchen took pity on me, and made me a muslin cap, with a broadish frill round it, to cover defects.

"You will wonder, perhaps, how I come to recollect and tell you this; but the fact is, that cap affair was a more important event in my life than you would suppose, for it brought about my third change of name. *Rosabella* had been long forgotten, and among these children I was chiefly known as 'Dolly,' or 'Mother's Old Doll.' But no sooner had Gretchen put the cap on my head, than she jumped up and ran shouting about the passages for her sisters; for was I not the exact image of the new baby's nurse who had just left the house, *Mrs. Blackmore,* to wit? and the notion spread like wildfire; and even the boys agreed with their sisters for once, 'Blackmore to the life!' 'Blackmore all over!' 'Blackmore for ever!'

"And Blackmore I was henceforth called, and, considering my eyes and hair, a more inappropriate name might easily have been found. Yes; and it was as Blackmore I became the darling of that youngest child with the hair like a flaxen doll, the last of really loving mistresses I ever had. For, for the rest of my life after that, I degenerated into a sort of object of universal fun, everybody's favorite, to do whatever they liked with, and to like whatever they did.

"Three days a week, for instance, for a month together, one year, after the family had been to the sea, I was bathed in the mill-dam with a rope tied round my neck—an unnecessary precaution, by the way, for it was always my nature to swim.

"On another occasion, I had a series of shower-baths under the pump for a week, because the doctors had ordered it, to keep off an attack of brain-fever. After which a spine complaint obliged me to be driven about in a little machine called a *drug* (well known to children in English north country villages) whenever the day was fine; the only inconsistency of the proceeding being that the drivers ran so fast, I used to be thrown out half a dozen times in the course of the excursion. But this did them great good from the exercise, and me no harm, so I took it quietly, thinking to myself when the upsets came, 'What a mercy I'm not a Waxy with eyes that open and shut! *I* can afford to fall on my face.'

"The History of Aunt Sally"—Mrs. Blackmore's Grave.
(*Original illustration*)

"One day at last, however, I was supposed to have
been killed by one of these overthrows; and after
being carried home on a flat piece of wood, as if to a
hospital, my funeral was ordered, and my grave was
dug; and the next day they popped me in, covered
me up, and left me alone. Now, when one is alone

one can't help thinking, unless one happens to be asleep. So I began to think, 'Here's an end, then; I wonder how far I've been useful in the world?' And then—I can't tell where it came from, a horrid idea seized me that in this life among the boys, though I had been patient enough, I had been of no use at all; merely something to be kicked about and destroyed. But what a foolish fancy that was, I found out when I had thought a little longer. For of course I had set them a good example of patience, and of course if they had not had me to kick about and destroy, they would have kicked about and destroyed the furniture, or something else, and perhaps of greater value. I reflected accordingly on my broken limbs and battered frame with great comfort, for, thought I, 'I have saved my mistress's furniture, and that's something.'

"And so thinking, I determined on taking a long sleep and thorough good rest, which I did; for it was the boys who buried me, and I never woke again till their holidays came round once more, when the very first thing they did was to dig me up, drag me to the lawn, make a circle of stones round me, and dance an Indian war-dance outside, in imitation of the Ojibbeways whom they had seen as they passed through London. After which the girls came to my rescue, first washed and scrubbed me in a tub, then dressed me in a nightgown, and put me to bed between warm blankets; and soon after they made their two younger brothers come in, in hats and coats, the one as an Allopathic, the other as a Homeopathic, physician, to prescribe for my case. Between these, of course, a tremendous tussle ensued, but it ended in my being ordered Dulcamara and Antimonial wine, alternately every three minutes, the effect of which combination was that at the end of a quarter of an hour I was pronounced perfectly recovered; whereupon the doctors fell to squabbling again as to which of them had cured me! I, meanwhile, was declared well enough to take a dancing lesson, which, considering that in the course of so many carriage accidents, and the burial, both my legs had come off, was rather peculiar. But they held me up, and I got through it pretty well; and it was then that my mistress, being asked by the children if they might send Blackmore to the carpenter for a pair of new legs, said she was tired of getting her new legs, they were always being broken off to light fires with, or do something preposterous, so she would make me a pair herself.

"It seemed a strange idea at first, and I confess I felt a little offended; but the legs turned out better than I expected. Nicely cut for calves and feet, and well stuffed with closely packed cotton-wool, there was something about them quite novel and attractive. And I believe they would have lasted till now, but for that bathing fancy, which returned upon the children in hot weather, and made the unfortunate legs so spotty and nasty, that an impatient hand one day cut them entirely off; after which the old stump was thrown into a rubbish-closet and forgotten for at least six months, when cold, wet Winter weather made the young folks want occupation indoors, and the elder ones took it into their heads to clear out that very rubbish-closet where I lay.

"Wonderful things, forgotten, and therefore as good as new, are sure to turn up for the younger olive-branches on all such occasions, and among others out came Blackmore herself, *sans* arms, *sans* legs, *sans* everything, almost, but the old solid stump covered with half an inch of dust.

"No sooner was I beheld then I was received with a general groan, which turned, however, somehow into a laugh very soon, and Gretchen suggested that the poor old thing should be treated with proper respect, and once more buried in the garden. But she advised that this time a stone should be placed over the grave, to mark the spot where I was laid.

"It is needless to describe the universal approbation with which the proposal was received and carried out; and when I knew that the third boy had spent a whole hour in carving my name, 'Blackmore,' on the stone, with the date of the day of burial below, I thought to myself, 'This is really the end, I'm sure. Nobody will disturb me any more now. Well, I shall sleep quite happy, having been useful as long as I could, even up to the very, very last moment.' And so thinking, I composed myself to rest.

"But it didn't last long. At a very early hour next morning I felt a tapping and scratching outside the grave, the stone was lifted up, and thwack! came the edge of a spade across my face. Nobody but myself could have borne it, I believe; but the spade was not very sharp, and the hand that held it was not very heavy. It was the youngest boy of all, a mere child then in petticoats, but as bold in taking his own way as any among them.

"As soon, however, as he felt the spade hit my

face, he laid it on the ground, and kneeling down, scraped the earth away with his fingers, till he could see me quite plain. I wonder what he thought when our eyes met? I shall never know, but I have a suspicion, from what I have since heard, that he half expected to see a skull, instead of my poor old head. Be that as it may, he looked very grave and inquiring, and it seems to me he must have wished to find out whether anything had happened to me in the night; a point about which he was evidently satisfied at once, for he lifted me out, laid me down while he replaced the earth and stone, and then taking me in his arms, carried me to the barn, where he made a sort of nest for me in some old hay in a corner, put me in, covered me lightly up, and went away.

"It was an amazingly comfortable bed in cold weather, and I was quite satisfied, and rested as well as I had ever done in my life, if it had not been for the rats, who disturbed me a little at first by running across my face; but I soon got used to them, for they did me no harm, not even tickled me as they went; so I dozed off by degrees into one of my long rests, and I believe my last thought was, wondering what use rats were of, for that was always what I wanted to know of everybody: what use are they of to other people? And here, where the rats and I were alone together, it was quite natural to inquire. But one can't find out everything, even about that. It's a very interesting question, nevertheless, and one that everybody ought to put to themselves about themselves.

"But was it not odd that I was woke up at last in the Summer-time that followed, by the arrival of a rat-catcher, who came to lay poison trains in the barn to kill those very rats? I mightn't have known much about it, but that the holidays had come round again, and the boys were helping the rat-catcher, and poking about in all directions to find traces of rats, so they came upon me in my nest; and, oh, dear! what a shout there was when they found me! I really believe the rat-catcher himself, who, with that horrible rat-skin cap on his head, looked pretty well seasoned to anything, was startled when he heard the schoolboy cry, 'Why, here's Blackmore, I declare! How on earth did she come here? I thought we buried her last holidays? Who in the world dug her up? What fun!'

"Whereupon my former little friend came forward with a rather timid grin on his face, and announced that it was he who had done it; he had wished to know how I was, he said; besides, it was such cold weather then to be in the ground. (Wasn't that a kind thought of his?) He added honestly enough that after a day or two he had forgotten all about me. But now he would have taken me under his protection again if the second boy had not interfered and suggested what a noble scare-crow I should make, and as the birds were taking all the peas and currants in the garden, what a capital thing it would be to set me up there to frighten them away.

"Here was a new line of life indeed, and I dare say many of you, my dears, may be inclined to think I was very hardly used in being made a scare-crow of; but that is because you are not old enough to know life as well as I do, and to appreciate the comfort of being of use to other people. The fact was, I had lived to be afraid of only one thing in the world, and that was being of no use at all; (if such a thing is possible, but I have great doubts on the subject; one must always be of use, either as a help or a warning, I suspect); and my mind had been a little uneasy on the subject when I was left alone in the barn with the rats. Imagine to yourselves, therefore, the delight with which I heard that very proposal which seems to you so cruel and disgraceful. A thousand times better be a scare-crow and frighten birds from peas and currants, than lie idle and useless in the prettiest four-post bed that ever adorned a nursery! So I entered on my scare-crow duties, with a battered hat on my head, and long sticks for arms, with proud delight; and if nobody knew how happy I was, no matter. I knew it myself.

"And a scare-crow I remained till the peas were gathered and eaten, and Autumn weather set in; when just as my old fever of wondering whether I was of any use was beginning to return, Gretchen and my last dear little mistress came strolling into the garden together; and Gretchen, happening to look my way, stopped and exclaimed, 'Oh, that poor old doll! What a shame it is to see her swinging about in the wind and wet! Do let's take her into the house once more! She may come in of use yet on a wet day, and she certainly has nine lives, like a cat.'

"Didn't it seem now as if she had read my thoughts, and here was the answer? And the little one came and undid the fastenings, and threw the hat on the ground, and cuddled me in her arms, as she used to do in old times, and declared she would dress me up quite comfortably, and make me a crinoline, that I might be like other people.

"Really, girls are worth their weight in gold, for they always think of something pleasant and kind; and by what I heard remarked afterward, my little friend's efforts were most successful, for I turned out a most respectable-looking matron under her management. The thick bishop sleeves she made in my dress looked as if there must be good stout arms underneath, though there were none at all, and the crinoline and plenty of petticoats entirely hid the want of legs, as did the close-fitting cap the absence of hair. To casual observers, therefore, I presented a thoroughly creditable appearance, and no one could have suspected me of having played scare-crow so short a time before. Indeed, when I found how well they thought I had turned out, I had a half-fright lest they should do by me what they were just then doing by several of their other old dolls and play-things, viz., give me away into some strange family. Of course I knew that if I had gone I should have been of use, but I had no fancy for so great a change, even to get out of the way of the holidays and the boys.

"And I don't think I should have altered my mind, even could I have anticipated what those creatures were to do to me when they next came home. For, as I said before, their mischief was really sometimes so comical, I could not help being amused by it.

"Now if you were to guess for half a century, I don't think you could guess what their next dodge was about Blackmore.

"Well, it was a pouring wet day, and they had all been in the nursery doing carpenter's work with boxes of tools. One was making a bed for the dog to sleep in; another some shelves for fossils, and so on; when suddenly, 'I am so tired, I can't get on,' cries the third; 'I wish we could think of something fresh!' On which the rest left off work too, and there was a sort of general stare round the room, when it happened that the eyes of the third young gentleman met mine. One glance was enough, his face suddenly lighted up. 'I'll tell you what! It will be such awful fun! Let's have a trial, and hang old Blackmore! I've some pieces of wood here which will make a capital gibbet!'

"'All right!' answers the first boy, as coolly as possible; 'but what shall she have done?'

"'Murdered her husband,' suggests boy No. 2, with a smile on his face. 'Let's smash one of the old dolls for the corpse of the late lamented Mr. Blackmore. I'll be counsel for the prosecution.'

"'And I'll defend Mrs. Blackmore,' interposes the fourth young hopeful.

"'And I shall be judge, and hang her in spite of anything you can say!' says the eldest.

"'That of course,' remarks boy No. 3, 'for I'm making the gibbet on purpose.'

"This was a joke indeed, and they carried it out with an ingenuity I could not but wonder at and admire. The girls were sent for at once, and gave up an already half smashed wax doll, to be quite smashed for Mr. Blackmore's mangled remains; and this was laid on a fireboard, and covered with a sheet; and the trial was arranged, after a few suitable costumes, such as a barrister's wig and red jacket for the judge, etc., had been found in what was called the acting-box. I cannot half tell you how quizzical they all

looked, for it was just like a play, where everybody is
supposed to be somebody else than himself.

"Well! when they were all seated, the judge
shouted for the prisoner to be placed at the bar,
whereupon my little mistress, who acted as turnkey,
brought me forward and set me on a chair. And then
the judge made a flourishing speech, in which he in-
formed me I was charged with having deliberately
thrown myself upon the late Mr. Blackmore, with
the criminal intention of smashing him to pieces with
my weight, he being made of wax and I of wood; a
statement which was received by all present with a
groan of horror; after which the judge inquired if I
was *Guilty*, or *Not Guilty?*

"When I heard this, I wondered for a minute
whether I was expected to speak; but no such thing.
My counsel now stepped forward, in a coat which
trailed on the ground, and a hat which came nearly
over his nose, and called out, '*Not Guilty, of course;*'
for that Mr. Blackmore was a horrible muff, and it
was all his own fault.

"The company hissed at this, which obliged the
judge to call 'Order! Order!' and thump the table
with a stick at the same time. Indeed, I believe he
stamped with his feet, besides. Then the counsel for
the prosecution got up and made a few remarks,
something to this effect: 'What could such an elegant
man as Mr. Blackmore have been thinking about, to
marry such a coarse creature as I was?'—a sentiment
which was received with a general clapping of
hands; on which he proceeded to say, 'That this was
the worst case he had ever known. If I had offered
to fight him, and then knocked him down and killed

him, it wouldn't have been half so sneaking; but to take him out walking down a lane, and trip him up when he didn't expect it, and smash him all to bits, was abominable. The witnesses would tell us all about it, if the judge liked.'

"Of course, the judge liked; and two or three witnesses were called, one especially, a lady in a veil, who turned out to be Gretchen, who described herself as aunt to the late lamented Mr. Blackmore, and as having seen myself and him out walking together on the fatal night in question. She described also that unpleasant words passed between us on that occasion, and that a scuffle ensued, in which Mr. Blackmore fell on the ground, and I threw myself upon him, and dashed him in pieces at a blow.

"Here the judge inquired whether the mangled remains on the fireboard were, indeed, those of the late lamented Mr. Blackmore or not? Whereupon the turnkey lifted up the sheet, and requested witness to look; which she did, but was so overpowered by the spectacle, that after uttering a smothered 'Yes!' she was supported to her seat in a supposed fainting fit, but I heard her splitting with laughter all the time.

"Then came another witness, who said he had been looking through a telescope for the comet that evening, but happening to incline it for a minute to the earth, had caught sight of the whole affair, just as the previous witness had described it, although at three miles distance.

"The judge shook his head on hearing this, and remarked that he considered the matter as quite settled by the telescope evidence just given. Nevertheless, if I had any excuse to make, or any objection to being hanged immediately—'that is,' added he, with a grin, 'as soon as the gibbet is finished'—I was to say so as quickly as I could, for he expected the dinner-bell to ring every minute.

"He paused for a moment; and up jumped my counsel again, but first whispered to the third boy, who had been hammering at the gibbet all the time of the trial, 'How soon shall you be ready? Because I'll go on talking till you are.' To which the gibbet-maker replied, 'Oh, I sha'n't be a minute. There's only a nail or two to be put in. Cut away as fast as you like.'

"Whereupon my counsel hemmed, and began: 'Mr. Judge, and you, gentlemen of the jury' (here he turned to the second and third girls, who were doing jurymen in coats and hats) 'it's all nonsense about Mrs. Blackmore murdering her husband. They used to quarrel, I know, but that was because Mr. Blackmore was such a muff, he couldn't walk straight, and was always getting under his wife's feet, so of course she couldn't help tripping him up sometimes. And that day he had been to a friend's house and got a little *fresher* than usual, so he stumbled about worse than ever, and upset her as well as himself. And when they tumbled down, it wasn't her fault that she smashed him to pieces, for how could she help wood being heavier than wax?'

"Again the judge shook his head. He had never heard, he declared, such a lame defense in all the course of his long experience. Mrs. Blackmore ought to have rolled on one side when she found herself falling. He hoped the jury would not be such geese as to pay any attention to the prisoner's counsel, but bring in a verdict of Guilty, and so end the affair. He shouldn't listen to any recommendations to mercy, so it was no good proposing them.

"The answer of the jury to this lucid charge was a shout of *'Very Guilty indeed!'* whereat all present in court clapped their hands once more, and the judge proceeded to inform me that I was to be hanged on the gibbet forthwith, and if it broke down with my weight, as he was half afraid it would, I was to be suspended from the nursery window, which would do just as well, and be firmer. Which sentence the turn-key, assisted by the lady in the veil and the two counsels, executed at once.

"And this seemed to be the natural end of the trial; but a few minutes after, as a couple of the children were chasing each other across the nursery, down came the gibbet, as the judge had foretold, and I lay sprawling on the floor. Whereupon the turnkey was summoned to complete the second part of his office, in which the judge himself conde-scended to assist. Doing so, however, in rather a hasty manner, the rope ran out further than he in-tended; I swerved with the sudden jerk, and in an-other instant felt myself dashing through the glass of the laundry window below. There was a dead silence above, when the noise of the crash was heard, and I was drawn up again with all speed, and found the young party a good deal sobered by the accident. But the blame was all laid on 'those boys,' so it didn't much matter; for most parents lay to their account a few broken windows at Christmas and Midsummer, or at all events ought so to do!

"Nevertheless, this business led to my third burial,

for my mistress herself suggested, on the painful occasion, that in her opinion nothing further would be done with the old doll, except that she would be flung about and do more mischief, so she advised her being once more returned to the grave, where, if I could be of no further use, I should at all events do no harm.

"So buried I was once more, but I felt rather sad about it for a time. It pained me so that my old mistress should have been the person to put the finishing stroke to my long career of usefulness. I had no doubt she did it for the best, but I own I thought her decision a little premature, and ventured to believe that had I been allowed to remain above ground, I might still have been useful in many a piece of fun and good-fellowship with those boys. Who could help liking their witty spirits, after all?

"And you see, dears, I was not so far wrong. True, I fell off into a doze, and then into one of my deep slumbers, even while I was thinking all those things over. But when the young folks came the other day, and routed me up and out again, I declare I felt as fresh as ever. Why they laughed so, I didn't understand, certainly, nor what they meant when they said I should make a splendid *'Aunt Sally.'* But I was going to be *something* once more, that was as clear as that they were lifting me for the third time out of my grave, and I was as much pleased as they were, and quite contented to wait for the explanation.

"It might have been a long time, though, before I got it, but that the youngest boy knew as little what was the meaning of 'Aunt Sally' as I did; and having listened in vain for any chance information, he called

"The History of Aunt Sally"—Dressed for a New
Character. (*Original illustration*)

Gretchen aside, and begged her to tell him who Aunt
Sally was, and what they were going to do.

"So in that way I heard all about it, and submitted, I am sure you must all own, with a very good

grace, to being scrubbed and painted up, and dressed and fixed on the stump of a tree for my new character. It certainly was a great consolation to hear, from my old mistress, that I had never before had so magnificent a complexion as the pink one they now made me all over. Moreover, when I was finished, a great treat came, for the young folks invited all the boys and girls from the workhouse to tea, and I and a swing and a swarming-pole were fixed in a field, and were their chief amusements. The poor little things had been up from three o'clock that morning, I heard, blacking their shoes and getting ready. And when they did come, they were so happy that it seemed to me there was more fun than ever in the world. And when the children were gone, and one of our young ladies remarked how useful I had been, thought I to myself, 'Yes, and in more ways than one! For are not *all of you* trying to be of use to other people, and mayn't I flatter myself that my example has had some——?' But I won't be vain.

"Well, the new game is a rough one, I know, as I said before, and I get some desperately hard blows now and then; but a loyal heart and a strong body are grand things, and I don't see why one shouldn't be of use as long as there's a scrap of one left. For my own part, I can look forward to the future with peace, for when the young folks are weary of Aunt Sally, there is a Christmas log to be found yet in the old worn-out stump."

"The History of Aunt Sally"—Useful to the Last.
(*Original illustration*)

J. H. PEARCE

THE PUPPETS

Puppets have often been the poor man's source of entertainment and education. In Eastern countries puppet plays regularly substituted for newspapers.

Puppets have an aristocracy of their own; the Greeks delighted in them, the Middle Ages developed them into "marionettes." (The word "marionette" comes from the movable wooden figures of the Virgin Mary that were carried in processions.) Finally, the Italian theater, called "commedia dell'arte," introduced a character called Punchinello, and the famous Punch and Judy show developed.

Writers have long been attracted to puppets: Shakespeare, Chaucer, Ben Jonson, Charles Dickens all extol them. Many writers, too, have bestowed them with a life of their own. This is the first publication in our time of this very remarkable story by the British writer J. H. Pearce.

THE TRAVELLING showman, his box of puppets slung across his shoulder, paused outside the window and looked in with a glance of enquiry.

The mother nodded, and the little lad, sitting on her lap, clapped his hands delightedly, his face radiant with happiness.

So the showman unslung his box and set up his table, and then, one by one, out came the puppets and played their parts, dropping so naturally into the game that it seemed to be shaped by themselves.

The master of the puppets was a squat, white-faced little man, with a long grey beard that fell halfway to his knees, and the mere sight of him—so old beyond memory did he seem—filled the child with wistful interest, and yet with a touch of fear.

"I'm glad he's outside the window!" said the child, snuggling to his mother. "I like his dolls, but not him. Will he ever come in?"

And the mother hugged him to her lovingly, and whispered, "N . . o, dear! . . . Not to-day!"

But presently everything else was forgotten in the interest of the show itself.

The daintily-painted dolls, with their gaudy dresses and their fantastic motions, obeyed the slightest touch of the showman with a promptitude that was delightful: dancing or drowsing, sad or merry, at the merest hint on the wires. For the woman, they mimicked humourously the puppets of daily life: the see-saw, the fatuity of the game heightening the illusion. But for the easily-excited child they were no more than so many playful mice. And as they frisked and gambolled merrily on the baize-covered table, their antics so amused him that he laughed until he was tired.

Above everything, now, the little lad desired to
have the puppets, that they might play about with
him and obey him even more tamely than the cat.

The Puppets. *Many puppets have had a
quality of the macabre. (Nineteenth-century
illustration)*

So the young mother, willing to please her first-born if it were possible, beckoned the showman to the window and struck a bargain with him for the puppets. They would amuse the child for a little while, even if presently he should grow tired of them: and what was a mother for (she argued) except to give with both her hands?

With the box of puppets at his bedside, the child went to bed contentedly, his little brain full of delightful plans for the morrow. And in all his plans the puppets were to dance to him obediently and the game, from beginning to end, was to go just as he wished.

It was a cloudless moonlight night, and through the windows of the nursery the light streamed in with dazzling brilliancy.

Right opposite the panes hung the great yellow moon, so that when the little lad, tossing restlessly in his dreams, chanced to open his eyes in the quiet midnight, it was as if an illuminated lantern were hanging just outside the window; filling his little brain with odd suggestions of a fair.

For a while he lay staring at the big yellow disk, until presently it seemed to be staring back at *him;* as if suddenly in a lantern one should discern a smiling face.

The friendly smile was so distinctly like an invitation to a frolic that the little lad jumped out of bed laughing merrily.

"I'll play with you, Mr. Clown, if you want me to!" he cried.

And at this he was aware of a squeaking and scratching somewhere near him: as if a company of mice were at play behind the wainscot.

Suddenly he clapped his hands with a shrill burst of merriment. Why, of course, it must be the puppets crying to him from their box! They wanted to come out and play with him. And come out and play they should.

He lifted the lid of the box and threw it back with a bang, so that it snapped from the hinges and clattered on the floor.

And at the sound all the puppets began to clamber out of the box—pulling one another back, climbing, tumbling over each other—all eager, so it seemed, to get out and strut in the world.

The great round face looked in on the little company, as the child set out the puppets on the floor, and the glance, if touched with humour, seemed at the same time strangely sad: as if they all were puppets together, the child as much as the dolls.

"As father and mother are in bed," said the little lad to it, "please will you be Mr. God and see that we play fair? Will you, *please,* Mr. Clown?" he asked, with childish boldness; in his eagerness confusing the ideas in his little brain.

And the great face smiled consentingly through the window-panes: with a hint of the mother in it, and a hint, perhaps, of something more.

"Now we'll begin," said the mannikin, standing there in his little nightgown. "And you must only play as I tell you: all the game is out of my head."

So he began to frolic about with the puppets as if they were children like himself.

At the outset, the game went exactly as he wished: all the puppets humouring him and obedient to his whims. Whether he set them up, or knocked them down, or wished them to be sad or to be merry, so they stood or fell obediently and were merry or sad at will.

But presently a change of some kind seemed to be taking place in the nursery. The puppets began to disregard and jostle the little fellow as if they actually had wills of their own and wished to shape the game themselves. And at the same time it seemed either that the puppets increased in stature, or else that the night-gowned mannikin, after all, was no bigger than they.

Was it the puppets growing more animated, or the little lad growing more drowsy? He could scarcely hold his own against them, try as hard as he would. It was like a man, in the press of his fellows, giving and taking, taking and giving, yet losing ground persistently and being steadily pushed to the wall.

"I won't play with you, if you don't do as I tell you!" cried the mannikin, who at last was almost entirely thrust outside the game.

At which the puppets burst out laughing, no doubt rudely enough.

"Isn't it, shall *you* play with us?" the little voice squeaked. "Go and play by yourself, Poor Temper! *We* don't want you—don't think we do!"

Then the mannikin appealed angrily to the great face that watched the game.

But the smile on the face had vanished: it had now only watchful eyes.

"I wish you were back in your box!" the mannikin cried crossly. "I'm tired of the game, and I'm tired of *you!*" he pouted, stamping his foot fretfully.

"Put us back if you can!" the puppets laughed

mockingly. "We are as good as you, or better. Put us back, if you can!"

So the mannikin turned wistfully to the great face outside the window. "I can't make them play as I want to, they won't any of them do as I tell them. Please, they're not playing fair! Make them, *please,* Mr. God!"

But the great shining face, though it hung there watching him, seemed no more than a mere paper lantern, after all.

Then the little lad pushed up the window-sash tearfully. "Please, Mr. Showman, I want *you!*" he cried into the depths of the night.

And at this he was aware of the grey old showman squatting on the window sill and looking fixedly into the room.

"Yes!" said the showman, "here am I, my little friend."

"I'm tired of them all," said the mannikin, pointing to the dancing puppets. "They won't do as I tell them, any of them! Please, put them away in their box!"

"So tired, are you, my little fretful man?" asked the showman, stepping into the room and seating himself beside the bed. "Why not let them play their game to the end, if they want to? After all, to-morrow what will it matter to you or I? And besides," he added musingly, watching the antics of the puppets, "there is only *one* way to quiet them, when once they are out of the box."

"I'm tired," said the mannikin, "I want to go to sleep. And I can't go to sleep, with all of them playing except me. Please, Mr. Showman, will you put them in their box?"

The old showman took him up on his knee without a word.

"You are cold," said the mannikin, a drowsiness on his eyes.

"You will sleep none the less sound for it, my little man," said the showman tenderly as his great grey beard fell over the golden hair.

"Your arms hold me so tightly . . . oh, they hurt me!" gasped the mannikin. And then again, and more faintly, came a little tired, "oh!"

When the mannikin was still at last, with a face as white as the sheets of his bed the old showman laid him gently in the box on the nursery floor.

The puppets sat on the edge of the box and clicked their heels against it jovially.

"That's another of my puppets broken," squeaked a little voice from somewhere.

It sounded like one of the puppets speaking . . . but, then, what did they consider themselves?

Punch and Judy drawing—1802.
(Manley-Lewis collection)

SEON MANLEY

❖❖*❖*❖*❖*❖*❖*❖*❖*❖*❖*

THE CHRISTMAS OF THE BIG BISQUE DOLL

Many of the American Indian tribes, our true native Americans, did not paint the faces on any doll they made, be it in buffalo skin or corn husks. They believed that if they did so, they would give the doll a "spirit."

The great bisque dolls imported into America during the nineteenth century did indeed seem to have spirits of their own. Their beautiful faces were painted with only mineral pigments. Coat after coat of pink flesh was applied by master doll-makers; a steady hand applied the bloom of rosy cheeks, a firm stroke the deeper red of lips. When the eyelashes and

A very innocent child, but a very haunted doll, in a rare nineteenth-century engraving. (Manley-Lewis collection)

eyebrows had been drawn, the doll's head was returned to the oven. The doll's head had been in the oven first for a well-timed twenty-seven hours; this second cooking would be for seven hours more. Bisque comes from the French word "biscuit," which means to cook twice.

Metal crystal was then spread over the eyes to give a look that made them "human." Sometimes this look had a charming touch of innocence; at other times, it was almost one of malevolence. The doll had suddenly become "much more lifelike," and thanks to the mechanical knowledge of the period, the doll of this period had other abilities, as you will discover in this tale.

MIRANDA had never seen a doll like it. Why, it was nearly as tall as she was. Beautiful, and its curls were golden. She often was dismayed at her own dark hair. It had two china blue eyes that looked at you, that told you, "Take me home."

Miranda knew that doll wanted to speak to her, had something special to say to her. At the same time she felt her mother's agitation. Her mother, as she so often did, could read her mind.

"It's a very old bisque doll, Miranda. Valuable. It's not the kind of a doll you play with."

But Miranda said nothing.

She studied the store window carefully. She spelled out the golden words that were fanned out on the window:

The Magic Doll House
Antique Dolls and Toys

On the bottom of the window there was a cardboard legend that said: "We take consignments."

"What's that?" said Miranda. "What does it mean?"

"It means a lot of the things in the store belong to other people. They've left the toys and dolls to be sold to other people. To collectors," Miranda's mother said lamely, "not to little children. A doll like that isn't for a child."

"She wants to talk to me," Miranda said stubbornly. "She wants to go to Grandfather's house."

"Come on, Miranda, it's getting cold."

But Miranda just stood there. She had to take that

doll to Grandfather's. The doll was insistent. She would be a special gift. Different.

"It's Christmas," Miranda said. "It will be Christmas soon. You said this Christmas will be different than any other."

"That's true," her mother said begrudgingly. "But you've never known a real northern Christmas before. Grandfather thought you should see one." And then she laughed a little nervously. "Grandfather collects Christmas."

Miranda didn't know what she meant. She didn't much care. Right now she knew only two things. She didn't like Grandfather, and she wanted that doll. Or was it, that doll wanted her?

"Come along, Miranda. We've got the mistletoe to get." And Miranda moved along reluctantly.

"I didn't want to come, Mother," she said. "It's not like Christmas at all. I didn't want to come up here."

"Don't you like the snow? All this beautiful snow on the ground?"

"It's cold," Miranda said. "I don't think I like snow. I don't know why we couldn't have Christmas at home." Palm trees and the sun.

"Don't be silly, Miranda. Grandfather wanted you to see a real Christmas. Wait and see. He'll show you. He collects Christmas. He knows more about Christmas than anybody."

Miranda thought that this was ridiculous, but so much was ridiculous for children. She knew that. She knew sometimes she just wanted to grow up and buy a big doll of her own, and have her own Christmas anywhere she wanted to. At home.

"What's mistletoe?" she said. But she didn't care.

Then she stopped sharply.

"Listen," she said.

"Listen to what?" said her mother, without patience this time.

"The doll wants to go home. She says so."

"Oh, Miranda," said her mother, and pulled her so that her boots made a squeaking sound in the snow as though, as though, thought Miranda, a doll was crying.

It had all started with that letter from Grandfather. Christmas wasn't Christmas in Florida. But Florida was home. What did Grandfather know about it? He never came down. Never once. He didn't know the way they lived, nor care. Part of that she got just from the conversation between her parents. Something was wrong between Grandfather and her parents. He felt they shouldn't be there, that they had left the North where things were all right and had gone South to what evidently Grandfather called a strange, savage country. Nothing but alligators and sunshine.

Miranda was afraid of alligators, but she loved the sunshine, and besides there had been the best Christmas every year. Old Johnny McDonald had taken her out to the scrub and showed her where the wild turkeys hid. They had picked wild oranges and then old Johnny had cut down an old scrub palm for the heart of the palm. That was a great Christmas dinner. She didn't want anything else. There were candles that smelled briefly of palm oil, and guava jelly besides the wild turkey and things she wanted. And

Johnny McDonald wove her funny dolls out of palm leaves. Not like the big doll at all. They couldn't talk.

Grandfather's house was strange, old, large, the largest house she had ever seen. And the darkest. And it had a fireplace that you could walk into. Except, who wanted to walk into a fireplace? When they had told her that, it was frightening. A fireplace taller than you were. She supposed people could live in that. Maybe in the summer when they didn't have a fire you could play inside it like a little cabin. But she was afraid of that now. Grandfather had a fire going all the time. It was frightening with its great logs and its splashes of fire. He said you could look in it and see things, but any time she looked into it, it frightened her. And tonight was going to be the "best night of all," said Grandfather. Christmas Eve with the old Christmas customs. Grandfather was famous. That's what her mother had said. He knew everything. He knew everything about everything. And Miranda had a terrible feeling he knew everything about her. He could look deep in her heart and know she wasn't happy here. But she hadn't wanted to come.

What did it mean about collecting Christmas?

Christmas wasn't something you could just put in a box all wrapped up and then packed away for the next year. She knew that, but she couldn't tell that to Grandfather.

He talked funny too. "The child knows nothing about Christmas," he said. "And you know, Margaret," he said to her mother, "you know how much I like to celebrate it. One must be scrupulous about holidays. One must pass on customs; to disport ourselves."

Her mother had laughed. "Oh, Father, you're impossible! You're still trying to give us a Washington Irving Christmas with merry disports and the like. You can't really do it, Father. Do you remember when we were children, you forced us into your old antiquarian games, Hoodman Blind, Shoe the Wild Mare, Hot Cockles, Steal the White Loaf, Snapdragon, and Bobbing for Apples? Well, Tom and I only liked the bobbing for apples. We hated them. We hated those games.

"And you never gave us what we wanted. Books— that's all we ever had. Books, books, books. I wanted a doll one year. I saw a doll that I set my heart on. Did I get it? You bet I didn't. Now, Miranda wants one."

"Run along, Miranda," said her grandfather. "Little pitchers have big ears. Help Letty in the kitchen.

"Now, Margaret," said the old man, turning back to Miranda's mother, "now Margaret, you're overtired. Distraught. I gave you books because you wanted books."

"You wanted me to want books," said Margaret. "I wanted that doll—and now Miranda . . ."

"Margaret, don't be childish. Where is this doll that Miranda wants so much?"

"In that local shop. The Magic Doll House. She'd love it. Of course, it's an antique."

"An old doll," said her father. "An old doll. An old bisque doll. Blond hair. Pink ribbon."

"Oh, you've seen her?" said Margaret delightedly.

"Not that doll," said her father. "Not that doll. I won't have that doll in the house. No, no," he said vehemently and turned on his heel. "I won't have her in the house.

"Come, Margaret, come. We must attend to the Yule log. Get Miranda. She should know some of the old customs."

"That at least," said Miranda's mother grudgingly, "has a certain amount of sense. Certainly you've got the fireplace for it.

"If you take a nap, Miranda," her mother had said, "if you take a nap, you can watch them bring in the Yule log and see it burn."

Miranda wasn't at all interested, but she had learned rapidly that Grandfather liked questions. "What is the Yule log, Grandfather?"

"See, Margaret," said her grandfather to her mother, "the child *is* interested. It's an instinctive thing in each generation to recreate the old customs.

"The Yule log, my child, is a great log of wood brought in with ceremony on Christmas Eve. We'll lay it in the fireplace and light it with a brand of last year's log. It must burn all night, and if it goes out, it is considered ill luck. Now I shall give you a little verse. Try to remember it."

"No," said Margaret. "None of that poetry. Don't you even remember how often you gave us a verse, and we had to come down from our naps reciting it? Some old verse. No, not for this child."

Grandfather ignored Mother. How hard it was to do that. Miranda never found it easy. She wanted to put her hands over her ears. But Grandfather was booming out, " 'Come bring with a noise, my merry

boys, the Christmas log, inquiring, while my good
dame, she bids ye all be free, and drinks to your
heart's desire.' Do you think you can learn that,
Miranda?"

"I don't know," Miranda said shyly.

"I'll write it out for you and bring it up, shall I?"

"I don't read quite that well," said Miranda.

"Nonsense, Miranda," said Grandfather. "You're
my granddaughter."

Miranda didn't feel at all well. She was beginning to
feel feverish as she went up to nap, and then felt
chilly. Chilly and hot. Hot and chilly. Was that the
way you felt in New England? She never felt like this
at Christmas before. She needed company. She
needed that big doll.

The big doll was calling her again, "Miranda."

How did the doll know her name?

Way in the distance she could hear her mother
and grandfather quarreling.

Downstairs Margaret and her father were indeed
quarreling bitterly.

"I know all about the doll. I'm not about to take
it back."

"She seems so set on it." Margaret didn't know
who she was fighting for—herself or her child. She
remembered all the dolls she didn't get. But why was
her father so unbelievably upset?

"You see, Margaret, I put that doll on consign-
ment."

"But you never collected dolls."

"No," he said. "The doll was here when I bought
Elmwood. I had to get rid of it, don't you under-

stand? It acted like it owned the house. Don't you understand?

"Why, one day I picked that doll up, and it kicked me as though it was a demon. Yes, kicked me. Kicked me until I was black and blue.

"And I could swear it was trying to say something. Inanimate things can be terrifying, Margaret, absolutely terrifying—particularly when they can become animate, if you know what I mean.

"And I swear—the doll was trying to speak.

"Dolls used to be sacred images, you know. So many customs. Never was interested, though. Still, that doll kicked me. Very definitely. Had to get rid of her.

"And when I took it to the shop, it cried. Why, I had to cover its mouth.

"Believe me, a doll like that could seek its revenge."

"A doll?" said Margaret inquiringly. She looked at her father. Always eccentric; was he finally going completely potty?

Some dolls have a peculiar arrogance.

"I have her papers upstairs. Her provenance, history and all that in my desk drawer."

Completely potty, thought Margaret.

"Come on, old dear," she said, in a burst of fondness and concern. "Let's wrap presents."

"I'm coming. I'll be back. I must see my house again."

"Yes," said Miranda. "Yes . . . doll." She didn't know the doll's name, but she knew she'd be back tonight.

It was a Christmas Eve unlike anything she had had before. Grandfather was standing before the fireplace and reciting:

> *" 'Now Christmas has come,*
> *Let us beat up the drum,*
> *And call all our neighbors together.' "*

He raised a glass to Miranda as she came down all dressed up in her new black velvet dress with the Irish lace collar.

"And here is to you, Miranda," he said.

> *" 'And as she does appear,*
> *Let us make such a cheer*
> *As will keep out the wind and the weather.' "*

She was so cold and so hot, Miranda was.

There were presents now under the great Christmas tree. It was the tallest Christmas tree she had ever seen. She had never seen anything except for the little pine scrubs that old Johnny McDonald had brought in from the edge of the Everglades. Then

Beneath the Christmas Tree. (*Old drawing from the Manley-Lewis collection*)

they'd decorate it with things that she made herself. Circles out of palm leaves. One circle tied into the other circle. And some of the berries that Johnny McDonald had helped her to pick, so bright and vibrant on the little pine tree. The little pine tree had looked so much better to her than this great towering tree that was so frightening. It should have been in a forest.

There were all sorts of weird things on the tables. Great wax candles which Grandfather called "the Christmas candles," and they were wreathed with greens. There was holly and ivy all around, and mince pies. Imagine! Right on Christmas Eve. And the smell of too-rich everything.

"Don't tell me, Father," said Margaret. "Don't tell me. Not frumenty."

"An old tradition," said Father. "Don't you remember I always had it out for you and your brother when you were children? A dish made of wheat cakes boiled in milk with rich spices," said Grandfather, turning to Miranda.

He certainly talked funny, she thought. Ate funny, too.

"You can't recreate those old Christmases, Father. They weren't even real to us," said Margaret. The poor old dear had really lost touch with reality. Where did he get that crazy business about the doll?

"Nonsense," said Grandfather. "Of course, you can. It's important to keep on with custom."

But all the smells of spices and the tall towering tree and the raging fire from the Yule log had turned Miranda's stomach.

Now people were coming in from all over. All the neighbors, some with their children who didn't talk to her, and older people that talked to her too much. She wanted to go to bed.

"She is tired, Father. She should go to bed."

"Well, take her up then."

"At least she could put on her night clothes," said Margaret, "and perhaps come down and say goodnight."

"Why not? A charming picture," said Grandfather. "Children in their night clothes."

Somehow or other Miranda got undressed, put on a flannel nightgown which she had never worn before, and came downstairs.

"Oh, no," said Grandfather. "Not in front of the Yule log. Don't you know, Margaret? Didn't I tell you as a child? You never, never come barefooted while the Yule log is burning. It's an ill omen."

"Father," said Margaret. "Father, you're getting

worse than ever. An ill omen! What do you want to do? You'll frighten Miranda."

"What's an ill omen, Mother?" said Miranda, going back upstairs.

"Oh, something silly. Like bad luck, Miranda. Forget it."

She couldn't sleep. Which box held the doll? There were two boxes beneath the tree. Either could be the doll. One was flat on the starched white linen sheet in front of the tree; the other (you could barely see it) stood just behind the tree. Just as though it was out in some forest of Hansel and Gretel. Was the doll frightened?

Or maybe it wasn't the doll at all? Could it be that the doll wouldn't come? No, the doll was certain, very certain.

Had Mother been carrying the doll when she came in with that package? Mother looked happy. Was the doll happy?

She had to find out. She had been asleep, she guessed. Everything was quiet downstairs.

What was an omen?

She crept downstairs, her feet cold against the stairs. The Yule log (wasn't it supposed to burn all night?) had gone out.

"No, not in the box, Miranda," said the doll. "Those are books. I'm here behind the tree."

"Yes, doll," whispered Miranda.

"He can't keep me out. He can't. I've been here for eighty years. This is *my* house. *My house, my house!*

*   *   *

"My house," said the doll. "My house. You understand, it's my house. It's that man or me."

"Yes," said Miranda, groggy. The doll made perfect sense. She didn't like Grandfather either.

It was no surprise to Miranda that Grandfather didn't come down the next day, or the next. He died before they left for home. And Miranda's mother never was satisfied as to what the medical explanation was for all those minute black and blue marks that covered his body.

Miranda never understood quite why. Was it the omen? Was it the doll? It was funny how willing she was to leave the doll at Grandfather's house. "Thank you," the doll had said.

For what, Miranda wondered? It was a polite doll.

On the train going home to Florida, she hugged her mother close. Her mother seemed so hurt and tired.

"It wasn't my bare feet, Mother, was it? It wasn't the omen that made Grandfather die?"

"Of course not, Miranda. Of course not, dear."

She didn't ask her mother if it could have been the doll. No, that was really silly.

"Mother," she said, "the doll's name was Rosebud."

"Oh," said Mother. "How did you know that?"

"She told me," said Miranda, and she never once mentioned the doll again.

Neither did her mother, who, for some reason she did not understand, carried the doll's provenance in her purse. She knew what it said by heart:

"Rosebud: A Steiner bisque kicking and crying

doll, French, c. 1885. Very rare. Brought to this country for Elizabeth Perrault, the daughter of Thomas Perrault of Elmwood. Elizabeth Perrault died on Christmas, 1889. The doll has stayed at Elmwood ever since, and must remain there, according to the deed of Thomas Perrault."

Miranda's mother sighed. Everybody would be glad to be home again.

F. MARION CRAWFORD

✳❖✳❖✳❖✳❖✳❖✳❖✳❖✳❖✳❖✳❖✳✳

THE DOLL'S GHOST

How soon dolls become the ghosts of our childhood past.

Charlotte Brontë, for example, the author of Jane Eyre, *described in that very book what a doll meant (and can still mean) to a lonely child. She always took her doll to bed because "human beings must love something." Remembering her own childhood, she said, "I contrived to find a pleasure in loving and cherishing a faded graven image, shabby as a miniature scarecrow. It puzzles me now to remember with what absurd sincerity I doted on this little toy, half fancying it alive and capable of sensation. I could not sleep unless it was folded in my nightgown; and when it lay there safe and warm, I was comparatively happy, believing it to be happy likewise."*

This enormous affection and deep meaning between child and doll, indeed between child and any

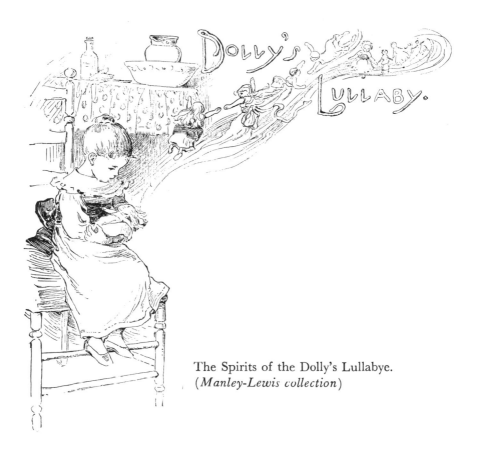

The Spirits of the Dolly's Lullabye.
(*Manley-Lewis collection*)

*toy, is so pervasive that it is not surprising that the
doll should take on so many supernatural overtones.*

*It is not surprising either that a doll should be
loved so much that it could indeed have significance
even when it had become . . . a ghost.*

I<small>T</small> <small>WAS</small> a terrible accident, and for one moment the
splendid machinery of Cranston House got out of
gear and stood still. The butler emerged from the retirement in which he spent his elegant leisure, two
grooms appeared simultaneously, there were actually

Intimacy with dolls was so strong in past centuries that it was easy for F. Marion Crawford to imagine a doll's ghost.

housemaids on the grand staircase, and Mrs. Pringle herself stood upon the landing. Mrs. Pringle was the housekeeper. As for the head nurse, the under nurse, and the nurserymaid, their feelings cannot be described.

The Lady Gwendolen Lancaster-Douglas-Scroop, youngest daughter of the ninth Duke of Cranston, and aged six years and three months, picked herself up quite alone, and sat down on the third step from the foot of the grand staircase in Cranston House.

"Oh!" ejaculated the butler, and he disappeared again.

"Ah!" responded the grooms as they also went away.

"It's only that doll," Mrs. Pringle was distinctly heard to say, in a tone of contempt. Then the three nurses gathered round Lady Gwendolen and hurried her out of Cranston House as fast as they could, lest it should be found out upstairs that they had allowed the Lady Gwendolen to tumble down the grand staircase with her doll in her arms. And as the doll was badly broken, the nurserymaid carried it, with the pieces, wrapped up in Lady Gwendolen's little cloak. It was not far to Hyde Park, and when they had reached a quiet place they took means to find out that Lady Gwendolen had no bruises.

Lady Gwendolen Douglas-Scroop sometimes yelled, but she never cried. It was because she had yelled that the nurse had allowed her to go downstairs alone with Nina, the doll, under one arm, while she steadied herself with her other hand on the balustrade, and trod upon the polished marble steps beyond the edge of the carpet. So she had fallen, and Nina had come to grief.

When the nurses were quite sure that she was not hurt, they unwrapped the doll and looked at her in her turn. She had been a very beautiful doll, very large, and fair, and healthy, with real yellow hair, and eyelids that would open and shut over very grown-up dark eyes. Moreover, when you moved her right arm up and down she said "Pa-pa," and when you moved the left she said "Ma-ma," very distinctly.

"I heard her say 'Pa' when she fell," said the under nurse, who heard everything. "But she ought to have said 'Pa-pa.'"

"That's because her arm went up when she hit the step," said the head nurse. "She'll say the other 'Pa' when I put it down again."

"Pa," said Nina, as her right arm was pushed down, and speaking through her broken face. It was cracked right across, from the upper corner of the forehead, with a hideous gash, through the nose and down to the little frilled collar of the pale green silk Mother Hubbard frock, and two little three-cornered pieces of porcelain had fallen out.

"It's a wonder she can speak at all, being all smashed," said the under nurse.

"You'll have to take her to Mr. Puckler," said her superior. "It's not far, and you'd better go at once." The under nurse wrapped Nina up again and departed.

Mr. Bernard Puckler and his little daughter lived in a little house in a little alley, which led out off a quiet little street not very far from Belgrave Square. He was the great doll doctor, and his extensive practice lay in the most aristocratic quarter. He mended dolls of all sizes and ages, boy dolls and girl dolls, baby dolls in long clothes, and grown-up dolls in fashionable gowns, talking dolls and dumb dolls, those that shut their eyes when they lay down, and those whose eyes had to be shut for them by means of a mysterious wire. His daughter Else was only just over twelve years old, but she was already very clever at mending dolls' clothes, and at doing their hair, which is harder than you might think, though the dolls sit quite still while it is being done.

Mr. Puckler had originally been a German, but he had dissolved his nationality in the ocean of London many years ago, like a great many foreigners. He still had one or two German friends, however, who came on Saturday evenings, and smoked with him and played picquet or "skat" with him for farthing points, and called him "Herr Doctor," which seemed to please Mr. Puckler very much.

He looked older than he was, for his beard was rather long and ragged, his hair was grizzled and thin, and he wore horn-rimmed spectacles. As for Else, she was a thin, pale child, very quiet and neat, with dark eyes and brown hair that was plaited down her back and tied with a bit of black ribbon. She mended the dolls' clothes and took the dolls back to their homes when they were quite strong again.

The house was a little one, but too big for the two people who lived in it. There was a small sitting-room on the street, and the workshop was at the back, and there were three rooms upstairs. But the father and daughter lived most of their time in the workshop, because they were generally at work, even in the evenings.

Mr. Puckler laid Nina on the table and looked at her a long time, till the tears began to fill his eyes behind the horn-rimmed spectacles. He was a very susceptible man, and he often fell in love with the dolls he mended, and found it hard to part with them when they had smiled at him for a few days. They were real little people to him, with characters and thoughts and feelings of their own, and he was very tender with them all. But some attracted him especially from the first, and when they were brought to him maimed and injured, their state seemed so pitiful to him that the tears came easily. You must remember that he had lived among dolls during a great part of his life, and understood them.

"How do you know that they feel nothing?" he went on to say to Else. "You must be gentle with them. It costs nothing to be kind to the little beings, and perhaps it makes a difference to them."

And Else understood him, because she was a child, and she knew that she was more to him than all the dolls.

He fell in love with Nina at first sight, perhaps because her beautiful brown glass eyes were something like Else's own, and he loved Else first and best, with all his heart. And, besides, it was a very sorrowful case. Nina had evidently not been long in the world, for her complexion was perfect, her hair was smooth where it should be smooth, and curly where it should be curly, and her silk clothes were perfectly new. But across her face was that frightful gash, like a saber cut, deep and shadowy within, but clean and sharp at the edges. When he tenderly pressed her head to close the gaping wound, the edges made a fine grating sound, that was painful to hear, and the lids of the dark eyes quivered as though Nina were suffering dreadfully.

"Poor Nina!" he exclaimed sorrowfully. "But I shall not hurt you much, though you will take a long time to get strong."

He always asked the names of the broken dolls when they were brought to him, and sometimes the people knew what the children called them, and told him. He liked "Nina" for a name. Altogether and in every way she pleased him more than any doll he had seen for many years, and he felt drawn to her, and made up his mind to make her perfectly strong and sound, no matter how much labor it cost him.

Mr. Puckler worked patiently and Else watched him. She could do nothing for poor Nina, whose clothes needed no mending. The longer the doll doctor worked, the more fond he became of the yellow hair and the beautiful brown glass eyes. He sometimes forgot all the other dolls that were waiting to be mended, lying side by side on a shelf, and sat for an hour gazing at Nina's face, while he racked his ingenuity for some new invention by which to hide even the smallest trace of the terrible accident.

She was wonderfully mended. Even he was obliged to admit that; but the scar was still visible to his keen eyes, a very fine line right across the face, downwards from right to left. Yet all the conditions had been most favorable for a cure, since the cement had set quite hard at the first attempt and the weather had been fine and dry, which makes a great difference in a dolls' hospital.

At last he knew that he could do no more, and the under nurse had already come twice to see whether the job was finished.

"Nina is not quite strong yet," Mr. Puckler had answered each time, for he could not make up his mind to face the parting.

And now he sat before the square deal table at which he worked, and Nina lay before him for the last time with a big brown paper box beside her. It stood there like her coffin, waiting for her, he thought. He must put her into it, and lay tissue paper over her dear face, and then put on the lid, and at the thought of tying the string his sight was dim with tears again. He was never to look into the glassy depths of the beautiful brown eyes any more, nor to hear the little wooden voice say "Pa-pa" and "Ma-ma." It was a very painful moment.

In the vain hope of gaining time before the separation, he took up the little sticky bottles of cement and glue and gum and color, looking at each one in turn, and then at Nina's face. And all his small tools lay there, neatly arranged in a row, but he knew that he could not use them again for Nina. She was quite strong at last, and in a country where there should be no cruel children to hurt her she might live a hundred years, with only that almost imperceptible line across her face to tell of the fearful thing that had befallen her on the marble steps of Cranston House.

Suddenly Mr. Puckler's heart was quite full, and he rose abruptly from his seat and turned away.

"Else," he said unsteadily, "you must do it for me. I cannot bear to see her go into the box."

So he went and stood at the window with his back turned, while Else did what he had not the heart to do.

"Is it done?" he asked, not turning round. "Then take her away, my dear. Put on your hat, and take her to Cranston House quickly, and when you are gone I will turn round."

Else was used to her father's queer ways with the dolls, and though she had never seen him so much moved by a parting, she was not much surprised.

"Come back quickly," he said, when he heard her hand on the latch. "It is growing late, and I should not send you at this hour. But I cannot bear to look forward to it any more."

When Else was gone, he left the window and sat down in his place before the table again, to wait for the child to come back. He touched the place where Nina had lain, very gently, and he recalled the softly tinted pink face, and the glass eyes, and the ringlets of yellow hair, till he could almost see them.

The evenings were long, for it was late in the spring. But it began to grow dark soon, and Mr. Puckler wondered why Else did not come back. She had been gone an hour and a half, and that was much longer than he had expected, for it was barely half a mile from Belgrave Square to Cranston House. He reflected that the child might have been kept waiting, but as the twilight deepened he grew anxious, and walked up and down in the grim workshop, no longer thinking of Nina, but of Else, his own living child, whom he loved.

An undefinable, disquieting sensation came upon him by fine degrees, a chilliness and a faint stirring of his thin hair, joined with a wish to be in any company rather than to be alone much longer. It was the beginning of fear.

He told himself in strong German-English that he was a foolish old man, and he began to feel about for the matches in the dusk. He knew just where they should be, for he always kept them in the same place, close to the little tin box that held bits of sealing-wax of various colors, for some kinds of mending. But somehow he could not find the matches in the gloom.

Something had happened to Else, he was sure, and as his fear increased, he felt as though it might be allayed if he could get a light and see what time it was. Then he called himself a foolish old man again, and the sound of his own voice startled him in the dark. He still could not find the matches.

The window was gray; he might see what time it was if he went close to it, and he could go and get matches out of the cupboard afterwards. He stood back from the table, to get out of the way of the chair, and began to cross the board floor.

Something was following him in the dark. There was a small pattering, as of tiny feet upon the boards. He stopped and listened, and the roots of his hair tingled. It was nothing, and he was a foolish old man. He made two steps more, and he was sure that he heard the little pattering again. He turned his back to the window, leaning against the sash so that the panes began to crack, and he faced the dark. Everything was quite still, and it smelt of paste and cement and wood-filings as usual.

"Is that you, Else?" he asked, and he was surprised by the fear in his voice.

There was no answer in the room, and he held up his watch and tried to make out what time it was by the gray dusk that was just not darkness. So far as he could see, it was within two or three minutes of ten o'clock. He had been a long time alone. He was shocked, and frightened for Else, out in London, so late, and he almost ran across the room to the door. As he fumbled for the latch, he distinctly heard the running of the little feet after him.

"Mice!" he exclaimed feebly, just as he got the door open.

He shut it quickly behind him, and felt as though some cold thing had settled on his back and were writhing upon him. The passage was quite dark, but he found his hat and was out in the alley in a moment, breathing more freely, and surprised to find how much light there still was in the open air. He could see the pavement clearly under his feet, and far off in the street to which the alley led he could hear the laughter and calls of children, playing some game out of doors. He wondered how he could have been so nervous, and for an instant he thought of going back into the house to wait quietly for Else. But instantly he felt that nervous fright of something stealing over him again. In any case it was better to walk up to Cranston House and ask the servants about the child. One of the women had perhaps taken a fancy to her, and was even now giving her tea and cake.

He walked quickly to Belgrave Square, and then up the broad streets, listening as he went, whenever there was no other sound, for the tiny footsteps. But he heard nothing, and was laughing at himself when he rang the servants' bell at the big house. Of course, the child must be there.

The person who opened the door was quite an inferior person, for it was a back door, but affected the manners of the front, and stared at Mr. Puckler superciliously under the strong light.

No little girl had been seen, and he knew "nothing about no dolls."

"She is my little girl," said Mr. Puckler tremulously, for all his anxiety was returning tenfold, "and I am afraid something has happened."

The inferior person said rudely that "nothing could have happened to her in that house, because she had not been there, which was a jolly good reason why;" and Mr. Puckler was obliged to admit that the man ought to know, as it was his business to keep the door and let people in. He wished to be allowed to speak to the under nurse, who knew him; but the man was ruder than ever, and finally shut the door in his face.

When the doll doctor was alone in the street, he steadied himself by the railing, for he felt as though he were breaking in two, just as some dolls break, in the middle of the backbone.

Presently he knew that he must be doing something to find Else, and that gave him strength. He began to walk as quickly as he could through the streets, following every highway and byway which his little girl might have taken on her errand. He also asked several policemen in vain if they had seen her, and most of them answered him kindly, for they saw that he was a sober man and in his right senses, and some of them had little girls of their own.

It was one o'clock in the morning when he went up to his own door again, worn out and hopeless and broken-hearted. As he turned the key in the lock, his heart stood still, for he knew that he was awake and not dreaming, and that he really heard those tiny footsteps pattering to meet him inside the house.

But he was too unhappy to be much frightened

any more, and his heart went on again with a dull regular pain, that found its way all through him with every pulse. So he went in, and hung up his hat in the dark, and found the matches in the cupboard and the candlestick in its place in the corner.

Mr. Puckler was so much overcome and so completely worn out that he sat down in his chair before the work-table and almost fainted, as his face dropped forward upon his folded hands. Beside him the solitary candle burned steadily with a low flame in the still warm air.

"Else! Else!" he moaned against his yellow knuckles. And that was all he could say, and it was no relief to him. On the contrary, the very sound of the name was a new and sharp pain that pierced his ears and his head and his very soul. For every time he repeated the name it meant that little Else was dead, somewhere out in the streets of London in the dark.

He was so terribly hurt that he did not even feel something pulling gently at the skirt of his old coat, so gently that it was like the nibbling of a tiny mouse. He might have thought that it was really a mouse if he had noticed it.

"Else! Else!" he groaned right against his hands.

Then a cool breath stirred his thin hair, and the low flame of the one candle dropped down almost to a mere spark, not flickering as though a draught were going to blow it out, but just dropping down as if it were tired out. Mr. Puckler felt his hands stiffening with fright under his face; and there was a faint rustling sound, like some small silk thing blown

*Haunted attics produced haunted dolls and
haunted toys.*

in a gentle breeze. He sat up straight, stark and scared, and a small wooden voice spoke in the stillness.

"Pa-pa," it said, with a break between the syllables.

Mr. Puckler stood up in a single jump, and his chair fell over backwards with a smashing noise upon the wooden floor. The candle had almost gone out.

It was Nina's doll voice, and he should have known it among the voices of a hundred other dolls. And yet there was something more in it, a little human ring, with a pitiful cry and a call for help, and the wail of a hurt child. Mr. Puckler stood up, stark and stiff, and tried to look round, but at first he could not, for he seemed to be frozen from head to foot.

Then he made a great effort, and he raised one hand to each of his temples, and pressed his own head round as he would have turned a doll's. The candle was burning so low that it might as well have been out altogether, for any light it gave, and the room seemed quite dark at first. Then he saw some-

thing. He would not have believed that he could be more frightened than he had been just before that. But he was, and his knees shook, for he saw the doll standing in the middle of the floor, shining with a faint and ghostly radiance, her beautiful glassy brown eyes fixed on his. And across her face the very thin line of the break he had mended with such care shone as though it were drawn in light with a fine point of white flame.

Yet there was something human in her face, like Else's own; as if only the doll saw him through them, and not Else. And there was enough of Else to bring back all his pain and to make him forget his fear.

"Else, my little Else!" he cried aloud.

The small ghost moved, and its doll-arm slowly rose and fell with a stiff, mechanical motion.

"Pa-pa," it said.

It seemed this time that there was even more of Else's tone echoing somewhere between the wooden notes that reached his ears so distinctly, and yet so far away. Else was calling him, he was sure.

His face was perfectly white in the gloom, but his knees did not shake any more, and he felt that he was less frightened.

"Yes, child! But where? Where?" he asked. "Where are you, Else?"

"Pa-pa!"

The syllables died away in the quiet room. There was a low rustling of silk, the glassy brown eyes turned slowly away, and Mr. Puckler heard the pitter-patter of the small feet in the bronze kid slippers as the figure ran straight to the door. Then the candle burned high again, the room was full of light, and he was alone.

Mr. Puckler passed his hand over his eyes and looked about him. He could see everything quite clearly, and he felt that he must have been dreaming, though he was standing instead of sitting down, as he should have been if he had just waked up. The candle burned brightly now. There were the dolls to be mended, lying in a row with their toes up. The third one had lost her right shoe, and Else was making one. He knew that, and he was certainly not dreaming now. He had not been dreaming when he had come in from his fruitless search and had heard the doll's footsteps running to the door. He had not fallen asleep in his chair. How could he possibly have fallen asleep when his heart was breaking? He had been awake all the time.

He steadied himself, set the fallen chair upon its legs, and said to himself again very emphatically that he was a foolish old man. He ought to be out in the streets looking for his child, asking questions, and inquiring at the police stations, where all accidents were reported as soon as they were known, or at the hospitals.

"Pa-pa!"

The longing, wailing, pitiful little wooden cry rang from the passage, outside the door, and Mr. Puckler stood for an instant with white face, transfixed and rooted to the spot. A moment later his hand was on the latch. Then he was in the passage, with the light streaming from the open door behind him.

Quite at the other end he saw the little phantom

shining clearly in the shadow, and the right hand seemed to beckon to him as the arm rose and fell once more. He knew all at once that it had not come to frighten him but to lead him, and when it disappeared, and he walked boldly towards the door, he knew that it was in the street outside, waiting for him. He forgot that he was tired and had eaten no supper, and had walked many miles, for a sudden hope ran through and through him, like a golden stream of life.

And sure enough, at the corner of the alley, and at the corner of the street, and out in Belgrave Square, he saw the small ghost flitting before him. Sometimes it was only a shadow, where there was other light, but then the glare of the lamps made a pale green sheen on its little Mother Hubbard frock of silk; and sometimes, where the streets were dark and silent, the whole figure shone out brightly, with its yellow curls and rosy neck. It seemed to trot along like a tiny child, and Mr. Puckler could almost hear the pattering of the bronze kid slippers on the pavement as it ran. But it went very fast, and he could only just keep up with it, tearing along with his hat on the back of his head and his thin hair blown by the night breeze, and his horn-rimmed spectacles firmly set upon his broad nose.

On and on he went, and he had no idea where he was. He did not even care, for he knew certainly that he was going the right way.

Then at last, in a wide, quiet street, he was standing before a big, sober-looking door that had two lamps on each side of it, and a polished brass bell-handle, which he pulled.

And just inside, when the door was opened, in the bright light, there was the little shadow, and the pale green sheen of the little silk dress, and once more the small cry came to his ears, less pitiful, more longing.

"Pa-pa!"

The shadow turned suddenly bright, and out of the brightness the beautiful brown glass eyes were turned up happily to his, while the rosy mouth smiled so divinely that the phantom doll looked almost like a little angel.

"A little girl was brought in soon after ten o'clock," said the quiet voice of the hospital door-keeper. "I think they thought she was only stunned. She was holding a big brown-paper box against her, and they could not get it out of her arms. She had a long plait of brown hair that hung down as they carried her."

"She is my little girl," said Mr. Puckler, but he hardly heard his own voice.

He leaned over Else's face in the gentle light of the children's ward, and when he had stood there a minute the beautiful brown eyes opened.

"Pa-pa!" cried Else. "I knew you would come!"

Then Mr. Puckler did not know what he did or said for a moment, and what he felt was worth all the fear and terror and despair that had almost killed him that night. But by and by Else was telling her story, and the nurse let her speak, for there were only two other children in the room, who were getting well and were sound asleep.

"They were big boys with bad faces," said Else, "and they tried to get Nina away from me, but I held on and fought as well as I could till one of them hit me with something, and I don't remember any more, for I tumbled down, and I suppose the boys ran away, and somebody found me there. But I'm afraid Nina is all smashed."

"Here is the box," said the nurse. "We could not take it out of her arms till she came to herself. Would you like to see if the doll is broken?"

And she undid the string cleverly, but Nina was all smashed to pieces. Only the gentle light of the children's ward made a pale green sheen in the folds of the little Mother Hubbard frock.

ABOUT THE AUTHORS

❋⟡❋⟡❋⟡❋⟡❋⟡❋⟡❋⟡❋⟡❋⟡❋⟡❋⟡❋

AGATHA CHRISTIE was born in 1891 in Torquay, England, of an English mother and an American father. Her first attempt at writing, toward the end of World War I, was rejected by several publishers. It was entitled *The Mysterious Affair at Styles,* and in this work she introduced the now famous Belgian detective Hercule Poirot. The book was eventually accepted and was published in 1920. In 1926, after averaging a book a year, she wrote what is still considered her masterpiece, *The Murder of Roger Ackroyd.* In private life she was Lady Mallowan, the wife of the noted British archaeologist Sir Max E. L. Mallowan, and often accompanied him on his expeditions, using the experiences as background for some of her books. In 1971, on her eightieth birthday, her eightieth book was published. She was created a Dame Commander of the British Empire in 1971. Agatha Christie died in 1976 at the age of eighty-five. In all she produced eighty-eight books—a little better than one for each year of her life—which have been translated into 103 languages. Her books continue to be made into films.

ROSEMARY KENYON TIMPERLEY, British author, was born in London in 1920 and educated at King's College, University of London. Her novels include *The Listening Child, Dreamers in the Dark, The Fairy Doll, Across a Crowded Room, People Without Shadows* and *My Room in Rome.* Her numerous ghost stories are mostly gentle ghost fantasies. She has written for numerous periodicals and for the BBC.

M. R. JAMES was born in England in 1862. He was educated at Eton and at King's College, Cambridge, where he was awarded many prizes and scholarships. In 1905 he was elected Provost of his old college, from 1913 to 1915 he was Vice-Chancellor of Cambridge and in 1918 he became Provost of Eton. He published books on biblical, historical and artistic subjects and had a special interest in archaeology. In a more popular vein were his two collections of *Ghost Stories of an Antiquary.* He died in 1936.

ALGERNON BLACKWOOD, novelist, born in Kent in 1869, son of Sir Arthur Blackwood and Sydney, Duchess of Manchester, was educated at Wellington and at Edinburgh University. At the age of twenty he went to Canada, where he was successively journalist, dairy farmer, hotelkeeper, prospector, artist's model, actor and private secretary. He had a great interest in the occult and has been called "The Ghost Man" because of his subjects. After two volumes of short stories, *The Empty House* (1906) and *The Listener* (1907), he made his reputation with the weird *John Silence* (1908). Other novels were *The Human Chord* (1910), *The Wave* (1916) and *Dudley and Gilderoy* (1929). *Incredible Adventures* (1914), *Tongues of Fire* (1924) and *Tales of the Uncanny and Supernatural* (1949) are collections of short stories. He wrote several children's books, and the nonfiction *Episodes Before Thirty* (1923), which tells of his early roving life. He died in 1951.

JEROME K. JEROME, English humorist, was born in 1859 in Staffordshire, England, and died in 1927. During his lifetime he worked as a schoolmaster, as an actor and finally as a journalist. In 1888, he published his first book. He had a genuine gift for highlighting the more ridiculous aspects of the society of his day, but always with tolerance and a style of humor that owed much to Dickens and Mark Twain. In 1889 he became popular as a writer with *Idle Thoughts of an Idle Fellow* and his most famous book, *Three Men in a Boat,* which sold over a million copies in America.

MARY DANBY, British novelist, short-story writer and editor, the great-great-granddaughter of Charles Dickens, was born in Dorking, Surrey, in 1941. In the horror and fantasy field she is noted as an anthologist and editor. She edits the original anthology series *Frighteners,* and also has compiled six volumes of the Armada Ghost Book for children and five volumes of the Fontana Book of Great Horror Stories. In her spare time she continues working on her own novels and short stories.

HANS CHRISTIAN ANDERSEN, Danish author, was born in 1805, in Odense, Denmark, son of a poor shoemaker. His father died when he was eleven years old and he stopped attending school, spending his time making a toy theater and puppets. Later, he was educated through the generosity of wealthy patrons. His novels are almost completely forgotten and his lasting fame is due entirely to his three series of fairy tales, produced between 1835 and 1872. Although some of the fairy stories are old tales retold, most of them, including *The Steadfast Tin Soldier,* were his own invention. He died in 1875.

NATHANIEL HAWTHORNE, novelist, was born in Salem, Massachusetts, in 1804, the son of a sea captain. A slight lameness shut him off from sports and led to a taste for reading which fostered his literary aspirations. He attended Bowdoin College, where Longfellow was a fellow student. He wrote extensively, had several Custom House appointments at different places, and was appointed United States Consul at Liverpool by his friend President Franklin Pierce. He died in 1864.

TERRY TAPP, British writer of fantasy, horror and science fiction, was born in 1940 and educated at a grammar school. He held a variety of jobs before his first story was publishd by the *London Evening News.* To date he has published over a hundred short stories, some of which have been used by the BBC. His stories have appeared in several of the British ghost and horror anthologies, and one story, "All You Need is Rhythm," was selected by the Arts Council of Great Britain to appear in the *New Stories Anthology.* Mr. Tapp is married, and has a schoolgirl daughter.

J. H. PEARCE, British novelist, essayist and short-story writer of the nineteenth century, published ten books. His story "The Puppets" was included in *The Little Crow of Paradise and Other Fantasies* and has not previously been anthologized. Among his other books are *Drolls from Shadowland* (1893), *Tales from the Masque* (1894) and *The Dreamer's Book* (1905).

SEON GIVENS MANLEY has been a historian of the supernatural for many years. She is the author of *The Ghost in the Far Garden* and other stories with supernatural and folklore themes. A writer, editor and anthologist, she has published books in many fields.

F. MARION CRAWFORD, American novelist and short-story writer, was born in Bagni di Lucca, Tuscany, in 1854. The son of sculptor Thomas Crawford, who designed and executed many of the statues for the Capitol at Washington, F. Marion had a cosmopolitan education. He wrote in French as easily as in English; he studied German, Swedish and Spanish at Cambridge; he also studied Sanskrit at Rome and Harvard and knew many Eastern languages. His first novel, *Mr. Isaacs* (1882), was a great success and was followed by more than forty others, mainly historical romances. His play, *Francesca da Rimini* (1902), was produced by Sarah Bernhardt in Paris. However, he is best remembered for his ghost and horror short stories, written mostly in the 1890s. He died in 1909.

SEON MANLEY and GOGO LEWIS, who have worked together on many books, are sisters and have been collecting supernatural stories throughout their lives. Mrs. Manley lives in Greenwich, Connecticut, with her management consultant husband Robert, their daughter Shivaun, two dogs and five supernatural cats.

Mrs. Lewis lives in Bellport, Long Island, where the mist comes in from the bay with all the atmosphere of a Dickens novel. Her daughters, Carol and Sara, are also devotees of the supernatural tale.